A LIFE RENEWED

SECRETS OF THE QUEENS • BOOK 1

OLIVIA RAE

A LIFE RENEWED
© Copyright 2020 by Denise Cychosz
All rights reserved.

Please Note

This is a work of fiction. Names, characters, places and incidents are either the product of the author's imagination or are used fictitiously, and any resemblance to any actual persons living or dead, business establishments, events or locales is entirely coincidental.

Published by HopeKnight Press

For information, please contact:
www.oliviaraebooks.com
www.facebook.com/oliviaraeauthor
www.twitter.com/oliviaraebooks
www.instagram.com/oliviarebooks

ISBN: 978-1-7320457-5-0

Cover Design by Robbi Standemo
Digital Formatting by Author E.M.S.

Books by Olivia Rae

The Sword and the Cross Chronicles

SALVATION

REVELATION

REDEMPTION

RESURRECTION

ADORATION

DEVOTION

Contemporary Inspirational

JOSHUA'S PRAYER

Secrets of the Queens

A LIFE RENEWED

A LIFE REDEEMED
Coming Soon

Contact Olivia at
Oliviarae.books@gmail.com

Want notice of upcoming books? Join my mailing list:
Oliviaraebooks.com
Facebook.com/oliviaraeauthor

For Mark,
The best man in the whole wide world and the only one in
my life, now, always and forever. A new series and a new
chapter in our lives.

And to the glory of God

PROLOGUE

February 12, 1554
Tower of London

John Feckenham, chaplain to Queen Mary, donned his heavy black cloak before clasping his sweaty palms together. He dropped to his knees and offered up one last prayer for the poor soul whose death this day would ease many minds. All this could have been avoided had Lady Jane Grey returned to the true faith. Perhaps then Queen Mary would have held off the executioner's blade. Yet, she had not.

He would miss their lively doctrinal conversations, for Jane did have a quick mind. A pity they could not continue in this fashion for another month or so. But he had failed to make Jane see the errors of her Protestant faith, and she would not give up the Church of her great-uncle Henry VIII for the true Catholic religion. Jane even made Feckenham promise to give her prayer book to the queen when all was over and done, the hope being that Queen Mary might see the light and turn away from the Pope and Rome, thus saving her body from the flames of hell.

John placed his cap upon his head and slowly made his way to Gentleman Gaoler's quarters where Jane had been staying since she had been deposed. Though a satisfactory place within the Tower, it still held an unfortunate view of the Tower Green where Jane's scaffold had been constructed.

Sir John Brydges, Lieutenant of the Tower, was waiting by Lady Jane's door. A grim line creased his lips. Within the house, the weeping and wailing of Mrs. Ellen and Mrs. Tilney, Jane's attendants, twisted Feckenham's heart. All knew their parts to play. The question was, did the fair Lady Jane?

John followed Sir Brydges into the room. "It is time, madam," Brydges said kindly.

The woman flinched as if Brydges's words were a hard lash. Dressed in the black gown and dark French hood Lady Jane wore at her trial, the dry-eyed woman finally nodded. In her hands she held a new prayer book and a crumpled piece of parchment, lest she forget the memorized words. As she departed the home and walked to the scaffold, her lips moved slowly, though no words could be discerned—almost as if she were rehearsing the lines to a tragedy.

Few were present to watch this spectacle unfold; after all, Lady Jane did have royal blood coursing through her veins and her death was not subject for public display. All walked on in silence until they stood at the scaffold steps. She turned; her gaze locked with his. "God grant you all your desires and accept my own hearty thanks for all your attention to me. Although indeed, those attentions have tried me more than death can now terrify me."

Her words swirled through Feckenham's head and tied his tongue. Before his voice returned, she had ascended the scaffold stairs. With haste, he followed.

She stood, her back ramrod straight as she fumbled with the parchment in her shaking hands. Slowly the woman began to address the small assembly. "Good people, I am come hither to die, and by a law I am condemned to the same. The fact against the queen's Highness was unlawful, and the consenting thereunto by me: but, touching the procurement and desire thereof by me, or on my behalf, I do wash my hands thereof in innocency before God, and the face of you, good Christian people, this day.

"I pray you all, good Christian people, to bear me witness that I die a true Christian woman, and that I do look to be saved by no other mean, but only by the mercy of God, in the blood of his only Son Jesus Christ: and I confess, that when I did know the Word of God, I neglected the same, loved myself and the world; and therefore this plague and punishment is happily and worthily happened unto me for my sins; and yet I thank God, that of his goodness he hath thus given me a time and respite to repent.

"And now, good people, while I am alive, I pray you assist me with your prayers."

Here then she knelt and turned once again, gazing into Feckenham's eyes. "Shall I say this Psalm?"

"Yea," Feckenham said and hoped the woman could read the words as practiced. She turned back to the prayer book and began to recite the fifty-first Psalm. He followed her English words with his Latin. When done, she rose and gave a timid smile. "God, I beseech Him abundantly reward you for your kindness to me."

Feckenham could feel a heat creep up the back of his neck even though the day was brisk. How had he been kind? Oh, if only there could be another way.

As instructed, the woman handed her gloves and handkerchief to her attendants and her prayer book to Thomas Brydges, the lieutenant's brother. She removed her hood and began to untie her gown when the executioner stepped forward.

Startled, she stepped back. "I desire you to leave me alone."

Had she forgotten that her clothing would become the executioner's property?

Quickly her attendants came to her aid and helped with the unlacing. At least this small disaster had been avoided.

Feckenham looked around the green, but none seemed to think the behavior odd. Perhaps they had written it off to nerves instead of a queen forgetting her duty before her executioner. He breathed a sigh of relief. All would continue as planned.

A cloth was given to the woman to fasten about her eyes. The executioner came forward and knelt down. "My lady, I beg your forgiveness."

"You are forgiven," she said in a soft voice.

There was nothing else to be done. "My lady," the executioner said, "please stand upon the straw."

She hesitated, and her eyes grew wide as she stared at the block. Feckenham thought for sure she would bolt. But she did not.

"I pray you dispatch me quickly," she whispered before kneeling. Again, she paused. "Will you take it off before I lay me down?"

"No, madam," he answered just as quiet.

With shaking fingers, she tied the kerchief across her eyes and began to fumble about with her hands, looking for the block. "What shall I do? Where is it?" she cried.

All about looked on in horror, if this did not conclude swiftly who knew what mischief would be had. Without further thought, Feckenham guided her to the block.

She lowered her head and uttered her last words, "Lord into thy hands I commend my spirit."

With a swift swing of the ax, by all accounts, Lady Jane Grey was dead.

Chapter 1

Late March, 1556
Outside of London

Asher Hayes dug his hands deep into the rich black soil and closed his eyes as the tiny moist particles of dirt seeped under his fingernails. Finally, after all these years, he had his reward. Perhaps most would think the small farm outside the city was a meager earning for his years of service to Queen Mary, but he was elated. Asher lifted his hands to his face and inhaled the sweet earth. No more blood. No more death. Now his hands were covered with life. He would plant beans, turnips, wheat, and more. His past crimes would be washed away by feeding his family and the poor. He would make amends for all the lives he had stolen and butchered in the name of Bloody Mary.

Now Asher's biggest worry was convincing his parents and younger sister to join him in the simple life. His mother was indeed ready, but she feared her husband would slip back into his gambling and outlandish ventures. But all debts had been paid with the blood of others.

Asher stood and brushed the dirt from his hands. How he wished he could as easily wipe away the screams of all the Protestants he had sent to their deaths. But that horrible business was done, at least by him. A fortnight ago he had declared his wish to leave the queen's services, and it had been granted. Now he would live quietly. Now he would create life instead of destroying it. Now, hopefully, God would grant him peace.

The huffs of a small lad running up the hill drew Asher's attention. The boy approached with a parchment in hand. "Sir Asher, Sir Asher, I have a message for you."

Asher took the note, reached into his coarse brown doublet, and tossed a coin to the child. "Who gave you this missive?"

"Them down there, sir." The lad pointed to a pair of the Queen's Guard. "They did not wish to leave the comfort of their horses, so I offered to do the task for them." A wide smile broke on the lad's face, clearly he had been paid by the guards as well.

When the men saw that the message had reached Asher's hands, they turned their mounts and swiftly made off toward London. An action he had seen often when the queen was ready to send him on another secret undertaking. Asher looked at the wrinkled note in his hand, but his service was done, so what would the queen want with him now?

The lad looked on expectantly as if he thought Asher would share the contents. Youth, so curious and often impetuous. He had been the same way. How often had he carried a message to gain a pittance or a few scraps of information just so he could fill his belly and that of his sweet sister, Audrey? Thus were their lives with a father who always chased a pot of gold with a farthing in his hand. Yet, had it not been so, Asher never would have gained a skill that caught the eye of a queen.

"My thanks," Asher said to the boy without another glance at the parchment.

The lad reluctantly shuffled down the hill, glancing over his shoulder wondering if he could garner something from Asher's expression. When the child was out of sight, Asher unfolded the message and quickly read. The queen wished to see him this eve. The note ended with words he had seen often. *Come in your usual manner.*

The sentence curled his stomach. Surely, this was not yet another mission. He had made it plain. He was done sniffing out Protestants and sending them to the flames. Had she not publicly praised his service and released him? What then would the queen want of him?

Asher crushed the note in his hand and looked up at the fading sun. Dread filled his soul. He had only a few hours to wait, when the earth was covered with blackness, to discover what Her Majesty would have of him now.

The latch on the hidden wooden door slid open easily, and Asher stepped into the cool, damp tunnel that led to a dark set of stairs. He used to count how many times he snuck into the queen's chamber, but as the scaffolds were built, and young and old alike were hung, burned, or chopped to pieces, he stopped. No longer did he believe he was sent to do God's work, for surely not even God would want heathens to die in such a gruesome way.

At the chamber door he paused and made a hasty vow. No matter how much she offered, no matter how much she screamed and shouted, he would not lift his hand against one more Protestant. The few years of service to Queen Mary had seemed like a lifetime. She would have to find someone else to do her bidding.

With a swift knock and the soft words that bid him to come hither, Asher entered the room. He bowed low to the dark shadowy figure near the window silhouetted by the moonlight. "Your Majesty, it is Asher Hayes."

The silhouette turned and blended into the blackness of the chamber. "Of course it is you, who else slinks about like a demon in the night?"

Asher wanted to point out that he only hid in the shadows upon her orders, but with his dreams finally realized, to voice such thoughts would not be prudent. "I thought our private meetings were finished, since in the light of day you proclaimed my service to you was over."

Queen Mary stepped forward. The glow of the fire in the hearth defined her features—tiny, thin, and timid-looking. No one would ever believe this fragile sickly woman could have caused such carnage. But then again, she did all in hopes that her beloved husband, King Philip II of Spain, would return to England. But her dreams were in vain. Once the Holy Roman Emperor, Charles V, abdicated most of the empire to his son Philip, there was no reason for him to return. Mary loved her husband so much; he could control her from whatever country he resided in.

She brushed past Asher and picked up a flagon of wine with her bony hands. "A warm drink?"

The hair on his neck pricked. Only blood followed when their meeting started out with such cordiality. "No thank you, Your Majesty."

Mary gently placed the flagon back on the ornate table and lifted her watery-blue eyes to meet his. Her lips twitched, and her jaw released slowly. "You know I would not be queen today had it not been for you."

Why after all these years would she remind him of the one act that had started all the pain and suffering? Yet, she talked to him as she always did, without the royal 'we.' Her true familiarity was a gift he readily accepted and, at times, dreaded.

"Had you not warned me that Lord Northumberland sought to harm my person when poor Edward died, who knows where this kingdom would be now. Without you, England would be deep in the hands of the Protestant reformers. Dare I say it, we could all be infected with the words of that heretic John Calvin or of those who follow the blasphemous doctrine of Martin Luther."

Asher used to enjoy Mary's rage against the Protestants for his family too had suffered when King Henry VIII created his own church out of lust for a wicked woman. The annulment of his first marriage to Catherine of Aragon split England in half. Asher's family remained loyal to the true Catholic faith; others embraced the new Church of England. The decision swallowed up Asher's father's successful textile and spice trade, leaving him with few prospects. It was folly to oppose the king who could grant and decline trade routes with the stroke of a quill. Yet William Hayes would not conform.

"I believe Luther thought he was reforming the Church not creating a new religion," Asher said dryly, hoping Queen Mary would explain why he was here, instead of dwelling on the past.

A fury flared in Mary's eyes, and her body began to shake. "Then he would have done well to stick to the true teachings of the Church instead of clinging to the insane ramblings of reform." She inhaled deeply and closed her eyes, obviously digging for a patience she could not hold. Her eyes flipped open. "I did not summon you to discuss religion."

Asher kept his distance and folded his arms across his chest. "Nor do I think you brought me here to sing my praises."

"No indeed." She turned her gaze to the fire popping in the hearth, her straight features taking on a menacing glow. "But what happened back then affects what we must discuss this eve." Her voice did not hold the drama of one of her fits of anxiety. Nor did it have the wheeze of one of her mind-driven maladies. Nay, her voice held fear and regret…and sadness.

"My Queen?" Asher stepped closer, but she did not look his way. "What is troubling you?"

"Without you, Lady Jane Grey would be sitting on the throne."

Why rehash the old? She had never done so before, and he had not the stomach for it. His father had become desperate making risky ventures and gambling, hoping to regain his fortune. But it just sent the family further into debt. Asher's older brother, Robert, stubbornly chose the Church years earlier and was more interested in prayer than in helping the family to survive. So, the task fell on Asher's shoulders. He did whatever it took to keep a warm meal on the table. He'd lied, cheated, stolen, but mostly he had collected information that could be sold for a good price.

Asher bowed his head. "This is in the past. Let us not think on it. I did what any faithful servant would have done."

Without wanting, that fateful day flooded Asher's mind. He had been waiting in a dark alley to hear from one of his court informants. For weeks, there had been wagers and discussions on the sickly King Edward's health. If Asher could get a reliable tidbit on the situation, it could be most profitable. That July night his informant was late. When the man did show up, he was staggering and using the stone building to steady his gait. At first, Asher had been irritated thinking the man had stopped off at a tavern for drink, but when he got closer, Asher saw the man had been stabbed through the gut and, no doubt, left to die. Just before he passed on, the informant handed Asher a very important letter. King Edward was dead and John Dudley, Duke of Northumberland, planned to put his daughter-in-law, Lady Jane Grey Dudley on the throne, but he needed to capture Mary Tudor in order to control the Privy Council. At the time, Asher thought good fortune had returned to the Hayes family with this piece of information.

He stumbled out of the alley and hastily left the city. By the grace of God, Asher met Mary's entourage en route to London under a summons she believed to be from her alive brother, King Edward. After being bashed in the head several times for his insolence, Asher was allowed to speak. At first, many guffawed. But then he held out the missive he had collected from the dying informant, laying out all the details of Lord Northumberland's diabolical plot.

The rest became history. Mary became Queen of England, and in private, she knighted Asher, making him her secret eyes and ears into the Protestant world. Not once did he show his face at court or dance with the nobles. As Queen Mary often said, his dark eyes, black hair, and nondescript features were perfect for hiding in the shadows, collecting information and names so she could conquer all her enemies.

Mary snapped her gaze to his. "Nay, you are worthier than most. You remember Wyatt's Rebellion, do you not?"

Again, she dug up one of the most painful times in Asher's life. When she had decided to marry Philip, all hell broke out in England. Philip, being a foreigner, was the last person the English people wanted sitting in the throne room. Thomas Wyatt, a good Catholic, could not stand the thought of having a Spaniard as King of England. He foolishly contacted Henry Grey, Duke of Suffolk, who would only join Wyatt's rebellion if Lady Jane, his daughter was given the crown once again. They marched on London. Asher's pious brother thought he could reason with Wyatt's mob and wound up dead. Thankfully, the rebels were defeated.

Perhaps Lady Jane Grey did not have a part in the rebellion, but she lost her head along with her father and Thomas Wyatt. An action Asher heartily supported. However, none of these deeds could bring his brother back to life.

"My Queen, again, this is all in the past. You did the right thing and squelched the rebellion with a few heads."

Mary cocked her own gaunt head to the side and raised her brows. "Did I?" She waved her hand to a chair. "Sit, Asher." Though she made no attempt to do the same.

"Your Majesty, it is not proper. If you stand, then I shall stand."

She rolled her eyes. "Suit yourself. Though do not hold formality on my account." With a quick turn, Mary began to pace. "Not all lost their heads because of that rebellion."

"Aye, you were merciful to many who followed the orders of their betters." His words were meant to soothe, but Mary paused her pace, and her eerie blue eyes grew wide with a wild glare.

"You do not know the truth." She resumed her pace and continued as if each step would help her telling. "I never wanted to kill Jane. She was not like her father or that insufferable John Dudley. When he met the ax, I thought for sure this nasty business was over. I even gave Henry Grey his freedom. And how did the fool repay me? He marched on London with Thomas Wyatt. I had no choice then. Jane and her father had to die or there would be more unrest. Besides, Philip refused to come to England while Jane drew breath."

Asher almost laughed. Killing Jane Grey had made her a martyr for the Protestants. Nonetheless, he would have done the same thing if he were in Queen Mary's place. Perhaps if Lady Jane had not taken the throne, then many would have accepted Mary without all the bloodshed—his brother might still be alive.

"Do not torment yourself with this. You did what had to be done." Asher stepped in Mary's path and stopped her pace. "Come. Rest by the fire. This overexertion is not good for the body."

Her lips thinned, and her gaze flipped across Asher's form. Instead of heeding his advice, she stepped around him and began to pace the room again. "There is where you are wrong. I did not take off Jane Grey's head."

What? Could the queen be losing her wits? Or was she playing with words? "No, my Queen. The executioner took off Lady Jane Grey Dudley's head."

Mary stopped and turned her cold, icy eyes on him. "Do not make sport of this. That she married one of John Dudley's sons does not change the royal blood that courses through her veins."

"You mean that *coursed* through her veins. For she is dead and so is her husband, neither can harm you now." Asher should have held his tongue for Mary's face twisted up with a rage he had never seen before.

"That stupid husband of hers is dead, but Jane lives and breathes just as you and I." A film of perspiration above Mary's lips glistened in the firelight. Deep folds creased her forehead, and her body shook. "But thanks to you, I now know her plan. She wishes to take my crown once again. Though she swore she never would do so."

Thanks to him? What nonsense did the queen utter? Asher gently stepped toward her. "Perhaps you should sit. I will call for your physician."

Mary let out a cackle. "I am not ill. Nay, maybe you are right. For it is the softness of my heart that I let the girl go. Only a person suffering from a vile malady would have done so."

A spark of apprehension niggled between Asher's shoulder blades, not because of her claimed illness but because of her words. "Let her go?" he asked softly.

Mary nodded. "After the conviction of high treason, I allowed Jane some freedoms while living in the Tower. I knew she had only been a pawn in this game of intrigue. I thought actually to make her an ally. She was such a smart and articulate girl. I thought if I could turn her to the true faith, she would happily voice her love for Catholicism to the people. Herein calming all English souls."

Asher had to agree if fate had chosen that path, then surely all in England would have fared better, but alas, it had not. "But Lady Jane went to her death singing the praises of the Protestant faith."

"Aye, so her eloquent words were spoken, just not by her."

The tension expanded between Asher's shoulder blades and started to seep down his back and curl around to his gut. He was not sure he wanted to hear the rest of the queen's story. Still, his lips moved. "What do you mean?"

"Do you know of my most excellent chaplain, John Feckenham?"

"Aye, who does not?" Though Asher had never met the man.

"I sent him to change Jane's thinking. If I could not save her in this world, I thought surely she could be saved in the next if she confessed her sins. Feckenham regularly reported on their progress, or should I say the lack thereof. The girl had been so deeply educated by Protestants in her youth that she could not even abide God's teachings without hearty debate. But even so, Feckenham was fond of the girl, as was I. So, we began to hatch a plan."

A strong heat swept up Asher's body and tore at the dark places of his soul. Nothing good ever came from a secret plan, and well he should know, for he had devised many. "A plan, Your Majesty?"

Mary twisted her hands together and dropped her gaze to her toes. "It was not hard for Feckenham to find a woman of dire need that looked like Jane. The woman was deeply in debt and could not support her bastard child. Dare I say, the child was upon death's door, but through much intercession and care, we were able to heal the babe."

"*We?*" Asher managed to squeak out.

Mary looked up, narrowed her eyes, and answered his question with only a nod. "Feckenham offered to put the boy with a very *good* family where the lad might prosper and gain a mite of wealth and property."

"God's blood, you gave the boy to a noble family?"

Again, Mary nodded. "The woman only had to do one thing."

Asher stared at his queen and hoped she spoke out of a malady that addled her mind, but he knew that was only a wishful thought. "What did the woman have to do?"

A hard line sharpened Mary's lips, and she gave out a loud huff. "Surely you are not that dim-witted? The woman would do anything for the child. She took Jane's place. I sent Lady Jane to the eastern border of France to a nunnery, hoping the good sisters could make her see reason, but that had not happened."

Asher's pulse kicked up as Mary stood before him like a squawking raven. "You sent her to France—to our enemies?"

Mary waved off. "I could not send her to Spain or Flanders. If Philip had found out, it would have been disastrous. And the Scots...if Jane fell into the wrong hands...there could have been an uprising. Nay, Feckenham swore that she would be safe tucked away in a remote part of France, near the southern German border. Only the abbess knew who she was, or so I thought. However, not long after Jane's arrival, a few German lords showed up and absconded with her. I was in a fit when I heard this. My poor head." Mary touched her temple and then gave a slight cry. "Lady Jane sent me a letter, professing never again to challenge me for the crown." Mary shrugged. "So I let her be."

God's holy blood, what had Mary done! "And you believed her? Where did she go?"

The queen huffed. "I did not know. I thought, let the Germans have her. After all, even Charles V gave that forsaken country to his brother, Ferdinand I. All was fine for a year, but then word came that there was a rebellion brewing in the northern German principalities. No doubt caused by that ungrateful girl."

More than likely it was brought on by Mary's butchering of Protestants that so many fled to places where they could be safe. Whatever the reason, Lady Jane lived, and a woman who would happily sneak away and let another take her place at the block was indeed a vile villain.

Asher lowered his head and gazed at the dancing flames. "This is most unfortunate, my Queen. Are you sure your information is reliable?"

"Quite. The details came from the last group of Protestants you apprehended."

Asher tried to picture the Protestant followers in his mind. They were naught but a few older women, a man, plus a few spindly lads. 'Twas their pathetic state that had sealed Asher's desire to leave Her Majesty's service.

"That is why you are here," she continued. "We have learned these rebels are in a small principality north of Frankfurt. I want you to go and gain favor with the retched group. After which you will shatter their plans and find and destroy Lady Jane Grey Dudley. Return with only her head so I know she is truly dead. You must do all of this before Philip finds out the girl is alive. He will never return to England if he discovers the truth!"

As much as Asher wanted to see Lady Jane dead, for in his mind had she not been greedy for the crown, his brother would still be alive. Still, Asher was done with these nasty affairs. This was not his fight anymore. He shook his head. "Nay, I am finished. You gave me your blessing and your word that my service was over. I have seen too much. I cannot, nor will I, do this. Find another."

Mary lifted her chin in a most regal fashion, though her hands shook like a woman with palsy. "You can and you will. I trust no other with this task. If you did not want this involvement, then you should have let the old woman, Mrs. Ellen, in her home instead of dragging her to my cells."

One of the women gave the queen this information? Preposterous. He vehemently shook his head. "Nay, I cannot be part of this."

A cruel smile splayed across Mary's lips as she gained her composure. "Such a pity." She shrugged. "I guess your father, mother, and sister will have to be sold into servitude."

Dread and wariness flooded Asher's body. "I have long paid their debts."

Mary made her way to the table and poured a goblet of wine but did not lift the glass to her lips. "Aye, but your father could not resist the temptation to enter into an unsavory transaction with Lord Allerton. Unfortunately, the deal did not turn out as expected."

Asher fisted his hands as anger infused every muscle in his body. "You did this. Why? Have I not served you faithfully? Why would you do such a revolting thing?"

Mary pressed her back into the table. "I knew you would refuse me. I could not publicly force you to continue your service without raising eyebrows. I want no more scandal. Do this for me and I will release your parents and raise your sister to prominence at court. I will find her a good and profitable match. I promise, before God, this will be done. All you have to do is bring back the head of that traitor Jane."

Asher's legs weakened; his anger changed to defeat. He knew when he had been bested. He sat down in the queen's presence. "I think I will have some wine now."

With a chalice in hand, Mary drifted toward him. She handed him the goblet, flashing a wicked smile. "I dare say, Asher, *we* would be lost without you."

CHAPTER 2

Early April, 1556
Hanenburg, a northern principality in the Holy Roman
Empire of the German Nation

One would think it would be impossible, but Otto Werner had managed to slice a good piece of healthy skin off the inside of his palm. Ella examined the wound and clicked her tongue. "How did you do this?"

The good preacher shrugged. "I was skinning a rabbit. I thought to have a nice stew this eve."

Sitting across from the man, Ella reached for some clean linen. She patted the blood away and breathed a sigh of relief when she noticed the wound would not need a stitch. On the table sat a fresh beer. The pastor licked his lips when she reached for the brew. With a smile, she poured the drink on the torn flesh.

"Ack, such a waste," he cried.

Without breaking her care, Ella laced a dab of honey on the wound, then quickly bound it. "I would think God would want you to continue to do His work with two hands instead of one."

"*Ja*, for sure, but God would not want a man to die of thirst either."

Ella arched a red-gold brow and reached for a pitcher of beer and poured some into a mug, placing it in his good hand. "Indeed, Master Werner. We would not want you to die before you have finished your earthly duties." She smiled, knowing it was safer to call him Master Werner than *Herr Doktor* when speaking out loud. Even though they were the only two present to hear.

The ruddy-faced preacher with wiry red hair lifted his mug. "To my good nurse, Ella Brandt." He followed his short salute with a wink for he knew well that was not her true name. They both carried secrets, which made them dear friends.

Perhaps she never should have confided in him, but he was her only source to get her hands on the written word. For months she had nothing to read but her prayer book, which when opened only brought back bad memories. As much as she loved her so-called aunt and the simple life, Lady Jane Grey swore madness would set in shortly if she did not find something else to read. Hence, she struck up a friendship with Otto Werner and his shelf of spiritual writings.

Oh, she knew the risks, Prince Nikolaus von Hoffbauer and her Aunt Hildegard both lectured her on the importance of secrecy. But Otto Werner was a man of God. Surely, he could be trusted. Nonetheless, Hanenburg was a town of gossip; even so, she loved the small hamlet. She never ever intended to leave. Though their modest cottage sat on the prince's lands, Jane thought of the place as hers. She loved the cluck of the chickens in the morn, which were housed in a small shed along with their cow, Matilda.

A freshwater stream was a short walk from their abode. An abundant source of trout. Large evergreens protected their home in the winter months and kept it cool in the summer. This simple life held so much more contentment than her previous life ever had.

Otto Werner took another drink. "Ah, this is good."

"Slow your drinking. You have lost some blood, and it has been my experience that those who drink too much or too fast after such a loss tend to act unwisely."

"Have no worries. I am not one to drink more than what is right in God's eyes, and how many times must I ask you to call me Otto?"

His request had become a game with them, and she hoped the banter would continue for a long time. "You are our spiritual leader. It would be improper for me to use such a familiarity." Jane rose from her seat and wiped her hands on her apron "Come tomorrow and I will change the dressing. Promise me you will not go out hunting until your hand is healed. You know you are always welcome to eat here. I am sure Aunt Hildegard would be pleased to have you."

Otto Werner's ears turned pink at the mention of the widow's name. He quickly emptied his mug and rose from his seat. His donkey brayed in the yard. "I shall think on your offer, Ella. Now I must go, I need to feed the beast and then... I have much to do." Without another word, the good pastor rushed to the cottage door, mounted the donkey, and was gone before Jane took another breath.

She shook her head. The poor man. His wife died of the sweating sickness five years ago. Three years after that he became smitten with Hildegard Brandt. All in town knew, and the gossips had told Jane the story when she arrived.

During one of *Herr Doktor's* many winded sermons, somewhere between the fires of hell and the saving grace of Jesus, his words stalled and his gaze hung on the gentle face of the widow, Hildegard Brandt. It was said the whole congregation turned to see what or who had distracted their preacher. There, fresh from Frankfurt, stood Hildegard. For a woman of middling years, she had a gentle face and a very fine smile. Clearly, *Doktor* Werner was smitten. To all it seemed to be a match made in heaven. Regrettably, to this day, the man had yet to exchange more than a few pleasantries with Mistress Brandt, mostly at the Sunday meeting hall.

Jane put the honey back into the cupboard. "How the man ever married in the first place is a wonder."

"Who are you talking to?"

At the familiar voice, Jane spun about. "Hildegard, I was not expecting you back so soon. We had a visitor this morning. He just left. Did you not see him on the road?"

Hildegard frowned and hefted a small bundle onto the table. "*Nein,* I saw no one. But then I came through the fields. It is a mite shorter than taking the path. There were few at the market this day, so I have returned with most of our cheese and little coin." She walked over to the cupboard and pulled out a cracked pitcher, dropping a few coins within. "Prince von Hoffbauer had a messenger this morning who wore the Queen of England's colors. Many decided to spend the day near the castle gate just to gain a little knowledge instead of buying goods."

A prick of uneasiness settled in Jane's chest. "Did you

hear anything? Are you sure the messenger was from England and not somewhere else?"

Hildegard smiled tenderly. "You must stop worrying about these things. Prince von Hoffbauer would never betray you. As long as you are in Hanenburg you will be safe."

How Jane wished it were so easy to believe. In her youth she had heard about awful forms of torture that could change a good Christian soul into confessing despicable things. What would happen if Prince von Hoffbauer were ever waylaid by such villains? Would he give up her hiding? *Heavenly Father, protect the good man.*

Quickly she pushed the thought out of her mind. If God wished her to be caught, then so be it. But for now, He willed her to be here, doing the prince's mending and being a helper to Mistress Brandt, who was known for her wise apothecary skills. Jane reached out and gave Hildegard a hug. "I wish you were my real aunt and that I could stay here with you forever."

"I would think you would wish to live in something grander than this small cottage." Hildegard raised her head to the loft that served as her bedchamber.

Jane pulled back and pointed to her own pallet, which lay in the far-right corner of the room, where a makeshift drape was drawn for privacy. "I have splendid quarters here." She then grinned. "Of course, I would not mind if Master Werner joined us as your husband. I think there is enough room up above to accommodate him."

Hildegard blushed. "You are a naughty girl. He is our spiritual leader and has far greater duties. Besides, I have had one husband and that was enough. Now stop this talk. We must set our minds on other things."

"The prince's visitor?"

"*Nein.* I am thinking we need to visit Mistress Meyer's house. That babe she carries should be coming along very soon. Her last birth was so hard I fear she will not have the strength to deliver another."

Jane stepped back and rubbed her hands over her upper arms. She had remembered the last birth. It was the first time Jane had ever accompanied Hildegard on such a task. Mistress Meyer labored for days, and in the end the babe had been still at birth. Thankfully, she had three others, all boys. Unfortunately, here she was again, little over a year later, trying to have another.

"We must pray God eases this child from her womb," Jane said.

Hildegard grabbed her birthing bag from the floor next to the wooden table. "I would much rather that God would have Master Meyer leave his wife alone in the future."

Jane's cheeks began to warm, but Hildegard just laughed. "Can we not speak of something else?"

"Let me see." Hildegard pursed her lips. "Master Klein's gout is acting up, and Mistress Gunther has the most interesting wart growing above her left eye."

"Ack, please. Is there nothing else you gathered from the village this day?"

"*Ja.*" A twinkle entered Hildegard's green eyes. "Hans Mueller said he will stop by this afternoon with his ax to cut some wood for us."

Jane took the cheese off the table and placed it in the larder. "Oh my. Why did you not say we have enough firewood already? I do not know why he always comes to visit."

Hildegard laughed once again. "You know why. He has had his eye on you ever since you strolled into our village."

"I did not stroll. I came in by cart in the dead of night."

"To me, *ja*. But to the town's people, you came as my niece whose family had succumbed to the sweating sickness. To these fine people you are one of them and not a deposed queen. Do not be surprised when a handsome young man takes notice of a pretty maid."

Jane dropped down into a chair by the table. "I am not pretty. Thankfully, I am ordinary in looks for I do want to spend my life as a commoner. I am so happy here. No rules to follow, no decorum to uphold, just freedom to be myself. I shall never marry again. I have no desire to put another in harm's way. And if there were a child..." She shook her head. "I dare not think what would happen if he or she were discovered."

Hildegard knelt in front of Jane and grabbed her hands. "I know you have had a tough life, but you must forget the past. You are German now, and once in a while it is okay to laugh."

Jane knew Hildegard's words were meant to soothe, but that did not take away the guilt she felt. A couple of years past, she had been prepared to die. Her speech written and memorized. When John Feckenham suggested another could take her place on the block, she quickly nullified the notion. She even desired that Queen Mary be given her prayer book.

Nonetheless, when the fateful day arrived, her dear nurse Mrs. Ellen suggested Jane take a draught to ease her nerves. The next thing she remembered was waking up in a cart, gagged and tied, her worn prayer book next to her.

She had not heard what had happened until she reached France and the abbess informed Jane of "her good fortune."

There was nothing good about it. A poor woman had died in Jane's place. Plus, from that day forth, she had been forced to study papist doctrine. But Jane endured out of guilt and shame for she did not want the woman's death to be in vain.

Rumors that she still lived swept the countryside. Perhaps the French sailors who brought her to the convent had told others who she really was or maybe God had been merciful, for six months later, two Germans, Lord Kraus and Lord Reinhardt visited. 'Twas like water splashed on dry bones, she was able to discuss her religious views freely without reprisal. When they suggested that she could possibly return with them to a northern principality in the German Nation, she jumped at the chance. Three days hence, she disappeared from France and from her perilous past life.

For months, she moved from one northern principality to another until one day she met Prince Nikolaus von Hoffbauer. The prince promised her a free life with no dogmatic ties. A place where she could stop running. There had been only one condition: she would have to live as a commoner. The whole idea sounded grand, and Jane accepted the offer.

However, her new freedom did not quiet her nerves. She still always looked over her shoulder, and of course, she was beholden to Prince von Hoffbauer. Oh, he had asked for nothing, except that she mend his clothing and those of his servants. Plus meet with him once a week to debate religious principles. But other thoughts niggled in her mind…someday he might want more. For experience had taught her one thing—no one gives a kindness freely.

Except Hildegard Brandt, who opened her home and gave Jane a new identity without question. "All right." Jane tossed a cape about her shoulders. "Let us check on Mistress Meyer and then let us have a quiet evening at home."

Jane tucked her dyed-brown hair under her white cap and lowered her head. One could not be too careful. No matter how safe her surroundings may be, she could not shake off the premonition that the future would be anything other than quiet.

And she had been right.

CHAPTER 3

The glowing sun shone bright in the morning sky, and Jane could not hide her giddiness. Finally, spring had come and soon the meadows would be resplendent with green grass and wildflowers. Humming a merry tune, she covered her head with a cap, then grabbed the prince's mending before heading out the door.

Sparrows flitted in the air, and Matilda's moos could be heard from the shed. Along with Hildegard's usual words of encouragement. "Come on now, girl. Just one pail of milk, that is all I am asking for." This ritual went on twice daily. Mostly with Matilda's cooperation, but never with certainty. Matilda was an old cow, and her milking days were soon coming to an end. Without her milk, they could not make cheese, and without cheese to sell, their livelihood could be jeopardized.

Jane thinned her lips and squeezed the bundle of mending to her chest. Today she would muster up the courage to ask the prince if he could provide them with another cow. Hildegard would protest such begging, but there was nothing for it—a new cow was needed or they would starve the next winter. Had not *Doktor* Werner preached almost every Sunday that God knew our needs and we need only to ask in Christ's name?

With reverence, Jane closed her eyes. *Lord, I know we should not set our minds on earthly things, but is it not better for us to support ourselves than to always rely on the prince's charity? Please grant us this small blessing.*

She opened her eyes, a new resolve filling her soul. "I am off, Aunt Hildegard," Jane called from the yard.

Hildegard poked her head out of the shed. "Good, I shall see you later. Give my greetings to the prince." With that, she was back to her challenge. Dear sweet Hildegard, she never gave up on anything without a fight.

Guilt pricked Jane's heart as she strode along the dirt road. She should be as bold and stand firm in front of the prince. After all, it was only a cow she sought. "Quit being such a ninny," she said out loud. "It is not as if you are asking for the Crown of England." She sucked in her breath. Where had that thought come from? She looked about, but no one stood on the path or lurked in the brush to hear. Yet, her heart thundered loudly. *God, forgive my foolish words.*

The past was gone and all that remained was the present. At least fifteen times a day she would mentally say, "I am Maid Ella Brandt." And each day that passed she believed the lie a little more. Lady Jane Grey Dudley died long ago at the Tower. Another wave of guilt crashed onto Jane's chest. She should be dead instead of some poor misguided soul.

Taking a deep breath, Jane wiped away the recurring thoughts. She could not change what had happened. She must focus on the future. Her steps became lighter, the few furlongs to the castle passed quickly, and before she knew it, she was standing outside Prince von Hoffbauer's castle. Hanenburg Castle at one time was owned by a family named Hanen, but somewhere in the fifteenth century, the Hoffbauer's took control of the castle in a most sinister way. The tale is still told among the villagers today.

At that time, Master Hoffbauer was the steward of the Hanen family. Good with numbers and managing accounts, he simply swindled the less intelligent Prince von Hanen. When the deceit was discovered, Hoffbauer was dragged in front of the magistrate, where Prince von Hanen demanded swift justice. But the events that unfolded did not follow normal practice. During the trial, a prince from a neighboring northern principality, who had been an enemy of Prince von Hanen, appeared with a very old document carrying the supposed seal and signature of Henry VII, the Holy Roman Emperor at that time. The document stated that it was Master Hoffbauer's family who were the true heirs to the principality.

Of course, this all seemed preposterous, yet the magistrate ruled in favor of Master Hoffbauer. Not long after, the magistrate received a windfall from the death of some obscure relative. The new Prince von Hoffbauer swore allegiance to the now friendly prince, who had found the old damning document. Poor Prince von Hanen was left with nothing and spent the rest of his life, which was short, trying to uncover the deceit.

To this day, the town still carried the name of the former prince. And by all appearances, the present Prince Nikolaus von Hoffbauer was not as sneaky and underhanded as his ancestors.

The gate opened as Jane approached, and she gave her greeting to the gatekeeper before making her way to the old great hall. She expected to find the prince breaking his fast, but he was nowhere to be found. She was led by one of the servants to the prince's private quarters. A prick of apprehension twisted through Jane as the prince bid her to enter.

Within, Jane found the prince and *Doktor* Werner perusing some parchments. A huge smile spread over the preacher's face, and with a wink, he chased all of Jane's fears away.

"Ah, Maid Brandt," the prince said, looking up from the document. "Come, come have a seat. I am almost finished with Otto." The prince motioned to a chair, then quickly rolled up the parchment and handed it to the preacher. "Make sure this is taken care of. We will speak more on the morrow."

Otto Werner bowed and then turned his attention to Jane. "You have quite the bundle there."

"The prince had a few more shirts than usual this week, some with long tears."

Both men looked at each other before the preacher cleared his throat. "*Ja*, well, I must be off. Much to do this fine day."

Jane looked at the bandage on his hand. How had he managed to get it so dirty in less than a day's time? "Perhaps you should stop by later so that I may have a look at that cut again," she called after him as he made his way to the door.

Otto Werner paused and looked down at his hand. "If there is time, I will. Busy day. A very busy, busy day."

On that he was gone, leaving Jane to contemplate his quick departure. Her thoughts did not tarry there long as the prince came and lifted the bundle from her hands.

"Many thanks on finishing these quickly. Come now. Do sit and have a bite for I have not broken my fast yet." Placing the bundle on a nearby chair, the prince softly took her fingertips and led her to the table.

An array of food lay there. More than one man could eat. White bread, dried apples, steamy meaty pottage, and large portions of cheese. Uneasiness and caution returned and swept through Jane as she slipped into a chair across from the prince. "My lord, this is quite a hearty meal to start the day."

"Ah, I know better than to try and fool you. I wanted you to join me." The prince moved to his chair and sat.

"But, Prince, I have already eaten." No sooner had the words left Jane's lips than her stomach growled.

The prince lifted a dashing eyebrow. "But perhaps not enough, eh?"

Dressed in a fine velvet doublet that showed off his muscular build, the prince graciously poured heavy rich milk into Jane's cup. His slightly greying temples did not distract from his firm features. Nor did his greying goatee from his looks. If he came with no title, his strong presence alone would command respect. "We rarely spend much time together, but I thought perhaps today." He paused and looked over her head to the open window where bright beams illuminated his face, giving him the most enthralling look. Perhaps earlier he had been praying, for only an angel would look thus. After a moment, his gaze shifted back to hers. "I have some news from England that I think you would wish to hear."

Jane's breath hitched and her heartbeat ticked upward. He handed her the milk, and she could feel her lips tremble as she raised the cup, but she could not make herself drink. She lowered the cup and placed it on the table. "Then they have found me."

"*Nein*," the prince said with a quick shake of the head. "The messenger has come with some other tragic news."

The only tragedy that Jane could think of would be the death of Queen Mary, but such news would have been announced far and wide. If so, Princess Elizabeth would be queen and the Protestants would be free to worship publicly. Of course, Elizabeth becoming queen would not change Jane's circumstances. So then, why the private meeting? Did he wish to inform her, out of kindness, before the crier was sent to the village? Was that what the document held that he gave to Otto Werner? Jane peered at the prince's face. His grey eyes gave no hint.

He popped a piece of dried apple into his mouth and chewed, but he did not offer up any further explanation.

"Is the queen dead?" she finally asked.

A tight laugh left his lips. "The queen is alive and well. The messenger brought another word. Perhaps you wish to eat before the hearing?"

Jane did not move a mite. "There is nothing you can say that will cause me such a fright that I would swoon. If it has to do with my mother, then worry not, we were never on good terms."

The prince washed the apple down with a healthy drink of milk. He reached over and grabbed Jane's hand. His palms were sweaty and sent a hot trail of foreboding down her spine.

"My dear," he began slowly, "this has nothing to do with your mother either. Over a fortnight ago, another group of Protestants were imprisoned."

Jane closed her eyes and wished she could close her ears as well. Every week carried such dreadful news—

Protestants being rounded up in England and falsely accused of many repulsive things. Why was this news any different that it warranted a private audience?

"One of the persons was your lovely Mrs. Ellen." The prince put his other hand on top of Jane's.

"Nay," Jane's voice cracked. Mrs. Ellen, her dear nurse had been with her…almost forever. If it had not been for her nurse giving her that sleeping draught, Jane would be dead now. Could that be why? Nay, Mrs. Ellen did only what Queen Mary ordered. "What has Mrs. Ellen done to warrant such cruelty?" Jane pulled her hand away from his as the smell of the meaty pottage made her nauseous.

"There needs to be no offense. Only a whisper of an accusation. A lie can bring someone to the gallows or the flames." The prince offered the plate of cheese.

With a wave of the hand, Jane dismissed the food. "But surely there will be a trial. Mrs. Ellen always held the highest level of civility even though she had different beliefs. Her life was dedicated to the service of others. I cannot believe anyone would wish to harm such a good woman."

The prince placed the plate back on the table and greedily filled his own plate. "It does not matter if she lived the Godliest life, all it takes is one so-called witness to wipe away years of impeccable service, destroy her good name, sealing her fate. She is accused of witchcraft and heresy."

Jane shot to her feet. "That is a lie!"

"The truth is not the goal. You of all people should know this." The prince exhaled before popping a piece of cheese into his own mouth. He smacked his lips as the cheese rolled down his throat. "She will burn, and the crowd will cheer."

"We have to do something." Jane walked over to the open window and observed a pair of birds making a small nest. How could they be so merry in their task when this day had brought the blackest news? Tears began to cloud her vision, obscuring the fluttering birds. "We must save her." She turned and lifted her pleading eyes to the prince. "Surely there is something you can do?"

"Oh, my dear, I have very little influence in England. Why, I believe if I ventured there, I might suffer the same fate." He shook his head and let out another heavy sigh. "I fear Mrs. Ellen is as good as dead."

Jane rushed to the side of the prince's chair and fell to her knees. "Please no. You are a powerful man. Can you not speak to Ferdinand, King of the Romans? He is King Philip's uncle. We all know Queen Mary does whatever her husband wants. If Philip made an intercession, the courts would have to let her go."

A snigger escaped his mouth. "We can trust no one in the Habsburg Dynasty. They only mean to gratify themselves. If you have not noticed, they are all Catholics. Ferdinand would never listen to an openly Protestant prince."

"Some say he is secretly a Protestant. Perhaps he could be persuaded to save Mrs. Ellen out of sympathy to the faith."

Her words were met with a shake of the head and more smacking of his lips as he devoured the cheese. "He does not care about some English nurse. Such a request would only raise more questions. That is not the answer."

Jane's stomach churned as her mind could not come up with one viable way to save Mrs. Ellen. She curled her chest to her knees; tears of defeat poured from her eyes. "There must be something…"

Gently, the prince touched the top of her head. "Hush now. Do not weep so. Come. Come. Look at me, *Jane*."

Rarely did he call her by her real name, for if he did so now, then all must be truly lost. She lifted her chin, and he pushed back his chair and bent down, wiping her tears away with his thumbs. She grabbed his hands. "Please, I cannot let her die...perhaps if I went back and offered an exchange. My life for hers."

"Queen Mary would have both your heads. Mrs. Ellen would be convicted of treason on the spot. She was a known participant in your escape."

A seed of anger flared in Jane's chest. "A plan that had been devised by the queen and John Feckenham. I was ready to die."

"And are you ready to do so again?" Prince von Hoffbauer stood and lifted Jane to her feet, squeezing her hands. "You cannot stop the butchery if you return to England like a beggar, bargaining one life for another."

"I have to try," Jane answered feebly. "I see no other course."

"Perhaps there is..."

His words were said so softly Jane wondered if her mind played a trick. "Come again?"

He dropped her hands and played with his goatee. "Maybe you should return to England."

Her spirits rose and fell faster than the waves sweeping a seashore. Without a doubt, Queen Mary would happily take Jane's head, but that did not mean Mrs. Ellen would go free. Jane took a deep breath, not seeing another answer. "Then I shall leave on the morrow."

Prince von Hoffbauer raised both hands. "Let us not be hasty. No plans for Mrs. Ellen's trial have been set. We have some time. Besides, I think there may be another choice. A way to save your nurse and your neck."

Elation shot through Jane's heart and brightened her spirits. "What is your thinking?" she asked eagerly.

"Come sit." He gestured to her chair. "Eat something. Ideas come more easily on a full stomach."

The smell of the food assailed her senses once again and made her stomach tumble. Cautiously Jane took her seat, but she did not lift a morsel of anything to her mouth.

"I am certain you have heard of the Champions of Christ?" Prince von Hoffbauer slurped the steamy pottage.

Her insides rolled again. To Jane's thinking, the Protestant rebels were no better than the Catholic butchers in England. For the Champions of Christ had been known to beat up and harass those who did not profess the Protestant faith. Many were bitter Englishmen who had lost their property and livelihoods when Mary came to power. "I am not fond of the group. For all their bluster, they are as bad as the Catholics. Force and mayhem are never the answer."

Prince von Hoffbauer wiped the dripping soup from his chin. "Normally, I would agree with you, but these are not normal times. The blood of reformed martyrs is running in the streets of England and in the southern German principalities as well, with no signs of abating. Many nobles in the north fear if we do not stand up for God's true words, then soon we will all be kissing the Pope's ring!"

"I do not doubt what you say, but surely there must be another way than bringing in that rebel group. Why, just last week they dunked Master Fischer in the well for aiding a Catholic traveler. Nothing good has ever come from associating with the Champions of Christ."

The prince picked up an apple and squeezed it between his fingers. His eyes became a dark tempest. "My dear, it is some of those very men who risked their own necks to save yours. Lord Kraus and our own fine *Herr Doktor* come to mind."

"*Herr Doktor!*" Did he know who she was all along? Before she told him? Was no one honest with her?

"Why are you surprised? Who do you think arranged for you to live with Mistress Brandt? You have been here a short time. We have suffered much under the control of the Habsburg Dynasty. Even with the Peace of Augsburg giving us religious choice, there are those south of Frankfurt calling for our Protestant bodies to be burned. Many have sacrificed much for their faith and for your freedom as well. You should be thanking these men and women, not snubbing your royal nose at them."

Since she had known Prince von Hoffbauer, he had never chastised her so severely. A sting of shame swept over her body. He and Hildegard had given her a new life, free from worry, and Otto Werner was ever so diligent in guiding her spiritual care. Lord Kraus and Lord Reinhardt had risked their lives smuggling her out of France. How many others had done the same to protect her?

Jane folded her hands and bowed her head. "I am sorry, my Prince. I have forgotten the charity many have given me."

He placed the apple back on the table and reached across, lifting her chin with a single finger. The storm in his eyes receded. "It is all right, Jane. You have come from a life of prosperity and indulgence. It is always hard to know the sacrifices others have made."

She wanted to clarify that her life had been anything but easy. Her mother had been ever so severe, and her father only saw her as a means to gain power. But then, perhaps that was indeed nothing compared to the sufferings of others. Jane swallowed hard. The words she had spoken so often in her youth settled hard upon her chest and constricted her throat. Finally, her voice came forth. "What would you have me do?"

A wide smile sprung forth on Prince von Hoffbauer's face. He picked up two cups of milk and handed one to Jane. "It is simple. With you as the head of the Champions of Christ, we will create a great army. One large enough to march on England and southern German principalities."

Jane could not believe her ears. This explained the strange cuts in the prince's shirts and Otto Werner's dirty bandages. They had been building and drilling an army.

"We will crush Queen Mary, her husband Philip, and the whole Habsburg Dynasty with a single blow. There will be singing in the streets of London, Frankfurt, and Hanenburg when the tyrants are gone." He raised his cup high. "To Queen Jane, may she sit on the throne of England once again."

Cursed is the blood that flows through my veins!

She did not want this. She wanted to live the quiet life of a commoner. But she could not let Mrs. Ellen die. God forgive her, but if blood must flow, she wanted it to be her own.

Chapter 4

Asher took off his boot and shook out the annoying pebble that had bothered his heel all afternoon. This country had more stones and rocks than the whole of England did. The hard ground gave little rest for a weary traveler, but tonight that would all come to an end.

He would enter the hamlet of Hanenburg as he did most London streets or small villages, under the cloak of darkness. Queen Mary had been correct, his dark looks were meant for blending into the night. Thus, every overture to a stranger or enemy of the Crown had always been made in the shadows, and tonight would be no different.

For a week, he had surveyed the comings and goings of the town from afar. Similar to many, this village was built around a stone well that stood in the middle of a cobblestone square. There were a few merchants' shops that sold textiles, cookware, farming tools, and other interesting bobbles. There was a blacksmith, a weaver, a master carpenter, and a makeshift meeting hall, which may double for a Protestant church.

The village received and owed its existence to Prince Nikolaus von Hoffbauer, who lived in Hanenburg Castle.

The high vantage point of the keep would dishearten any invader. By all accounts, Hanenburg was impenetrable. Perhaps for an army, but not for a single man on foot.

The most attractive place in Hanenburg was the Growl Bear, an inn and tavern frequented by most of the farmers and villagers. Queen Mary had planted the seed of gossip when she sent a mysterious messenger to the castle. Since then, there had been a lot of activity at the tavern. Asher smiled. Loose tongues full of drink would lead him to his prey. Without a doubt, the rebel group, the Champions of Christ, were busy debating the news the messenger had shared. Now, hopefully, they would take the bait. If all went well, he would have the head of Lady Jane Grey by week's end.

How he would find a woman he had never met would be the hardest part of the venture. Queen Mary offered up little information—Jane looks like a Tudor, maybe her eyes were green, or perhaps blue. As if those vague words would be enough to go on. Especially in a town of Germans where many had light skin, red hair, and eyes of many colors. There were no miniatures, no poems, no great accounts of Jane's beauty to go on. When he had asked Feckenham about the color of her eyes or the shape of her nose, he just blinked and spoke about her intelligence. All men and women see what they want to see.

One thing Asher had learned over the years was that a lady was easy to spot because they could not act like an uncouth maid even if they tried. So trained on proper manners, they could not hide their breeding—haughty and full of themselves. Lady Jane Grey would be in the castle, heavily guarded, ordering her inferiors to do her bidding.

Asher clenched his fist. One less noble in the world would be a good thing.

A soft cry drew his attention to the road near the castle. A maid carrying a small bundle kicked the dirt and mumbled like a madwoman. His curiosity piqued, Asher followed along hidden by thick foliage.

"I want nothing from you. Ha. What a lie. They all want something. And I did not even have the courage to ask for a new milk cow! Poor Hildegard, how will she survive the winter? I should let you mend your own shirts," the woman ranted before she dropped and kicked the bundle she had been holding. The object flew through the air and landed less than a quarter furlong from where he had been hiding. She gave out a gasp and ran to pick it up, slapping off the dirt. "Now I shall have to wash everything as well."

Asher could not help but chuckle at her lament. Such worries were the life of a common maid.

"Ah? Is someone there?" The maid peered into the brush, her head bobbing back and forth like a hoot owl.

He took a step back, then thought better of it. This woman had come from the castle, perhaps she held useful bits of information. Slowly Asher left the protection of his hiding place. "Forgive me, Mistress," he said in choppy German, "I did not want to frighten you."

A small screech left her lips. Her copper eyes widened, and her bundle fell to the ground when she brought her hands to her mouth. "Sir, you should have made your presence known sooner." The fear in the woman's lovely eyes did cause concern, for the last thing he needed was to have a hysterical maid go running for the magistrate.

Asher took a tentative step forward, then stopped. No wonder she trembled; the petite woman's head barely came to the top of his chest. "Please, you have nothing to fear. I am a stranger who has come to seek work, nothing more."

"You have a strange way going about it, creeping in the brush like a madman." She tucked a lock of brown hair under her white cap.

How odd to call him mad when she had been carrying on a conversation with no one in particular. He reached down, picked up her bundle, and handed it to her. She snatched it from his grasp without a thank-you.

"I am wondering… I saw you come from the castle. Is the prince in need of an extra hand? I am good with horses."

The lovely maid lifted her delicate nose into the air and lifted a brow. "You say you are good with horses and yet you come to Hanenburg on foot. I find that a bit strange. Besides, I do not know what goes on in the castle."

Her eyes shone fear as she added that last bit of information. Ah, she knew more about the workings in Hanenburg Castle than she was willing to share. If he could give her a little more push, then perhaps her lips would loosen. "I only thought that a pretty maid as yourself would hold some sway with those within the castle. If you could vow for me—"

"Vow for you? I do not even know your name," she cried.

Clearly not a vain woman for she did not acknowledge his words about her beauty. Nor was he ready to reveal his identity. Asher raised his hands. "Please forgive me. I am desperate. I am a long way from home. I have not eaten in days. I only seek honest work. Please, I have no coin."

The woman bit her lower lip, and her gaze darted about. "We have many strangers living among us. The more that come, the less the villagers like it. Work is hard to come by for all—German or..." She narrowed her gaze. "Nonetheless, I will not have your sad soul on my conscience." She reached into a small purse tied around her waist and pulled out a coin. "I cannot help you get into the castle, but I can give you this."

She held out the coin, and Asher's gut rolled. He had a heavy purse filled with more coins than this woman would probably see in a lifetime. He would have to use a different tactic. The maid was young, but not too young to not be married. Perchance she had a husband who was deeply involved in the Champions of Christ.

Asher shook his head. "I cannot take that from you. That would be too much. However, a warm bowl of pottage would be nice. I do not think your father or husband would mind."

Her eyes grew wide, and her face filled with horror. Had he muddled the translation?

The maid began to shake. "I am not married, and my parents are dead. You cannot..." She threw the coin on the ground. "Here. That is all I can give you." She lifted her skirts to show delicate, well-formed ankles before she dashed away down the road.

Perhaps he could have handled that better. Usually the women would lap up his sad story, but then, he was not German, and as the sweet maid said, the town was overflowing with strangers. English Protestants to be exact. Hopefully, none that he knew. Asher lifted his eyes to the heavens. "Lord, let all here be unknown to me for I do your work. Let your mighty Church stand forever."

He then bent over and picked up the coin, tossing it into the air before tucking it into his doublet. Certainly, they would meet again for there was something intriguing about the lovely woman.

Jane rushed away from the handsome, tall, and terribly frightening man. A foreigner to be sure. Perhaps it was just by chance that he sprung out of nowhere and engaged her in conversation, or perhaps it was by design. After what Prince von Hoffbauer told her, anything was possible.

Of course, she should have invited him to break bread with her, but her fear and caution turned her thinking. The man could have been from England, a spy or worse yet an assassin come to finish her off. Why, even when she asked about his name, he changed the subject and talked about a long journey and an empty belly. He also could have been a villain, running away from some dastardly crime.

Guilt niggled in her mind. Or he could just be a poor fellow seeking honest work as he said. He did not want her coin…yet that could have been a ruse to get into her home, hoping to gain more. Oh, her head ached with the possibilities.

All her worry made her feet fast, and before she knew it, she was standing at the cottage door. Matilda mooed from the shed, and a few chickens strutted about the yard. Nothing was amiss. She had been a ninny, letting the prince's words get the better of her. Still, her mind did worry and played out every possible scenario.

Jane tossed the bundle of mending onto the table and stared out the window at the setting sun. Where was Hildegard? Surely, she would have some answers once she heard what the prince said. In Jane's mind there was only one thing to do—leave, the sooner the better. Every day there were more strangers coming to Hanenburg, and now the prince had put out the call for fighting men. Queen Mary's spies might be lurking here already.

Jane made a fire in the hearth and jabbed the logs with an iron poker. She would have to be more cautious. She closed her eyes and muttered familiar words. "Trust no one."

The moment Hildegard returned, the whole conversation with the prince poured from Jane's lips, and the tale did not stop until she came to the part of the strange man on the path. There Jane paused. If she said much more, then perhaps Hildegard would think every word uttered was a young woman's hysteria.

"What shall I do?" Jane cried. "I cannot reclaim the throne, I gave Queen Mary my word, but I cannot let Mrs. Ellen die either. Do you know how many lost their lives trying to keep me on the throne? I have seen enough bloodshed for a lifetime."

Hildegard untied a slim knife she wore hidden in her skirt and searched in the larder for some dried pork. "I do not know what to say, the prince's plan does sound foolish, but he is an intelligent man."

"Poor Mrs. Ellen, she suffers on my account. If I do not do something, she will die." Jane turned and slammed her hands on the table. "Why? Why does God keep testing me so?"

Hildegard jabbed the thin knife into the meat and then rested her hands on the table. "We cannot question God's will. We can only seek to understand His plan."

"Then tell me, what is your understanding? For I have none."

Hildegard wrinkled her brow, letting her hands slide to her side. "Perhaps the prince is doing what God wants."

"Inciting a war? Do you truly believe that God wants a war with England?" Jane's blood boiled, not out of anger at God but because she could not find a solution that would not harm someone. "I wish I had never been born."

Hildegard reached across the table and grabbed Jane's shoulders, giving them a shake. "Do not say such nonsense. God has given all life a purpose, and yours more so than others. This is not about you and what you want. This is about Mrs. Ellen and others who may die trying to carry out the prince's plan."

Hot tears rolled down Jane's cheeks "You are right. I am being selfish."

"Oh child, you are not. Things are beyond our control, unless..." Hildegard dropped her hands and cast her gaze to the thin roof.

The single word dried Jane's eyes and lifted her spirits. She looked up hopefully. "Unless..." she encouraged.

"Prince von Hoffbauer wants you to march back into England and take control, but what if you go along with his plan to a point? I do not think he wants to march on England as much as he would like to strip away Habsburg control of the German principalities. Prince von Hoffbauer sees you as a way to build his army, to force the Habsburg hand. The knowledge of such an army coming Queen Mary's way might well make her relent.

Perhaps let Mrs. Ellen go if a proper demand is made without issue."

"You truly believe this? I could see the whole Habsburg Empire, England, and the southern German principalities making a strong alliance against us. Nay, that is not the answer." Jane rubbed her temples. "I must go back to England alone and hope for the best."

With a heavy sigh, Hildegard sat down. "I will go with you but wait before you do thus. We have some time. You said yourself Mrs. Ellen's trial has not even started. I am sure God will give us another answer. Wait on the Lord. Come, let us pray."

Jane sighed inwardly and kneeled next to her aunt. Daily prayers were affected, but at times God did seem so far away. *Heavenly Father, give me a sign. For I know not what to do.*

Chapter 5

Asher lifted his keen eyes to the Growl Bear, the sound of merry voices within drifted across the village square. If this German establishment was anything like English publick houses, then this would be a good place to make a few good rebel friends.

He pulled his worn red cap over his dark eyes and adjusted the drab, moth-eaten doublet on his chest. For good measure, he knelt down, spit into his hands, and scooped up a fair amount of dirt, rubbing it into his cheeks. An inkling of trepidation snaked down his back. Unfortunately, Asher spoke the German language terribly. There were so many different dialects. He could not pretend to be a good German Lutheran—his speech would give him away. As usual, he would play the zestful English Protestant hiding from the queen as he did back in England.

If he were humble, he might gain the trust of the town's people and slowly infiltrate their Protestant meetings as he had done so many times back home with great success. Surely, there was not that much difference between a German Protestant and an English Protestant? A rat in any country is still a rat.

Asher hefted his satchel over his shoulder and made his way to the inn. He had the true faith on his side. The Blessed Virgin Mother would help him and keep him safe. He could not fail.

To his surprise, when he entered the Growl Bear few conversations stopped or even dwindled. Both German and English were spoken freely among the patrons. A small number of merrymakers looked his way, but none lingered on his presence long. He walked to the small bar situated in the back of the inn and dropped his satchel near his feet. Standing behind the bar, a buxom, blonde-haired maid smiled but did not offer further greeting.

"I seek a place to sleep," Asher said in broken German.

Her smile drooped as her hazel eyes scanned the room behind him. "Can you pay for it?" she rapidly fired back in German.

A man who lived in the shadows always knew when trouble stood near. Asher leaned sideways against the bar as he scanned the room. Perhaps ten men sat at a handful of tables. Most of whom were well into their cups. Certainly, most carried a blade or two. Asher could hold his own in a fight, but he was no fool, these odds were not to his liking.

Perhaps he should use the coin the German maid had given him earlier or he could use a different approach. Asher rounded his shoulders and tucked his chin. "I have come a long way, I seek your charity for I gave all I had to escape..." His English words were met with a stony stare, and the room grew quiet. Out of the corner of his eye, Asher saw a man with a grizzly brown beard nod.

The woman cleared her throat, wiped her hands in her apron, and came around from behind the bar. "You can have the room at the top of the stairs," she said loudly. She knitted her brow, and she glared at the man who had given the nod. "For one night only." She grabbed a tallow off a table and headed up the stairs with Asher in tow. A shabby wooden door stood at the top, which the woman pushed open with her foot. "I suppose you are hungry as well?"

Asher nodded, keeping his eyes averted. "Aye."

"I will send up some food and a brew." She looked over her shoulder toward the room below. "Be very careful, sir. Though there are many English here, strangers are always greeted with suspicion. Especially those who come without knowing a soul in the village?"

The hope in her eyes faded when Asher shook his head.

She pointed to a small rickety chair that sat next to an equally broken-down wooden table. "Use that to secure the door." She placed the tallow on the table and left.

Asher slid the chair under the latch. He then made his way over to the bed and sat. He pulled out his own dagger, placing it in the folds of the tattered blanket. The meal may or may not come, but one thing was certain, this eve would bring trouble to his door, and he would be ready.

The noonday sunlight streamed into the room through a lone window, and Asher gave out a loud yawn. The night had not been what he expected. The mistress of the inn, Liesel, a young widow, had indeed returned with a steamy plate of stew and a tankard of beer. He thanked her like a modest man and added a few words about her beauty, which she lapped up like a thirsty dog. Her favor won, he learned she was the owner of the Growl Bear, but she was guarded when he inquired about seeking work and possibly meeting others of his Protestant faith.

After Liesel left, he stared at the food without taking a single bite. How easy it would be to poison a stranger and dump his body in a nearby woods. Especially a man asking questions. Asher pulled out a little wooden cup from his satchel and added some of the brew. He then placed a small amount of the stew on the floor. He returned to lie upon the bed. The smell of a fine meal left unattended always brought unwanted furry visitors, and Asher had not been disappointed. In no time, a rat scurried over to the scraps on the floor and gobbled them up and finished off the small amount of beer as well. His nose twitched in the candlelight as he reared up on his hind legs, trying to figure out a way to get to the rest of the food on the table.

The rat scampered to the right and then to the left and then began clawing at the table leg, inching his body upward. Asher threw his blanket over the rat. The creature tumbled to the floor, squeaking and viscously tearing at the material. This relentless struggle went on for a few minutes until Asher was satisfied the rat would not die and the food was safe to eat. He stabbed his dagger into the thrashing hump hidden in the blanket. The rat stilled.

Asher kicked the blanket and the rat to the corner and then greedily ate the stew and drank the brew. When finished, he smacked his lips and wiped his mouth with the back of his hand. A finer meal he had not had in a long time. Now, with a full belly, he would wait for his two-legged visitors.

But they never came.

As the hint of dawn's light peeked through his window, Asher thought it was safe to close his eyes. Rarely did the devil's henchman work in the brightness of the day. He slept soundly and was surprised that Liesel had not been banging on his door a few hours later— unless keeping him here was part of the plan. Swiftly, he grabbed his satchel and made his way to the door. It swung open easily. He headed down the stairs to an empty tavern. Wariness pricked the back of Asher's neck when he called out and no one answered.

Seldom had he found an establishment that served spirits to be empty and certainly not at noon. The only time he had ever known such a thing to happen in London was during a hanging or burning. Even though the room was cold, Asher broke out into a sweat. He knew the Germans had such punishments, but he did not think they were prevalent in a small village like Hanenburg. Nor had he witnessed any preparations for such an event in the town square.

With long strides, Asher made his way to the door. The voices of merry villagers greeted him and settled his fears. Small tables with fluttering canopies circled the square. People hustled about and gathered around the tables. Men and women alike called out, hawking their wares. An active town market had sprung up around the well.

Perfect. God truly must be behind this plan.

What better place to pick up information? He strode around the square, examining the contents on each table. Bread, fish, chickens, squirrels, marinated kraut, and dried fruits were being sold. Along with blankets, tapestries, eastern spices, wooden wares, and tools. Never had he seen such a rich market, not even during a festival, let alone at the beginning of spring. How did a small town come upon such things? Even in Frankfurt, one would be hard-pressed to find such goods.

Asher's stomach growled when he spotted a handsome woman of middle years selling loaves of bread, cheese, and a strange-looking poultice. "Good day, Mistress, I would like a small piece of bread and a hunk of fine cheese," he said in broken German.

Her eyes lit up when he pulled out the coin the maid had given him yesterday. "*Ja,* of course. Would you like some fresh milk to wash it all down?"

He shook his head when the woman held up a pitcher. "The food is fine. Is this a festival day?"

It was the woman's turn to shake her head. "*Nein.* At the end of every week from early spring to late fall the farmers and some merchants bring their food and goods to the town square." She glanced around. "Some days are more active than others. We barter, sell, and trade. This way, no one starves when the winter winds blow."

"A smart practice to be sure, and how does your prince feel about this?" Asher popped a large piece of cheese into his mouth as he watched the woman's gaze shift to the castle rising above the town.

"He profits the most." She pointed to a man of wide girth sitting at a table underneath a budding tree. Two guards flanked him. "That is the prince's tax collector. None leave this square without settling with him first."

"I had heard things might be different in the northern German principalities, but perhaps they are the same as in England. The nobles always profit."

"So that is where you are from. Now I see why you speak German so badly."

They both laughed, but she eyed him cautiously. Asher cast his gaze to the ground. "I grew up on a small farm, we were obliged to pay taxes often if not to our lord, then to the Church. We were always left with the scraps." He spat out the last words and then sheepishly raised his eyes. Her own gaze softened. How easy it was to sway the women.

"I know how hard it is to scratch a living from the soil, but that is in the past. My fortune changed when I came to Hanenburg." She leaned over the small table and patted his hand. "And your circumstances can change too, if you are a hard worker."

There. That was the entry he had been seeking. "Oh, I am, Mistress. Do you know of a place where I can get some work?"

She gave a short laugh. "First off, I think an introduction is needed. I am Mistress Hildegard Brandt, and just who might you be?"

Who might he be, indeed. He had always thought it better to keep it simple. The closer to the truth you were, the fewer mistakes you would make later on. What harm would there be in using his name? At least his first name. "I am Asher Blackwell, and I have come seeking a new life away from the Church's tyranny."

"Shh. Even here, we do not speak of such things out loud." A hand went to her throat, and her eyes quickly scanned the square. "Though most are enlightened in Hanenburg since the Peace of Augsburg, which gave us religious freedom, we still keep our beliefs somewhat private. There are plenty here who would happily slit your throat for such bold talk."

Asher slumped his shoulders and placed a look of contrition on his face. "If we remain silent, then the Catholics have won."

Once again, her gaze swept the market before she offered up another word. Her cheeks blushed when she spotted a ruddy-faced man of wide girth and a hearty smile coming their way. He raised a hand in greeting, and Mistress Brandt patted her own auburn locks. "Oh dear."

"*Hallo,* Mistress Brandt," the man called. "A fine day for our market, do you not agree?"

Her cheeks pinked all the more as she let out a strained giggle. "*Ja,* 'tis a beautiful day." Her eyes narrowed when she spotted his bandaged hand. "What happened?"

The man held up the appendage. "I cut it gutting a rabbit. But it is fine. Did not Ella tell you? She was the one who tended to my wound."

"She told me you had stopped by yesterday, but she did not say why. I thought it was to give her another boo..." Mistress Brandt stalled her words, a look of fright briefly splashed over her face. She turned to Asher. "Forgive me. I forgot to introduce you." Mistress Brandt then motioned to the older man. "Master Werner, this is Master Asher Blackwell. He comes from England."

The burly man removed his cap and gave a slight nod. "A pleasure to be sure. What brings you to our fine village?" he asked in English.

Asher opened his mouth to speak, but Mistress Brandt filled Master Werner in on all the details. Well, almost all the details. She did not say a word about fleeing the tyrannical power of the Church. Could this man be a Catholic sympathizer? If so, then perhaps he could be of help someday. However, it was too early to seek a friend among the wolves.

"Are you staying with relatives?" Master Werner asked.

The man fished for information. Asher dropped his gaze and tried to look guilty. "I do not know a soul in Hanenburg. But I had heard it was a safe haven for English Protestants. I am staying at the Growl Bear, but I fear I was not honest with the owner. I told her I had no coin for a room and food, but she gave me both anyway." A lie, but one that could not be helped. His full purse pressed against his chest.

"You came on foot?" Master Werner asked.

"I sold my mount to buy bread." A half-lie. He sold his mount in a neighboring town so he could observe Hanenburg from afar for a few days without notice.

"Ah, but you had coin for my bread and cheese," Mistress Brandt piped in.

"It was my last," he added quickly. "And I knew it was not enough for a room."

She stepped back and crossed her arms. "Methinks you are a shrewd young man, playing the timid soul."

Perhaps he had been too sure in his thinking when it came to this woman. Asher bowed his head. "I can assure you, I am without further means." Surely, God would forgive such falsehood since Mistress Brandt was clearly a heretic.

"Do you speak French?" Master Werner asked.

A mild sweat broke on Asher's back. He did indeed and fluently. A language he had picked up in the merchant trade. *"Oui, un peu,"* he said, stiffly in to hide the truth of his knowledge. "I care not for them or their language either."

"*Ja*, your French is as bad as your German," chuckled Master Werner.

Mistress Brandt's smile broadened. "*Willkommen* to Hanenburg." Asher sighed inwardly; he had won her trust. Still, he would keep his sheepish ways for a while anyway.

"*Vielen Dank,*" Asher responded, which brought a hearty nod from Master Werner. Victory! Approval from all. Oh, they were like young children so easy to please. Asher gave a humble smile and curled his shoulders a little more. "Do you know of a place where I can find work?"

Mistress Brandt and Master Werner exchanged a readable communication, and Asher could not be more satisfied. "Go to the blacksmith," she said. "Tell him I have sent you and that you are in need of work. I am certain he has a task or two for you to do." She then returned the coin he had given. "Here. You will need this. Tell Mistress Sommer at the Growl Bear that I said this should be enough for another night's stay. Good day to you, Master Blackwell."

Master Werner put his hand on Asher's shoulder. "I will introduce you to Master Schmitts, our smithy. He is a fine man and always in need of help. Do you know how to wield a hammer?"

"Aunt Hildegard, Master Werner!" the maid Asher had met yesterday called from across the square.

Master Werner tightened his grip on Asher's shoulders. "Ella," the older man said softly.

Mistress Brandt placed her hands on her hips. "What is she doing here? I told her to stay home and make another batch of poultice."

"Come along, Master Blackwell," said Master Werner, pulling on Asher's sleeve. "We best be getting on. We have no time for more women talk."

Why ever not? Asher would indeed enjoy talking to the fair maid, but Master Werner seemed adamant on leaving. Asher relented, but not without reservation. Why didn't they want him to talk to the young maid? What did she know?

Master Werner tugged on his sleeve again. "Come, we must go."

Not wanting to miss out on a golden opportunity, with rigorous steps Asher followed. Yet he could not help but look over his shoulder at the petite maid with longing. Perhaps God would grant him a few hours with the girl in the future. Once again, his gut tugged. An instinct that told him his prey was near.

CHAPTER 6

Days stretched on and still Hildegard would not give her consent to leave Hanenburg. Pieces of worrisome information drifted in daily, filling Jane with anxiety. Yesterday Hans Mueller added to her stress. Apparently, Prince von Hoffbauer had told the Champions of Christ that Lady Jane Grey was alive and was living nearby. Thankfully, the prince did not say where. However, the group was anxious to meet her. Once the rebels knew, the whole village would know. She wouldn't be surprised if the prince announced her identity at Sunday meeting.

Jane wondered what Hans would say if he knew it was her. The thought of telling him had some appeal—he might stop trying to woo her. So far nothing had worked to prevent his attraction. Even scolding him for being part of the Champions of Christ had not scared him away. Hans just laughed and said half the town was part of the rebel group.

Time was running out. The prince wanted to meet again and discuss just how to introduce her to the Champions of Christ without causing a town uproar. Through it all, Jane would listen to his plan and nod her head like a docile maid, but come next Sunday, she would leave and return to England without the prince, his army, and if necessary, without Hildegard. If God was merciful, Queen Mary would take one life for another. And this whole talk of marching on England would die with her. Jane took a deep breath. Once again, she would prepare for her death.

The heavenly angels must be smiling upon him. Asher sat in the Growl Bear with a full plate of pork, kraut, and a large mug of beer in his hand. At the mention of Mistress Brandt's name, the blacksmith, Master Schmitts, gave him work and Mistress Liesel Sommer gave him the best seat in the inn. Asher silently congratulated himself. In a week's time, he had become an accepted man in the community, even without family ties in the area. The success was beyond his own expectations. Rumors swirled that the prince was secretly building an army in the countryside. Indeed, the prince had ordered a large amount of weaponry to be forged. Asher alone had hammered more axes, daggers, and rapiers than he could count since starting his employment.

A strong wind blew in a heavy rain, and the Growl Bear had few visitors this eve—a drunk, resting his head on the bar, and a couple in the middle of a lover's quarrel. No matter, tomorrow he would gain more information from the blacksmith as he had every day. Oh God truly did give favor to those who were patient.

The door to the inn blew open, bringing in the rain and a man draped in a dark cloak. Asher recognized him immediately as the man who sat at the corner table the night when he arrived. As the man removed his cloak, Liesel brought him a tankard of beer. He nodded to her before he took a healthy swig.

Let it never be said that Asher passed up an opportunity when he saw one. He picked up his own mug and plate of food and made his way to the man's table. "Terrible weather," Asher said in German, placing his food and drink down before pulling out a chair. "Name's Asher. Asher Blackwell."

The man rubbed a hand over his grizzly beard without uttering a word. His beady black eyes held no greeting. Slowly, he picked up his beer and took a drink.

Asher did the same and smiled. "You live in the village?"

Again, the man said nothing and just glared at Asher.

Perhaps he had been too zealous. Better to move slowly than to rush and risk exposure. "Not much to say, eh?" Asher picked up his plate as he would gain no information here or at least not yet. "Then I shall let you be."

The man's hand snaked out and grabbed Asher's wrist. "Sit back down." The gruff words were followed by a rough cough. The man wiped his hand across his mouth and then took another swill of his beer.

Asher eased into the chair and waited.

"You speak terrible German, Englishman."

Asher smirked. "So I have been told." He then pushed the food toward the man. "Would you like some?"

The man picked up a spoon and dug deep into the pork before shoveling it into his mouth. "Liesel is a good cook," he grunted.

"Better than I have seen in a while. Master..." Asher smiled, and the man did the same.

"Karl. The blacksmith tells me you are good with a hammer. Is that so?" The man took another mouthful of food.

"Aye. My father's farm was far from the nearest village. You learn to do a lot of things when you are on your own."

"And just where in England would this farm be?" asked the man.

"North of Norwich in Norfolk. I am sure you have heard of the area?"

"I have lived here all my life. What do I know of England?" Karl averted his eyes.

He lied. German, for sure, but his dialect was thicker than the others in Hanenburg. If Asher were a betting man, he would suspect Karl came from the south. Probably fled persecution years ago. If that were the case, then Karl was probably a member of the Champions of Christ.

"Perhaps if the blacksmith keeps me on, I can make this my home too. How are the women here?" Asher winked.

Karl laughed. "There be none that would be interested in you, Englishman."

Asher shrugged and took another drink while Karl ate the rest of the pork.

"They butchered my father and carried off my mother and sister." Asher let Karl digest his words. If this man were a true Protestant, he would know who "they" were.

Karl nodded, shoveling in the last bite of food. "I have a few friends that might want to meet you."

Asher could not believe his ears. This eve he would infiltrate the rebels. These Germans were bigger fools than he had thought. Slowly Asher nodded.

With a belch, Karl pushed away from the table and motioned with his head to have Asher follow him. By the Holy Mother, Karl meant to lead him to the group now. Swiftly, Asher grabbed his cloak and followed Karl into the pouring, cold spring rain. Without looking back, Karl took off; Asher followed as best he could. The thick mud slowed his pace, and the heavy droplets clouded his vision. Still, straight ahead sat the meeting hall.

Jubilation blinded his mind, and Asher did not see the first punch that landed across his jaw. Two men, maybe three, jumped out of nowhere and pummeled Asher to the wet earth. Each kick brought searing pain, and each punch brought him closer to oblivion. A swift kick to the head sent him into the blackness.

CHAPTER 7

A musical chorus of chirping birds serenaded Jane as she quickly packed her satchel. She had to work fast before Hildegard returned from Mistress Meyer's home. As much as she did not want to leave, Jane could not stay another day. Last night, Hildegard again tried to stall her departure. Who could blame her? Hildegard was a German, why would she want to leave her native land to go live in a strange country?

But alas, the prince was steadily building his army and perhaps soon he would introduce her to the Champions of Christ. Once her identity was known, she would never be able to flee with anonymity. She picked up an old brown gown and her mind flipped back to another stressful time in her life. When the gown she had been wearing was made of silver and gold, beaded with pearls and diamonds—her wedding gown. What an awful time in her life, being forced to wed a man she did not love.

A short laugh left her lips. Here she was again, being forced to do something she did not wish to do. Jane jammed the gown into the bag. Not this time. Never again would she be led about like a mule tethered to a grindstone. She reached for a pair of boots when she heard a rap on the door.

Not now. No doubt it was Hans come to cut some more wood they did not need. However, when she opened the door, she was surprised to find Otto Werner, out of breath, his brow heavy with sweat.

"What is the matter?" She stepped back from the door. "Come in and sit."

Vehemently he shook his head. "*Nein.* You must come with me." He pointed to a cart that stood outside the cottage. "I did not know what to do. So, once I told Master Schmitts, he lent me his cart. We thought you and Hildegard might be able to do something."

Hildegard. Never had the preacher used such a familiar address. It had always been Mistress Brandt.

He pulled at her arm. "Come quickly."

Jane rushed to the cart and gasped. In the bottom lay a man covered in mud and blood.

"I found him lying face down in the muck between the meeting hall and the weaver's shop. I shouldn't have brought him here, but Hildegard is the only healer in the village." Otto Werner shook his head. "This should not have happened. A beating this bad was unnecessary. I thought he was dead, but then I heard a gurgle from his throat."

She wanted to point out that a gurgle could be a death rattle, but the stress on *Doktor's* face stayed her words. Clearly, he knew more about what happened to this man. No doubt his rebel group was involved. "We need to get him into the cottage."

"*Ja,* we can try. Is not Hildegard about?"

"She went to Mistress Meyer's. We will have to manage on our own. You take his shoulders, and I will take his feet."

With care, they tried to lift him up. The man moaned, confirming that he was indeed alive. A tug on his legs also established that he was heavier than he looked. They pulled him from the cart and placed him carefully on the ground. The man cried out but did not open his eyes. Blood caked the corners of his mouth. This could mean his injuries were deep within his body as well as on the outside. Jane feared the man would soon meet his maker.

She brushed back her hair. "We must get him inside."

A red-faced Otto Werner nodded and grabbed the injured man under his arms while Jane lifted his feet. Again, the man let out a painful scream. Jane lifted her eyes to the heavens. *Please, God, give us strength.* They shuffled to the doorway and managed to place him on her pallet.

Otto plopped into a chair and wiped his brow with the back of his arm. "You think he will live?"

She did not answer. A wave of metallic sweat oozed from the wounded man. She grabbed a cloth and tried to wipe the blood from his face. She paused; this was the man she had met outside the castle. Obviously, someone in Hanenburg did not want the stranger about, but to beat a man to such a state…it was unchristian.

The man moaned again and started thrashing about. "Quick, come here and hold him down," she called over her shoulder.

The preacher sprang to his feet and placed his hands on the man's arms. "He's bad off."

Jane nodded and made a quick assessment. "His face is badly battered, but his jaw looks to be intact. I think some of his ribs may be broken, but I cannot be sure until I remove his doublet and shirt. I am positive there are many more injuries we cannot see. His gut could be twisted since he has been punched senseless."

"Just what Hanenburg needs, another village idiot," Otto grumbled.

"Do we have one now?" she asked, glad to have something else to talk about besides the poor broken man. She swiftly finished wiping the blood from his neck and face.

"What are you doing?" another familiar voice called from the doorway.

Otto Werner looked up. "Hans. I was just thinking about you."

The humor was not lost to Jane, but they did not have time to laugh and debate Hans's mental abilities. "Go fill up a bucket with some water and bring it here. Then go to Mistress Meyer's house and get Aunt Hildegard," Jane ordered.

The muscular blond did not budge. He stood like stone, his ax over his shoulder. "What is going on?"

The man in the bed thrashed again. Jane rose and threw open a cupboard, grabbing a poultice and some strips of cloth.

"Did you not hear her? Go," shouted *Doktor* Werner.

That got Hans moving.

"And hurry up," Jane called before grabbing a knife.

"What are you going to do with that? Finish him off for good?" the preacher asked.

"Nein." She tore the knife through the man's doublet. "Help me get this off of him."

The pastor assisted without comment.

Within moments, Hans returned with the water. He stood in the doorway, his eyes wide. "Where should I put this?"

Jane sat down on a stool next to the injured man. "Next to me." Hans complied and then stood like a rooted tree.

"Go get Mistress Brandt," Otto roared. Hans jumped once again and hastened out the door. "He has to be the most witless man in all of Hanenburg."

"Do not let Aunt Hildegard hear you say that. She thinks he would be a good match for me." Jane dunked a cloth into the water and gently cleaned the man's chest. At least four ribs protruded against his bruised skin.

"You can do far better than Hans. Besides, I think Prince von Hoffbauer has other plans for you."

The mention of the prince and his plot caused her heart to race even more. She needed to leave, but she could not while this man struggled for his life. Oh, she hoped Hans would return soon with Hildegard. But even if she walked through the door at this very moment, no one would be going anywhere anytime soon.

At the very same time, Mistress Meyer decided to have her babe and Hans returned to the cottage alone. With no help from Hildegard, Jane patched up the man the best she could and prayed that God would do the rest. Otto Werner stayed for moral support, and Hans did what he always did best—chopped wood.

Jane rose from the stool and rubbed the small of her back as the sunlight faded away. "I think it would be best if you go home and take Hans with you."

The preacher frowned. A while ago he had found a small pitcher of beer and poured himself a cup. He also found some salted meat and dark bread. "*Nein*, that would not be proper to leave you alone with a strange man. Here, come sit by the table and eat something while I send the fool away who is hacking up all the yonder trees."

"Hans means well," Jane said weakly.

"Maybe so, but it is getting late, and you and this poor man need rest, free from all the noise." Otto left the cottage, and Jane took a seat near the table. It had indeed been a trying day. The easy rhythm of the injured man's breathing eased her nerves. The draught had worked. Now, hopefully, the healing would begin.

She wondered what this man had done to warrant such a beating. Once again, she marveled at his long legs and dark crop of curly hair. A day's beard covered his swollen chin. *"Please, God,"* she whispered. *"Do not let him die."*

"Hans is gone. Though he did not go easily," Master Werner announced as he entered the cottage. "Now you must eat, if not for yourself, then for that poor fellow who lies over yonder. For without you as his nurse, he will surely die."

A half-hearted laugh left Jane's lips as she watched the injured man take shallow breaths. "I think not. Aunt Hildegard would have better skill and knowledge."

Otto poured her a drink and pushed the plate of meats toward her. "I disagree. You handle all with such care and tenderness. I think God has called you to this type of work."

Really? If that were so, then why would He put such obstacles in her way? She ate in silence while the preacher watched the injured man intently. His interest was almost too keen. Could he have met the man earlier? A tingle of apprehension rode up her spine. 'Twas not interest that flooded his eyes, 'twas guilt.

Perhaps he could be persuaded. Jane took a small sip of her brew and stood. "A word with you outside."

With a nod, he stood and followed her out into the cooling late afternoon air. Large, dark shadowy clouds formed in the west. An omen of things to come. Jane shuddered.

"I can tell you nothing more than what you see. Strangers with no relation are never easily accepted in Hanenburg." Otto did not look at her as he spoke.

His firm stance and immediate explanation without a question made Jane pause. She cast her gaze to the sky above her, searching for the right words. "As sad as this man's situation is, that is not why I have brought you out here."

The preacher arched his brows but gave no comment.

"Have you forgotten that Prince von Hoffbauer has other plans for me? You know he is building an army."

"*Ja,* a grand plan, but I am thinking not a wise one."

Jane touched the pastor's arm. "You are our spiritual leader. Could you not sway him from such madness?"

"It is not all madness. The prince is right that if we do not stand up for our beliefs, Ferdinand and King Philip could well gather their own army to snuff us out. They are Catholics after all. However, I am not sure that Prince von Hoffbauer is following the will of God."

"You think this is all for power?" Otto's eyes softened. "My dear, no matter how noble the prince's principles are, power and pride always get in the way of a man's thinking. Very few walk away from it like you did."

A sting of guilt pricked at Jane's heart. "I did not walk away from it... I should have, but I was not strong enough."

He took her hand in his. "In England you are praised as a martyr."

His words did not soothe; Jane dropped her head to her chest. "And many died believing so. The true martyr was the woman who took my place at the block. What will the good people of England say when they find out I am alive? I tell you, I will not be loved and accepted with open arms as the prince thinks. They will curse me for the coward I am." She raised her gaze. "Please, can you not try? Talk to the prince."

Otto patted her hand. "All right, child. I will try, but do not get your hopes up. When pride grabs the heart, it is hard to wrestle free."

Oh, she knew that better than any other for at the English court there was no shortage of conceit.

Chapter 8

The next morn Jane awoke with not only a pain in her back but a crimp in her neck. Sleeping on a hard chair with a table to rest her head was never good for the body. Otto Werner had retired to the loft. Jane smiled. She wondered what Hildegard would say when she found out. A groan from the man lying on her pallet drew her to her feet. He had survived the night. The Lord was most merciful.

She made her way over to his side and sat on the stool next to the bed. More and more she wondered of this man's past. He said he was good with horses. Yet when she picked up his hand, there were a few calluses but not many. These were not the hands of a man who spent his life in stables.

He groaned again, then muttered something. Jane bent near to hear his words. "Save Audrey. Please do not harm her."

French words! She gasped. Perhaps her earlier thinking had been correct. A spy would definitely incur a beating. But a Frenchman in Hanenburg was as rare as a visit from the Pope. If he were French, his heritage alone might provoke others to violence. Most who lived here sought religious refuge. 'Twas why there were so many English about. But a Frenchman? Never.

A knock at the door stalled her thinking. "Come hither," she called.

The door swung open, and Hans and his ax filled the entry. *"Guten Morgen*, Ella."

Her spirits fell. She could not handle him stumbling about this morn.

"I was just wondering how the injured man was doing?" Hans briefly glanced at the bed with a concerned eye before he turned a bright, crooked smile on her.

"He is doing as well as can be expected. 'Tis terrible what men will do to another."

A sheepish look crossed Hans's face before he dropped his gaze and his ax to the floor. *"Ja."* He then lifted his head, a livelier look in his eye. "Do you need some help? Perhaps I could chop some more wood for you?"

The Lord save us. No more wood. "I think we have enough. The days will be getting warmer, and we will not need as much until this fall. Does not your father need you to turn the soil for planting?"

Hans shrugged. "He has said nothing. I think he means to wait until the ground is softer. Are you sure you do not need some wood chopped?"

Jane had to resist rolling her eyes. The firewood pile stood higher than their cottage. "We have plenty wood, but perhaps you could go down to the stream and do a little fishing. We have not had a good trout in a while, and I am sure Master Werner will be hungry when he awakes."

Hans frowned and shifted his gaze to the loft. "He should not have stayed here with you. People will talk."

Jane rose and put her hands on her hips. "Shame on you, Hans Mueller. He is Hanenburg's spiritual leader. No one would think such a thing, nor would anybody know unless you open your big mouth."

Hans opened that mouth and gaped like the fish she suggested he catch. His eyes all but bulged from his head. "I did not mean—"

"Now, go and get us some fish." Jane waved to the man in the bed. "I have much to attend to here."

Without another word, Hans nodded and took off toward the stream. At least she would not have to put up with him for a while. She turned her attention back to the man on the pallet. This Englishman or Frenchman clearly has a sweetheart named Audrey. In truth, there was something about him that did not sit right.

Jane spied the doublet she had cut from his body yesterday. She glanced at the loft above her, long low whistles drifted in the air. Good. *Herr Doktor* slept. Quickly she picked up the doublet and began rifling through it. Nothing. She tried again. Her hand paused on a lump. Two pieces of cloth had been sewn together to form a secret compartment. Jane took a knife and cut open the lining. A small bag popped out. She opened the bag to find it filled with coins: German, French, and English. Her insides dropped to her toes. What is this? He told her he had naught.

"Is this the man Hans spoke of?" Hildegard swept through the doorway, dropping her apothecary bag onto the floor. "How does he fare?"

Jane swiftly tucked the man's purse into the folds of her skirt. "He is breathing. How is Mistress Meyer?"

"She has a fine son. Let us pray it is her last, but I fear Master Meyer may have other plans." Hildegard sighed and placed her cloak on a peg near the door. "Now then, let us have a good look at this man." A long gasp escaped her lips when her gaze fell upon his form. "May God have mercy." Delicately, she pulled back the blanket. "I see you have bound his ribs."

"*Ja,* and I have put a herbal poultice on the wounds on his face and body." Jane pointed to the man's bruised belly. "But I fear what we may not be able to see. His middle is quite sore."

Hildegard let out a deep breath before placing a hand on the man's brow. "He is warm as well. Only time will tell us more. Has he said anything at all?"

The man moaned; Jane clenched the coin bag in her fingers. The eagerness in Hildegard's eyes made her cautious. "*Nein.* Nothing."

"Are you sure?" Her words were so intense. Could she see the lie in Jane's eyes?

"Mistress Brandt, is that you?" Two legs dangled over the edge of the loft before their owner descended the ladder.

Wide-eyed, Hildegard looked at Jane. "Is that Master Werner?"

Heat rushed up Jane's neck. "*Ja,* he offered to stay the night to protect my virtue."

"May the Lord help us. Others might not see it that way," Hildegard whispered.

With a thump, Otto's feet hit the floor. "Ah, Mistress Brandt. How are you this fine morn? I hope all is well with Mistress Meyer?"

Hildegard cleared her throat and turned a light pink before brushing a hand through her hair. "She is fine. She had another boy. I am surprised to find you here."

His gaze dashed between Hildegard and Jane. "Well, I did not think it would be proper to let your niece here alone with this…" He coughed and cast a glance to the man in the bed. "I mean with a man."

Hildegard cast a wary glance at the man on the pallet. "From the looks of him, I am sure she was quite safe. He took quite a beating. More than any man should have." Her words were sharp as if their preacher were the cause of this man's condition.

"It is a blessing that Master Werner found him," Jane defended.

"Indeed." Hildegard firm gaze never wavered from the preacher's anxious face.

"Hans was lurking about the cottage too," Otto blurted out.

"Hans! What goes on here when I am gone?" Hildegard huffed, folding her arms across her chest.

"He came by earlier this morn. I sent him fishing," Jane added.

"Indeed," Hildegard said again, narrowing her eyes. "Well, I am here now. So, you need not worry about Ella's virtue any longer."

Hildegard used Jane's false name in front of Otto. Obviously she feared the man in the bed could hear the conversation. Hildegard had always been cautious when it came to Jane's safety. Just like her dear Mrs. Ellen had been.

The preacher bowed his head, returned to the loft, searching for his shoes and hose. Once found, he descended the ladder again and stood with his cap in hand. "Well then, I bid you all a good day." When Hildegard did not offer a single word, he stumbled to the door and was gone posthaste.

Jane stared at the empty doorway. "He should have broken his fast with us. I think he stayed in hopes of seeing you. Why were you so agitated with him? It was not his fault that this man was beaten."

"Maybe not, but Hanenburg is a small place where very little happens, and any tiny morsel of gossip is readily gobbled up. He should not have brought the man here."

"Perhaps." Jane turned back to the bed. "I wager it was done by more than one man."

Hildegard remained silent. The dark circles under her eyes bespoke of a night without sleep while Mistress Meyer brought another babe into the world.

"Rest a bit. I will keep an eye on him," Jane said.

"And you have had a lot of rest last eve?"

Jane shrugged and looked at the tall man on her pallet. "I have watched him this long."

Hildegard sighed and nodded. "He is the first you have cared for without me. I understand." She made her way to the loft ladder. "All right. I will go and rest for a few hours, then you shall. By the looks of him, if he makes it, he will be here for some time."

The man flipped an arm above the coverlet and groaned. Oh, he had to survive, and Jane planned to be here to make sure he did. *Dear Lord, you have said all life is important. Please place your mighty healing hand upon this man, your servant. For surely you have brought him here for a reason. Heal him so he may fulfill his destiny.*

When Jane's turn for sleep had come, it was fitful. At first, she blamed her restlessness on being overtired, then she accused the moaning man below. She tossed and turned, muttered and complained, but sleep evaded her. Finally, she must have dozed for when she did awake streams of late afternoon sunlight filtered through the cottage windows.

Her foul mood had not improved with rest. The truth of her trouble lay before her—she had lied to Hildegard. The injured man did speak, and she took a purse filled with a great deal of coins that did not belong to her. Jane's past had taught her to be careful, but Hildegard was not the enemy.

There was only one thing to do. Jane brushed her hair and then placed her white cap on her head. She hurried down the ladder with the bag of coins in hand. The man slept peacefully on the bed, but Hildegard was not present. Voices from the yard drew Jane to the door. She stopped when she saw Hildegard talking to Hans near the woodpile.

"How could you and Karl have been so careless?" Hildegard spat. "He was supposed to be roughed up so he would leave. Not beaten to death."

"*Ja, ja*, it is all wrong. Wilhelm joined us. He would not stop." Hans kept shaking his head.

Hildegard took a deep breath, ready to continue her reprimand when she glanced at the cottage door. "Ella, you are awake. I thought for sure you would sleep longer."

They were party to this man's beating? Feeling like a mouse caught in a trap, Jane hid the coin purse behind her back. "I... I have slept enough." Her heart hammered in her chest as she stepped back into the cottage, tucking the coin bag into her cape that hung near the door. Once done, she moved to the doorway again.

Hildegard cast one last sharp eye at Hans before she hurried to Jane's side. "Did you see the fish Hans has caught for supper?" She touched Jane's elbow, ushering her back inside. "They are fine trout." Hildegard moved to the table to examine the fish. "We will eat like queens tonight."

Hans stumbled into the cottage holding his cap in his hands like a guilty child instead of the benefactor of the meal they were to have this eve. "'Twas easy fishing this day. I think tomorrow I will get some for my family and perhaps some more for you." He pulled out a long slender knife. "Would you like me to gut the fish?"

Hildegard grinned and pulled out an equally impressive knife. "*Nein*, I too have a nice blade that I carry with me all the time."

Laughter filled the cottage, and the man in the bed moaned and mumbled. Jane froze. Hans blanched. Hildegard gasped. Within moments, she began speaking to the man in English.

Pebbles of apprehension rolled down Jane's spine. "Did he speak before? In English?"

A warm, red hue settled on Hildegard's cheeks, and she forced a chuckle. "I—I thought I heard him mumbling in English earlier."

She's lying. Why? What is her part in all this?

"I best be going," Hans blurted, backing up to the door.

"Now?" Since their meeting, Jane had never seen Hans walk away from a free meal or her presence without being encouraged to leave. "But he is about to speak."

"*Ja*, but—but I have fish for my family…outside."

There was no fish outside. "Are you not interested in what he might say?"

Hans shook his head, twisting his cap over and over in his hands. Suddenly, Jane noticed the scrapes and bruises on his knuckles. Her throat went dry. Hans had beaten this man, and Hildegard was involved. Jane's heart cracked. 'Twas like being back in England where trust did not exist.

Chapter 9

Hans was out the door before Jane even had a chance to question him about his wounded knuckles. But that did not change the situation. Both he and Hildegard were hiding something.

The man's mumblings turned back into moans before he fell asleep once again. Hildegard shook her head and made her way over to the table. "I was hoping he was coming around. He is still not out of the woods."

"And he has never spoken before, has he?" Jane went over to her cloak and withdrew the bag of coins, throwing them on the table.

"What is this?" Hildegard opened the bag and clicked her tongue when she saw the silver coins. "He told me he was poor."

"You knew him and you did not tell me? Why?" Jane bit her lower lip at her accusatory tone. Was she any better? She had not told Hildegard about meeting the man earlier either.

Hildegard sat down, dropped the bag on the table, and rubbed her forehead. "I did not want to worry you. Your mind is always jumping to conclusions."

"And well it should. As it seems I can trust no one to give me the truth. But I must confess I have not been honest either. I met the man near the castle gate. He sought work and food. His eagerness made me wary. So I tossed him a coin with no charity."

"I first met him on market day. His name is Asher Blackwell, and he claimed to be fleeing Catholic cruelty in England. At first I thought nothing of it, but then later Master Schmitts, Karl Krumler, and Mistress Sommer said he had been asking a lot of questions about Prince von Hoffbauer."

Jane pondered her answer. This Asher Blackwell had said the same to her as well. "His actions are not strange. What peasant does not want to know what goes on in the castle on the hill? And if he truly is seeking protection, would not those questions be understandable?" Jane waved an arm in the air. "Think on it. How many questions did I have when I arrived?"

Hildegard averted her eyes. "He has no relation here. Why Hanenburg? He passed many a German town before coming here. Why did he not stop elsewhere? Others have said they saw him sneaking around the forest days before he entered town."

The hair on the back of Jane's neck pricked. He had sprung out of nowhere when she had met him lurking about the castle. She cast her gaze at the battered and bruised man lying on her pallet. A strong urge to protect him engulfed her. "Others. What others?" she asked.

"Some members of the Champions of Christ." Hildegard's last words came out like a whisper.

"The Champions of Christ!" Spirals of fear rose up Jane's back. Friend or foe, Asher Blackwell did not deserve to be beaten to death for being a stranger. "Oh, Hildegard, you above all should know not to believe everything you hear and especially from a group of zealots."

Hildegard's head snapped upward, and an affronted look entered her eye. "Take a look at this purse—English, French, and German coins. What peasant walks about with a full bag of coins and acts like a pauper? We cannot be too careful."

How true. The people of Hanenburg had heard the rumors that Lady Jane Grey was alive, but rumors were not facts, and many did not give them much weight. What would happen if they knew Lady Jane resided in a small cottage outside the village on the prince's land? All the more reason for her to leave.

Digging low, Jane fought for patience. "Whoever this man is, he did not deserve to be pummeled to death."

Hildegard's lower lip trembled. "*Ja,* you are right. Things got carried away. He was only supposed to be roughed up a bit. So he would leave."

"I cannot believe you were part of this. There is only one thing to do." Jane went over and took Hildegard's cloak off the peg. "I was supposed to meet the prince this eve. You will go and give him my apologies. Tell him I will not budge from this cottage until Asher Blackwell can walk out of here."

Pure terror rode over Hildegard's face. "I—I cannot. The prince will be furious. He could take this cottage away from us." She waved toward the man. "We do not know who this man truly is. He could be a spy. You could be in danger."

"Perhaps, however, that is how it shall be. And when you are done with the prince, you can tell the Champions of Christ that their lack of Christian charity may well have taken a man's life." Jane straightened her spine and held out Hildegard's cloak.

The older woman rose, sighed, and took the garment. "You should not be alone with him. He could be dangerous."

"Really? Do you think he will spring up and ravish me? I think not. The man cannot even lift his head without assistance."

With a nod, Hildegard wrapped the cloak about her. At the door, she turned back. "I am sorry. We are all just trying to protect you."

Jane nodded and then looked away. She could not bear the hurt in Hildegard's eyes. One thing was clear, both knew a strong friendship had been broken, and it would take a long time for it to repair. *Dear God, help me to not judge others but love them.* She looked at Asher's broken face. *This is all my fault. I should have stayed at the convent. This man may die because of me. Forgive me, Lord, for being so selfish.*

When Hildegard showed up at the castle with Jane's ultimatum, Prince von Hoffbauer was on his horse and at the cottage before Jane had a chance to sort out her thoughts. He dragged her outside, toward his horse. Jane locked her knees and stood her ground.

"You have no right to do this. I will not leave while a man's life hangs in the balance," she shouted.

"You will come with me immediately. It is not safe for you to stay here," the prince demanded through clenched teeth.

"Are you truly ready to reveal who I am to the world?" she whispered. "For surely that is what would happen if you cloister me in your castle. How long would it take for the news to spread? I wager that within a sennight Ferdinand and his nephew King Philip will know. Have you created a big enough army to march on the Habsburg Empire?"

The scowl on the prince's face clearly showed he did not. He pointed toward the cottage. "This man's presence is perplexing. If Queen Mary discovered our plans…"

Our? The prince's eyes became hooded, and Jane wondered what other plans were being hatched and by whom.

"Perhaps he should be moved to the castle where you and Mistress Brandt could care for him. None would think that to be odd. I shall send a—"

"Moving him will kill him, and I will not allow it. The man stays here and so shall I." Besides, she was not ready to reveal that he could possibly be French. She, too, had questions that needed answers.

The prince placed a gentle hand on Jane's shoulder. "My dear, that is not prudent. As he gets stronger, things will change. It could get far worse for you."

Jane pulled back. "I am not leaving, and you will not force me."

As if knowing things were only going to escalate into a damaging situation on all sides, Hildegard stepped forward. "I will be here and Hans too."

The prince's frown deepened. "Hans does not know who our dear Ella is, and I would like to keep it that way," he said quietly.

"Oh, worry not, Prince. We will take the utmost care Hans remains naïve of Ja… Ella's true heritage."

The prince did not look convinced, but wisely he did not force the issue further. Jane felt like adding that even if someone came right out and told Hans, the man would have a hard time believing it. As Otto once said, "Hans Mueller would have a difficult time finding his way out of a cottage with two doors."

"I want to know immediately when this Asher Blackwell regains consciousness and can speak with some intelligence. In the meantime, I plan to make some inquiries myself." With that, the prince headed for his horse. "I shall expect a report when you deliver my mending, before if he begins to make sense." The prince then turned to Hildegard. "If anything happens here, I will hold you responsible."

Hildegard flinched but then gave a stiff nod. After the prince left, she turned to Jane. "I told him nothing of the coins. I hope to God we have not made a huge mistake."

Indeed. Keeping Asher Blackwell at the cottage could prove fatal.

Days had passed since the prince's visit. Early April showers softened the soil and sent most of Hanenburg's residents to their fields, including Hans. It also became doubtful that their patient would ever gain his full faculties. Jane rarely went to the village and had not attended a Sunday meeting since Asher's arrival, which in hindsight was probably a blessing. How could the prince reveal who Lady Jane was without her being present? God truly did work in mysterious ways.

"I am going to town. I cannot make bread without flour." Hildegard sighed as she looked at the man who had taken nothing in but the draughts forced down his lips with a few sips of water. "I dare say, he will not last much longer. Perhaps I should go and tell the prince."

Sitting next to his bed day in and day out, Jane watched the cuts on Asher's face scab over and the bruises turn from a deep bloody purple to yellow. By all accounts he looked better outwardly, but he still cringed and mumbled when his stomach was touched, and his skin remained warm to the touch. "He may still recover."

Hildegard picked up a bundle filled with cheese and bread. "If he does, he will be daft in the head for sure. He's been in 'the sleep' for too long."

Last eve Jane had the same thought, so she cut the draughts by half. "He may still come around."

Hildegard grunted. "It is all in God's hands. I shall be a while. You will be all right alone? You know the prince would disapprove."

"I fear naught will happen this day." Jane picked up her mending. "We shall be fine."

Hildegard took one last look at Asher and nodded. "*Ja,* it would be a miracle if he woke up." On that she left, leaving Jane with her patient.

The steady patter of rain on the window and the crackle of the fire in the hearth lightened Jane's mood and sent her mind on a fanciful journey. She glanced at Asher and not for the first time noticed how fetching his features were. Oh, others might think he had a dark sinister look, but Jane thought them to be intriguing and mysterious. Would it not be grand if he were a dark knight come to save her from the prince's evil plan?

Together, they could jump on Asher's noble steed and leave all behind them.

She laughed inwardly. Asher had no armor, and there was not a steed in the yard. Nay, he was probably who he claimed to be, a peasant trying to escape Catholic persecution. Then she thought of the coins. More than likely, Master Blackwell was a thief running away from the owner of that rich purse. No matter, now she wished to pretend he was her husband and this was their simple home. The rain outside prevented him from working the fields, and thus he rested to gain strength to toil tomorrow.

A heavy sigh of longing left her lips. "Oh, if only it were true."

Asher mumbled, and his arms and legs began to thrash.

"You protest against my thoughts? You must be thinking of Audrey. Is she the one who holds your heart?"

His eyes fluttered open, then closed. Jane sucked in a deep breath. *Could it be?* She dropped her mending and placed a hand on his brow. Cool. *The Lord is good.* The fever had finally broke. Jane closed her eyes. *Thank you, Heavenly Father. Your mighty hand has done marvelous things.*

When she opened her eyes, two black orbs stared at her intently. A chill of fear whooshed down her spine. Jane adjusted her seating and grappled for her senses.

"Master Blackwell, I am glad you are awake. We were quite worried about you," she said in German. He seemed unfazed by her words. Perhaps… *Did she dare?* She repeated her words in French.

His gaze shifted to look about the cottage, only to come and linger on her face once again. Without offering a single word of understanding.

Perhaps if she tried English. "Master Blackwell, you have suffered some terrible injuries and have been asleep for a long time. But you are safe now."

He reached up and touched a tendril of hair that slipped from her cap. "Your name?"

She inhaled deeply but did not move. "I am Ella Brandt. We met outside the castle a few days past. Do you remember?"

His fingers slid down her face and then dropped at his side. "I thought maybe..." He closed his eyes and mumbled once again.

He must have thought of his love. Two things she had learned—he did not seem addled in the head from the beating, and he was, indeed, English. His speech was as good, if not better, than those at court. So, he could be a spy.

Quickly she picked up a mug of water and slowly lifted his head and shoulders. His eyes fluttered open again. "Here. Drink this," she ordered in English.

Again, his gaze cleared, and he parted his lips to drink. He reached out and cupped her hand, holding the mug to his dry lips. Another spark slipped down her spine at the warm touch of his hand. A satisfying sigh escaped his mouth. His eyes closed, and carefully Jane eased his head back to the bed.

He would live. Prince von Hoffbauer would want to know right away.

A rush of disappointment swept away her earlier musings. The prince would interrogate Asher Blackwell until the man was truly senseless. Jane reached over and tucked the coverlet under his chin. On all that was holy, she would not let that happen.

"Hush now. Say not another word," she whispered in his ear. "I will protect you."

CHAPTER 10

For a moment, after descending into hell, Asher believed he had found Jane. But alas, the woman was not the demon he was looking for. This woman, Ella, had given him a drink. From then on it was her face that loomed before him whenever he awoke. Her copper eyes, her shapely red lips, which seemed so familiar. Slowly, his memory returned, the pretty maid from the castle. Somehow, he had wound up in her care. When he would hear other voices in the room, she would whisper in his ear to keep his eyes shut—a sweet warning or a spell to keep him trapped in this unending purgatory.

When they were alone, she would sing and stroke his forehead like a tender lover. At those times, he wanted nothing more than to remain in her care. Then his gut burned and ached, and he knew he could not stay in this prison much longer. He opened his eyes and saw the woman tending a pot hanging in the hearth.

"El...la," he called.

Like a warrior called to the battlefield, her attention snapped to him. "You are awake once again." Her gaze flipped around the room and then fixed on the window, always checking, for what? "Are you hungry?"

"Aye," he said, trying to rise up on his elbows. "I think… I could try."

She scooped out a bowl of broth from the pot hanging over the hearth and brought it to him. "Do not eat too fast or too much. Your stomach may retch."

No doubt it would. Cautiously, he sipped the soup and let the warm liquid ease through his throat to his gut. He waited. When no complaint came forth, he tried yet another small slurp. This one settled nicely, removing the ache. "No…meat?"

She took the bowl from his grasp but did not move from the stool by his bed. "I do not think your stomach is ready for it."

"I cannot stay…here." Asher eased back down to the pallet.

Her lovely smile faded, and her gaze once again turned to the door. "I suppose not, but it would be best if you would rest and not speak for a while."

Possibly he had not been dreaming at all. This woman, this Ella, spoke with the authority of a woman of years, yet she could not be much older than eighteen or nineteen summers. Petite, with small delicate hands. If her hair was red and if this was a castle instead of a cottage, then he would think he had found his quarry. Then again, if he was hiding a deposed queen, this might be the perfect place.

Did she truly want him to stay and sleep his days away forever? Asher's gaze flipped to the bowl in her hands. Could it carry a poison or a draught that could suck the life from a man's body? But then a simple move brought an ache to his limbs and to his chest—he remembered. He had been waylaid by that man Karl and a few others.

"You saved my life." His simple words startled her.

A healthy glow filled her cheeks. "You owe your thanks to Master Werner. He brought you here. We just patched you up."

Ah, he remembered the portly man who seemed sweet on...what was the woman's name? He closed his eyes briefly. "We?"

As if the answer fell from heaven, an older woman walked through the door. Immediately Asher recognized her as Mistress Brandt from the market. "You are awake!" she said in German.

It was then that Asher realized he had been speaking to Ella in English and she had answered him in kind. His gaze shifted to Ella, her face pale and pleading. What the devil was going on here?

"*Ja,* Aunt Hildegard. Is it not wonderful?" Ella answered in German. "He even took some of your broth."

Mistress Brandt raised a brow. "And this is the first time he has awoken since—"

"That I am aware of," Ella lied.

Why would Ella hide the truth from her own aunt? But it had never been said that Asher was not cautious. He held his tongue.

"How was the market this day?" Ella asked, rising to her feet.

Hildegard dropped a small bag on the table without taking her eyes off him. "Was good. I sold all. Plus, I purchased some flour and a few seeds to plant in our garden. Has he spoken?" She pushed past her niece, hovering above him. "Master Blackwell, do you remember me?" she said in English.

Over Mistress Brandt's shoulder, Ella worried her lower lip. "Nay, I do not," Asher answered. Ella's face softened, putting Asher on further alert.

"I am not surprised," Mistress Brandt continued, this time in German. "Well, at least he seems to understand. Perhaps in time he will remember. I am not sure that is a good thing or a bad thing." She let out a heavy sigh and stared out the window at the pouring rain. "I think I can wait to go see the pr—"

"How about we bake some bread to celebrate! Our patient will live." Jane quickly pulled out a wooden bowl from a cupboard and began humming a merry tune.

Mistress Brandt watched Ella flitter around the small cottage, grabbing the flour and adding a bit of what looked like yeast. The older woman was not fooled by the tactic and neither was Asher. Where did Mistress Brandt need to go? Especially since she had just come home? And why did Ella not want him to know?

To avoid further questioning from Mistress Brandt, he closed his eyes. Possibly he could learn more when all thought he slept. Instead, they talked about the weather, who was at the market, and about the health of some of the villagers. Everything was discussed and nothing was discussed.

Finally, he did drift off and did not awake until the moon was full in the sky. From the loft above, he heard whispers. Try as he may, he could not make out the words. However, the rapid murmurs back and forth told him one thing: the ladies were in deep discussion, perhaps arguing. Answers were to be had here if he could be patient, and by the Holy Mother, he would get them.

The next morn, under hooded eyes, he observed a guarded household. Even though the day was pleasant and a cool spring breeze blew in through the open window, the room was steaming with anxiety. Once again Mistress Brandt and Ella talked in generalities, and every so often they glanced his way. When he fully opened his eyes, both women scurried to his side and stared at him as if he were the Divine Redeemer raised from the dead.

"Would you like something to eat?" Mistress Brandt asked in English, wiping her hands on her apron.

"A drink," he replied.

The older woman nodded and rushed to get him a cup of water from a small barrel near the cottage entry. "This was caught from yesterday's rain, so it should be safe to drink."

Asher raised himself up on his elbows. Immediately Ella propped folded linens behind his back, helping him to sit up farther. He nodded his thanks and then took the cup from Mistress Brandt's hands. The liquid sluiced down his parched throat and came to rest in his empty belly. "My thanks."

Mistress Brandt just nodded while Ella hovered behind her. The pair reminded him of two vultures sitting on a fence eyeing up a dying mule. Only these two wanted to pick his brain instead of his flesh. Well, they could wait a mite longer. He held up the cup. "More."

This time Ella reached past her aunt and refilled the cup. He drank it all and then handed the cup back to her before closing his eyes, but not his ears.

Mistress Brandt huffed but did not move for some time. When she thought that he slept, she stepped away and pulled the curtain that separated his pallet from the rest of the cottage. "Meet me outside," she whispered to Ella.

The girl said nothing, but the next thing he heard was a quiet click of the cottage door. In a flash, Asher opened his eyes and tried to sit up. His head swam. By the saints, he had to get out of this bed. Carefully, he swung his legs off the pallet and pulled back the drape. Instead of attempting to stand, he chose to crawl. Pain shot from his gut, his chest ached, and his thighs wobbled as he struggled on his hands and knees to the window. He clenched his teeth to still a groan with each move he made. By the hand of God, a small stool stood in his way. Sweat poured from every pore in his body as he used his forehead to push the stool toward the window. Once there, he heaved his body onto the stool and peeked out the window. As suspected, Mistress Brandt and Ella stood in the yard arguing. Asher turned his ear to the open window.

"We must tell the prince or there will be a high price to pay." Mistress Brandt huffed.

Ella put her hands on her hips and glared at the older woman. "I told you last night, if he is moved before he has the strength, he still may die. You know the prince will pound him with questions—the poor man could expire from pure exhaustion."

"Oh, you are being overly dramatic. The man is on the mend, anyone can see that. Are you forgetting all those coins? I say he is a spy and best we are done with him."

Asher placed his head against the cool cottage wall. Then he had not been robbed as he had first suspected. In his zeal to find Lady Jane, he must have gotten careless.

For here was the proof that he had been beaten because some thought him to be a spy. What made matters worse, these ladies had discovered his purse, though they said nothing of his dagger, which was missing too. Surely the villains that beat him took the weapon. Nonetheless, the ladies were overly cautious. Best he turned this situation around quickly or he could get his neck stretched by Prince Nikolaus von Hoffbauer.

"Wait a few more days. Allow him to heal. You said it yourself, he is probably witless. So where is the harm?" Ella pleaded.

"I am not sure on that anymore." Mistress Brandt threw her arms up in the air. "Ack, all right, but we must keep Hans away from the cottage. If he even thinks the man is awake, he will run to the prince."

"Perhaps not. Perhaps I can persuade him to keep quiet. There would be no reason for him to come here every day if Master Blackwell were gone. And you know how much Hans enjoys coming here to see me."

"You play a dangerous game. You know how that lad feels about you. It is wrong to give him false hope."

Ella placed a hand on Mistress Brandt's arm. "All will be fine. You will see."

A deep defeated sigh left Older woman's lips. "For you, I am doing this. But if I see one sign of danger, I will go to the prince. Do you understand? Only a few more days."

"Oh, *danke*. You will see. This is the better way." With a hug, the bargain was sealed.

The pair then turned and started coming back toward the cottage. Trying to hasten back to the bed, Asher toppled the stool and crashed to the floor. Even though his head pounded and his body screamed, he made every effort to crawl to his pallet before the door opened. He managed to make it to the side of the bed where he pulled himself up into a sitting position.

The door swung open. "Heavens. What is going on here?" Mistress Brandt asked in English.

Ella ran past her aunt and knelt down next to him, putting a gentle hand on his shoulder. "Are you all right?"

Her round copper eyes filled with concern. A light sprinkle of freckles graced her nose, and Asher wondered what they would feel like if he touched them. Unfortunately, he did not have the strength to do so nor did he have the vigor to answer her. He shook his head.

"Here, let me help you." Ella reached under his arms with her own. Her hair brushed his cheek, and a soft fragrance that reminded him of a spring shower filled his senses. She took a deep breath and leaned against him, trying to lift him onto the pallet. Being so tiny, she could not budge him.

"Oh here. Let me help." Mistress Brandt all but knocked Ella out of the way and hoisted him onto the bed with little effort. "There. Now maybe you can tell us what you were trying to do?"

Asher opened his mouth to speak, but Ella rushed to his side again, pulling a rough blanket across his body. "Do not badger him so. He has had a terrible ordeal." As if trying to protect him, she sat down on a chair next to the bed.

"Even so," Mistress Brandt said in German. "He was out of the bed and perhaps..." She glared at him and switched to English. "Why were you trying to get out of bed?"

"Go help, my—my father." He took an exaggerated breath and let it out slowly. "It is planting season."

"See. He does not remember where he is. He thinks he is back home in England."

The older woman folded her arms across her bosom and tapered her gaze. "Huh. I am not so sure. Master Blackwell, you are in Hanenburg. Do you remember why you came he—"

"Hallo," a loud voice boomed from the yard.

"Hans!" Ella jumped to her feet and made her way to the door. "I will distract him. You keep Master Blackwell quiet," she whispered to her aunt, but her eyes were on Asher.

The moment Ella left, Mistress Brandt hurried to the open window, peeking around the edge. From his bed, Asher could only make out a few words, but it what was clear that Hans was swallowing every single one of them. Men are such fools for a pretty face. Luckily, Asher had learned years ago that the more beautiful the face, the more wicked the heart. Yet, Ella did not seem to have a wicked bone in her body.

Asher tightened his jaw. He was not here to ponder on a young maid. He was here to kill a deposed queen, and the quicker he found her, the faster he could save his family and return to the simple life.

"I would love it if you would collect some eggs with me," Asher heard Ella ooze loudly.

"Oh sure."

The eagerness in Hans's voice made Mistress Brandt click her tongue and shake her head.

"But where is your basket?"

Within moments, Ella rushed back into the cottage, grabbed the basket off the table, and rushed out without a glance. The couple's laughter and voices drifted away while, once again, Mistress Brandt shook her head.

"She is playing a terrible game. All because of you." She turned an accusing eye on Asher, and he answered by closing his. He had no desire to be interrogated by anyone, and certainly not by the angry matron before him. Besides, he was not sure he could open his mouth without betraying any vital information. He needed rest to collect his thoughts and come up with a plan.

Mistress Brandt grumbled, then could be heard clanging around the cottage, but Asher did not dare look at her for he could feel her watching him.

It did not take long for Ella to return. "There was an abundance of eggs."

Asher peeked through his lashes.

Mistress Brandt focused her gaze on the basket. "We should send some home with Hans."

"*Nein.* Hans said they have plenty from their own hens. Perhaps we could give them to someone else."

"What is Hans doing now?" Mistress Brandt continued to count the eggs, putting some into a wooden bowl.

"I sent him fishing." Ella furrowed her brows. "I did not know what else to do with him. He brought his ax, and we certainly do not need more firewood. He also offered to fix the wobbly leg on our table. I told you you were busy making a batch of poultice to sell at the market, so it would be impossible to fix today."

"Which brings us back to the problem in the bed," Mistress Brandt whispered, casting a glance in Asher's direction. "What are we going to do when Hans comes back? He will be expecting us to feed him if he catches a lot of fish. How can we? What if Master Blackwell wakes up?"

Ella opened her mouth, but her words were interrupted by a shout in the yard. "Help. Mistress Brandt, please come and help."

Both women raced out the door, leaving it open. Asher had a clear view of the yard where an out-of-breath lad stood. "It is Mistress Meyer's boy," Hildegard said. The women rushed toward the lad. She squatted down to the boy's level. "What is it, Alfred?"

"Me *Mutter* is very sick, and me *Vater* wants you to come and look at her." The boy buried his head in Mistress Brandt's shoulder and began to cry.

She gave him a quick hug and then looked up at Ella. "Go get my apothecary bag."

Ella rushed back into the cottage, grabbed the bag, and lifted the basket of eggs off the table before she raced back out again. "Here. They might have use for these too."

Mistress Brandt nodded, taking the bag and basket. She motioned her head toward the door. "Are you sure you will be all right?"

"Of course. Do not worry. Hans is but a yell away." Ella tousled the boy's hair. "You better get going. Alfred's *Mutter* needs your healing."

With that, the pair took off toward the road. Ella walked to the cottage with slow, measured steps. It did not take a scholar to see that she was uncomfortable with the situation. Quickly he shut his eyes as she approached the doorway.

"You can open your eyes now," she said in English. "I know you are not sleeping."

Asher complied but said nothing. Patience. He had to exercise patience.

She sat down on a chair as far from the bed as possible, keeping her gaze fixed on him. "So, do not mix words with me. Are you a spy for Queen Mary?"

Interesting. She did not just ask him if he was a spy for England, she asked him if he were a spy for the queen. Was this whole village conspiring to hiding the traitor Lady Jane? He almost told her the truth, but the slight tremble of her fingers made him pause.

Instead he laughed and then winced at the pain that flowed from his ribs. "Why would Queen Mary send a spy here?" His words did not calm her but seemed to draw up an impenetrable wall.

"I do not know, sir. But the English among us claim she is a dreadful, bloodthirsty woman. They have made us suspicious of all strangers. Which begs me to ask, why do you have such a large purse filled with English, French, and German coins? I wonder why you lied to my aunt and me about being poor. For you are not. Are you French or English born? For you speak both languages well. Pray tell, can you answer these things?"

Damn his tongue. He must have spoken both languages in his delirium. A truthful answer had to be given even if the truth was slightly stretched.

Asher gave a penitent sigh and filled his face with remorse. "I am English. The French I learned from my mother who learned it from her mother, who was by birth French."

Ella said naught, her mind digesting his words. No doubt weighing the truth of them.

"I could ask the same of you. Are you German born? For you know English well, for a country maid."

Her cheeks flushed, and she dropped her gaze to the cottage floor. "Even poor German maids can learn other languages. I am not the one who has come to a foreign land for possible evil purposes." On that she raised her chin again, daring him to challenge her.

Truly she must have learned her English from a noble for it was clear with little accent. None of which is surprising for a maid who spent time in a castle. Yet, he could not shake the feeling that she was hiding something—something important. He slowly nodded and began to weave his story. "I will not lie to you. The coins belong to another." *Not totally a lie. The coins had been given to him by the queen, and some had been made when he sold his horse at a neighboring village.* "I left England because of the persecution. I feared I would be killed...like my brother." *Again, some truth. His brother did die, but it was Protestants that did the killing.* "I got to France. I ran out of money, so I stole the purse from a merchant. But it did not go well. I almost got caught. A hired henchman followed me across France. I feared for my life. That is why I told your aunt and you I was poor."

Asher was hard-pressed to find any truth in his last statement, but he had learned that the truth did not always set you free, but often true words could send you to the gallows. He closed his eyes.

"That is a nice tale, Master Blackwell, if that is your name, but methinks you have stretched the truth."

A sharp woman. Clearly Ella's solid heart was not easily swayed by sweet, sorrowful words. He opened his eyes. "That is the truth. What can I say?" He had uttered one simple sentence, and yet she seemed even less at ease.

"Mmm. We shall see." She placed her hand on the table, close to a sharp knife.

Holy Mary, Mother of God, did she plan to slit his throat? Perhaps another twist of the truth was needed. "I am a merchant's son. My father lost everything when he refused to convert to Catholicism. We were broke. I begged, borrowed, and stole to keep my family alive. I did not lie. They did kill my brother." All true except his father lost all long before Mary came to the throne, when he refused to become a Protestant.

Her fingers slid away from the knife. "Then you left England *after* you stole the purse?"

He nodded while he kicked himself inwardly; that is the tale he should have told in the beginning. "Aye. But I did not lie. The man wants my blood."

"Do you swear to this?"

His breath burned in his chest. These German women were not easily deceived. "It is a sin to swear. Do you wish to danger my soul?"

Acquiescence washed over her features. "Of course not." She rose to her feet and came over to the bed. "I have no choice but to believe you. Here. Keep your money. I am not a thief." She handed him the bag. "When you are well, you will leave, and I hope never to set eyes on you again. While you are here, I suggest you keep up the pretense of being addle a while longer."

"And why is that?" he asked as innocently as he could.

"You should know why. Unless you are ready to face the prince. Hanenburg is a Protestant... Lutheran village. We fight for our rights, for our souls against the papists that surround us." The copper in her eyes morphed into a bold bronze. "We protect and stand together. If you wish to stay in Hanenburg, you must give the people your loyalty freely. If you cannot, move on. For if you stay and are found to be a liar, I will be the first to help finish you off."

A large lump lodged in his throat. May the Lord protect him. He had no doubt she spoke the truth.

CHAPTER 11

The rest of the day proved to be uneventful. Asher Blackwell slept for most of it, but there were times Jane swore he watched her with those all-absorbing dark eyes. Now all that remained was to see if he was honest. Only time would tell, and only time would tell if he would stay in Hanenburg. Most that came here left within months. A dull ache settled within her. Asher Blackwell probably would be no different. This was a farming community. With the summer market, only a few merchants had managed to scratch out a living in Hanenburg. He had been working for the smithy, perhaps then he would stay—and get involved in the rebellion.

Jane sighed and tipped back her head, raising her eyes to the thatched roof. Why should she care one way or the other if Asher Blackwell stayed in Hanenburg? *Because he reminds you of home—of England.*

When Hans returned with the fish, she let him into the cottage. When he realized she was alone with a strange man, he railed at her like a Catholic priest. Through the whole lecture Asher kept his eyes closed and only opened and winked once when Hans could not see. Jane clenched her jaw and started preparing the fish for dinner, nodding as Hans's conversation turned to himself. He went on and on about how someday he would own his family farm, which was right next to the forest that had a lot of strong trees. Without a doubt, he was probably dreaming of cutting them all down. At times, his voice rose as if he were trying to make sure she understood what a fine husband he would make.

Asher Blackwell did not seem impressed either for he did not lift one eyelid. Truly she wanted to continue the simple life, she just had no desire to wed. One forced marriage in her life was enough. Still, her gaze drifted to the pallet in the corner.

Long after the evening meal, Hildegard returned home. Ella sent up a prayer of thanks. Hans on the other hand had the look of the devil. Unmistakably, he thought he would spend the night here in the guise of protector. Gad, what a juicy sweet that would have been for the villagers. They would be searching for the right log for the *Baumstamm sägen.* With Hans's fascination with wood, he would love sawing the large log in half with his wife. The thought curled like sawdust in Jane's mouth.

This eve did bring some happy news. Mistress Meyer collapsed because of exhaustion not because of some other illness. It seemed she had returned to taking care of her family too soon after giving birth. A problem that was easily remedied when Hildegard admonished the whole clan. Surely with all the strapping young men and boys in the Meyer family a few could partake in women's chores until their mother was fully recovered.

"I told the lot I would be back in the morning and their *Mutter* had better be resting or there would be some strong dealings for sure." Hildegard raised a fist.

"I told them I would live with them for a month if I had to."

Hans's countenance brightened at the prospect of spending more time at the cottage without a female chaperone.

Hildegard's face soured, reading the young man's thoughts. She quickly shooed Hans away, thanking him for his help, before slamming the door in his face. After he had left, she waved a finger at Jane. "I told you this was a dangerous game. On the morrow, I will send Hans to get Master Werner. It would be better for him to stay with you while I go to Mistress Meyer's."

A healthy heat rose in Jane's cheeks. "I do not need anyone to watch over me." She rose and went to the larder. "Are you hungry? I could prepare you a light meal."

Hildegard waved a hand. "*Nein*. I ate with the Meyers. I made a fine rabbit stew." Her eyes shifted to Master Blackwell. "You do need someone here. There are too many wolves around this hen house." On that Hildegard yawned, slapped her knees, and made her way to the loft ladder. "Do not stay up too late," she called over her shoulder as she ascended. "We have much to do tomorrow."

They would have the same amount of work as they did every day. Hildegard was just ornery because of her stressful day with the Meyers. Jane stoked the fire with a poker and then continued her mending, closely examining each stitch as she made it. As a child, she rarely sewed or worked on needlepoint, preferring to read and study. But she came to Hanenburg as a peasant, and a peasant girl did not read. Her gaze slid to the small trunk of books

Otto had given her. It had been days since she looked at those glorious words. Oh, how she would like to stick her nose into a little Plato tonight.

Jane's gaze snapped back to the man on the pallet, his stare on her. "You are awake," she whispered.

He nodded. His color looking so much better than it had earlier in the day. He pointed to the loft. A heavy rattle filled the air signaling that Hildegard was asleep. He then pointed to the door and tried to rise from the bed. Jane dropped her mending onto the floor and rushed to his side. She helped him put on his soft leather boots. Being a merchant's son must offer some benefits for every time she touched the fine leather she marveled at the quality. Had she noticed them when she first met him, she would have known he was not who he claimed to be. No wonder he suffered a beating, acting like a poor man when clearly his boots gave him away.

Jane wrapped a cloak around his shoulders. Then as slowly as possible, she helped him to his feet and out into the cool spring night. "This is madness," she whispered, guiding him to the woodpile. "If Aunt Hildegard awakes, we both will wish we were dead."

A low laugh left his lips as he rested his back against the timber. "I think I have been dead already and only now have been resurrected." He reached over and touched a lock of hair that had escaped her cap. "How fortunate I am that a beautiful angel was there when I awoke."

Heat shot to Jane's cheeks, and she hoped the moonlight did not betray her embarrassment. "You tease me, sir. I have never thought of myself as commonly, nor have others ever spoken such words. I have been told I am scrawny and too short."

"Nay, that is not true. You have high cheekbones and a noble nose. You are well portioned to your petite stature. In England, you would be a novelty. A beauty compared to the round or gangly females that comb the streets of London. Scrawny. Short. Who would say such things?"

Her mother, that's who. How often had she made Jane walk in the clunky high chopines to make her look taller? How often did Jane have to endure the pulling and stuffing of her bodice, giving her slight breasts an unnatural look? How often had her mother pinched and prodded Jane like an unruly mare? Too often. She would have gone mad if it had not been for her dear nurse, Mrs. Ellen. Jane tucked her chin and shrugged.

Asher placed two fingers under her chin, sending Jane's heart into a panic. "You may not look like most German girls, but you do have a loveliness in your own right."

Flames shot through her body. For surely he could feel her heart beat in his fingertips. Never had she been swayed by tender sentiments. Even when her husband, Guilford, tried to woo her, she had not been duped. Yet, here she stood drinking in this stranger's words as if they were the last she would ever hear. She stepped out of his reach. "Sir. You are too bold."

He rested his head back against the logs. "Aye, you are right. I have not been myself as of late. Forgive me."

Her shoulders relaxed. "It is understandable. Given what happened to you." She motioned to a large log on the ground. "Here. Sit."

With help, he sat down, his back still pressed against the woodpile. "My thanks, Ella."

Again, a warmth swept from her toes to the top of her head at his familiarity. However, she did not correct him for his impropriety.

"That is a lovely name. Is it your mother's?"

She snorted and regretted her rude act, after all, everyone believed her mother to be dead. "Nay. I was named after my dear... Aunt Ellen."

"Yet, you do not live with her? Is she dead?"

The thought of Mrs. Ellen dying in an English prison, or worse in a heretic pyre, brought tears to her eyes. She nodded and immediately regretted doing so; her simple lie might come to fruition.

He reached over and touched her hands. "I know how hard it is to lose someone you love. But take heart, God is merciful. We will see them again."

Oh, if that were true. If she could see Mrs. Ellen once more—on this earth instead of in heaven. Jane's throat clogged, and she knew she must change the subject or she would become a sack of tears. "You know Aunt Hildegard will turn you and your purse over to Prince von Hoffbauer. He knows of your beating and wishes to speak with you."

Asher made an effort to straighten his shoulders. "And I wish to speak with him."

"You do?"

"Aye. I want him to know I am not his enemy. I want to be part of the Champions of Christ. It is rumored the prince is their benefactor."

Jane pulled her hands away. All she wanted was peace, and here was another starry-eyed fool come to join the great Protestant cause to crush the Catholics and the Pope. Why could they not let well enough alone? "They are a dangerous lot."

"Aye. Methinks they are the ones who almost killed me."

"Then why would you want to become one of them?" She cringed when her words came out as an accusatory whine.

A small sad smile settled on his lips. "Have you forgotten? My brother was killed by papists' hands."

If weakness did not plague him, Jane would pummel his chest. She too at one time believed the best way of honoring and furthering the Protestant faith was to die for it. Instead, someone else died in her place. Forever that woman's blood would haunt Jane's mind and soul. "So, you would join a band of ruffians out of revenge? Tell me, once you have this revenge, do you think that will be enough? Do you think peace will miraculously appear in your heart and soul?"

Even in the moonlight she saw his features turn stony. His jaw clenched and his hands tightened into fists. "I am tired. Help me back inside."

He struggled to his feet and placed his arm around her shoulder as he hobbled back to the cottage. Not a word escaped his lips when he lay down on the pallet.

Jane stood above him, but he answered her presence by rolling onto his side, giving her his back. There was something dark that troubled Asher Blackwell. Perhaps in time, with kindness and goodwill, he would confide in her. If he did, possibly she could dissuade him from his deadly course. Maybe if he knew who she was...nay, it was too early for that. Way too early and probably never.

CHAPTER 12

Asher awoke the next morn in a foul mood. Once Ella had given up her watch and went up to bed, he spent the night tossing and turning. Her words played over and over in his mind. *Tell me, once you have this revenge, do you think that will be enough? Do you think peace will miraculously appear in your heart and soul?*

How well he knew there was no peace. That is why he did not want to do Queen Mary's filthy work anymore. Yet, here he was acting like a trained dog, doing her vile bidding. His family was counting on him; he could not let them down. His soul would have to endure more blood. Better he get on with the task, instead of hiding behind the skirts of the pretty Ella Brandt like an injured pup.

He breathed a sigh of relief when he found Mistress Brandt bustling around the cottage, preparing a meal to break their fast. "I was wondering when you would open your eyes. Did you sleep well, Master Blackwell?" she asked in English.

"Aye, I did." His gaze flipped around the room.

"She is not here. I sent her out to collect more eggs." Mistress Brandt wrinkled her forehead. "How fare you? Do you remember where you are?"

"I remember much." He struggled to a sitting position. "I am in the northern principality of Hanenburg. You came to my aid when I was set upon by ruffians."

She stopped stirring the pot of heated pottage and came to his bedside. "It was Master Werner that found you and brought you here. You were badly beaten. I am sorry. We are a small village. Many in Hanenburg fear strangers that have no tie to our hamlet."

"But you have Prince von Hoffbauer's protection. He is one of the most powerful lords in the north." He paused and intently watched—waiting for her reaction.

She dropped her gaze and simply nodded, offering nothing more.

"I came hoping to meet with him. I know that is almost impossible because I am only a peasant." Again, he waited as she slowly lifted her gaze and peered deeply into his eyes.

"Why would you wish to speak to him?"

"Because it is rumored he leads the Champions of Christ. I wish to join them." Sometimes the direct approach is the best, and Asher did receive his reward. Mistress Brandt clutched her hands together until her knuckles appeared white.

"I would not know about that. We have very little knowledge as to what the prince does and whom he supports. Though I suggest you keep your thoughts to yourself. They could be dangerous, and I wager your bold words were the ones that got you beaten in the first place. Mind your tongue. It could save your life."

Perhaps he had pushed too hard, too quickly again. "You are probably right. I just want to help the cause." He feigned a sad look. "A man can only hope."

117

She let out a huff. "Give it a few days and we will see how you are feeling. When Master Werner comes today, say nothing of the Champions of Christ. For now, let us keep that bit of information between us."

Truly, there were deep secrets here. Even Mistress Brandt seemed to be protecting him. What did she and Ella fear? Or what were they hiding? "All right." He looked toward the pot of soup over the hearth. "I am terribly hungry."

The tension seemed to ease from Mistress Brandt shoulders. She smiled. "I will get you some pottage. Would you like to sit at the table?"

"Aye. I would like to get off this pallet." With a sturdy lift, she guided him to the table. "My thanks."

The woman just chuckled and placed a bowl of pottage in front of him. "Eat. You will need your strength to heal."

Asher took a few slurps when the door opened and in swept Ella. Her cheeks pink and shiny from the morning air and her cap skewed to the right. What a lovely sight to begin the day.

She bit her bottom lip when she saw him at the table. "You are up," Ella said in perfect English.

He slurped more pottage into his mouth and nodded.

"It seems he has recovered his wits as well." Mistress Brandt placed a few slices of fresh bread by his plate.

"Has he?" Ella's eyes grew round and could not hide her disappointment that he did not heed her advice to act daft. The whole household seemed to think it was their duty to protect him.

"I told him not to do too much. He needs a few more days of our care," Mistress Brandt said.

Immediately, Ella's features relaxed. She placed the basket of eggs on the table and took off her cloak before sitting down next to him. "*Ja*. He needs rest." Mistress Brandt plopped a bowl in front of Ella, but she did not pick up a spoon. "When are you leaving to see Mistress Meyer?" she asked in German.

The prying query made Mistress Brandt frown. "When Master Werner comes and not a moment before," she answered in the same language.

"But that could be a long time. You know how Master Werner is, he gets involved with something and forgets the time."

The older woman sat down across from Ella and began eagerly eating her own pottage. "You are right. That is why you are going to go and find him."

"Me?" Ella's loud cry caused Mistress Brandt to purse her lips.

"*Ja*, you. I will not leave you here with this rogue," she said while pointing her wooden spoon to Asher. "Half-dead or not. Methinks he is a charmer and has already been working some of his talents on you."

Ella blushed from ear to ear, and Asher could not hold a smile. His German may be poor, but he understood their conversation perfectly.

"See there, that grin. He is no innocent. But you…" Mistress Brandt cleared her throat and stood, leaving her bowl of pottage on the table.

"I am not that hungry." Ella pushed her pottage away.

What the devil just happened? Granted, Ella had not lifted her spoon, but Mistress Brandt took to the meal like a sow at a trough. Suddenly neither of them had interest in their food. Perhaps it meant nothing or perhaps it meant everything, but for certain, the pair had more secrets than any king or queen in any realm.

Slowly Ella rose and took her cloak from the peg by the door. "Then I shall go." She raised her gaze to Asher's. "You should get plenty of rest. The more the better," she said in English.

"As soon as you are finished eating," Mistress Brandt pipped in, "I will help you back to bed. Rest. Sleep will make you stronger."

Clearly, neither lady wanted him to utter a word this day nor did they wish to see him on his feet. Well then, his questions would have to wait for the man who had saved his life. The faster Master Werner showed up the faster Asher would have some answers.

When he awoke again, a long curtain greeted his view and low voices pricked his ears. "I know not if he speaks the truth or if his tongue is filled with lies, but take every caution, there is more at stake here than the girl. If he is false, then the whole village may suffer," Mistress Brandt whispered.

"I wish to believe he is honest. For surely, God would not have saved him if he wished us harm," answered Master Werner. Finally. Someone who could bring sense to the secrets that swirled around this small cottage.

A creak of a chair and the shuffle of feet put Asher on alert. He could see under the curtain, the hem of Mistress Brandt's skirt moving toward the door. "I must go and speak to the others. Please be vigilant and say nothing to Ella. The less she knows the better." The door opened letting in a cool breeze, before it slammed shut.

Master Werner began to hum, tapping his foot to the tune. This lasted but a few moments, when he rose and could be heard rummaging through the larder. "Ah, here we are."

Asher followed the soles of his boots against the floor. He came to stand by the curtain, but he did not pull it back. He mumbled and then returned to his seat, placing a cup? A plate? Something on the table. It then sounded as if he were rifling through a bag. The man gave out another sigh of contentment when he seemed to find what he had been looking for.

"This might just be a fine day after all," Master Werner said to no one in particular. The chair creaked once more and then all became silent.

Anxious to end his boredom, Asher pulled back the curtain. Master Werner smiled. A frothy beer sat on the table and a small paper book rested on his lap. "Well *Hallo,* my fine fellow," he said in German. "Do you understand me?"

"*Ja,* I do."

The man placed the book on the table and then rushed over to help Asher sit up. "You look a mite better than you did when I brought you here."

"Then I am in your debt, for I would not have survived without the excellent care of Mistress and Maid Brandt," Asher replied in choppy German.

"*Ja,* they are a fine pair of women. As far as debts, I was only doing what any good Christian would do."

Asher looked around the cottage. "Where are the good women?"

"Mistress Brandt is going to visit friends and Ella is…in town."

Two lies? Perhaps. What a fine greeting, indeed.

The man's troubled gaze shifted about the room before he managed to control his features. "Would you like to join me in a nice brew?" His gaze slid to the table where his beer rested.

Asher nodded and maneuvered his legs over the edge of his bed. Master Werner helped Asher to a chair by the table. Before he could blink his eyes, an inviting beer was placed next to his hand. "My thanks, Master Werner."

"Call me Otto." He sat back in his chair and raised his mug. "To a future filled with smooth roads and pretty maids."

Asher raised his mug to his lips and enjoyed his first decent drink in a long time. "Ah, that is good, Werner."

The man seemed pleased on the use of his name without title. He winked and nodded. "*Ja*. Nothing heals the soul better than a little beer."

"Agreed." Asher gulped deeply, then wiped his mouth with the back of his hand. Even though the man might have lied earlier, there was something likable about him. Not only because he saved Asher's life, but Otto Werner was most hospitable. Asher placed his mug on the table and pointed to the paper book. "I did not take you for a man of knowledge. What are you reading?"

The older man frowned and then quickly smiled. "That, my friend, is called a pamphlet. Have you ever seen one?"

Of course, Asher had seen and read many, but never in a common household. The question was how did Werner come by it? "My father was a common man. We had no pamphlets or books. Nor would they do us any good since none of us could read. Only the priest had such."

Werner laughed. "I see the wary look in your eye. Fear not, I am not a Catholic priest, far from it."

That may be so, but an ordinary man of modest means did not spend his time reading. Asher took another sip of his brew. "Then who taught you to read?"

"When I was a lad, I worked in an old man's weave shop. His eyesight was slowly failing, and his hearing was not much better. Through bartering with my parents, I became the man's servant. He taught me what I needed to know in order to make his shop run smoothly. One of those skills was to read a little. Having no heirs, he left me his shop upon his death. I sold it and used the money to further my education."

There was no doubt the tale was true for he told it without pause. "So, then you are a scholar?"

With a slap on the knee, Werner let out a hoot. "You are the quizzical sort, aren't you?"

Asher shrugged. "It has always been so."

"No wonder you earned a beating." Werner leaned over the table and stared straight into Asher's eyes. "Then let us not mix words. Most think you are a spy come to root out Protestants. Is that so?"

"Nein. I am of the reformed faith."

A large smile split Werner's lip. "I believe you. For God would not have saved you if He thought you would do harm."

No indeed. God never intended harm on those who remained devoted to the true faith. "It would seem so. I believe I have been spared to help my fellow Protestant brothers, but I have yet to meet any who profess to be such since I have arrived."

Werner's brows shot upward. "Would you like to meet some?"

Would he! Asher's heart raced as he tried to keep his elation under control. *"Ja."*

"Then I think we should do something about that. If you are up to it, next Sunday I will have Hans come by with a cart and mule to bring you and the ladies to Sunday meeting."

"That would be *wunderbar.* I have lain in this bed long enough. It is time to get back among the living."

"*Ja*, if you stay here much longer, you will be mad in the head. Of course, with the attention of Mistress Brandt and Ella maybe you are living in paradise."

Aye, so it would seem and so it would be if he did not have his family rotting in an English prison. Werner lifted his mug and Asher did the same. Together they toasted their newly formed alliance. The trail was hot again, and Asher could not wait for the hunt to begin. Thank God for trusting men like Otto Werner.

Chapter 13

The morning had been trying. Jane's last attempt to sway the prince from his present course had proven futile. With the rumors of Lady Jane Grey possibly being alive, the prince's army was quickly materializing. Protestants from all over were flooding north. The prince proudly stated he had thousands of men promised by most of the northern principalities. There were rumors that Scotland, Ireland, and half of England would join the fight, so disillusioned were the people with the present queen.

Jane could not refute what the prince said for there were many new faces showing up in Hanenburg every day. Had Asher arrived a week later, no one would have been leery by his presence. As a matter of fact, he was forgotten already. By most, but not by the prince. He inquired about Asher's health, wishing to see him as soon as Asher had gained his senses. The thought of him communicating with the prince left her so melancholy she could not even think straight. So she lied to the prince, stating Asher was still addle in the head. Not very noble and it gnawed at her gut—God would never accept a liar in heaven, even if she did so for good reason. *Forgive me, Lord.*

The sooner the handsome Englishman was out of her life the better. For then she could continue on with her plan to leave. And yet this thought gave her no pleasure either. Why did Asher have to be so ambitious on becoming a member of the Champions of Christ? If he were not, then possibly she could persuade him to give up this folly. But she did not have the time. She had to leave. Once she was in Queen Mary's custody and properly killed, the better for all.

Jane entered the cottage to find Asher and Otto Werner deep in conversation, laughing as if they had been friends for years.

The pastor raised a hand in greeting. "Ella. How was your morn? I trust everything went well?"

The lazy grin on the men's faces and the mugs on the table meant both had been taking the liberty to drink whatever beer was left in the larder. After removing her cloak, Jane scooped up the two empty mugs from the table. "You should be ashamed of yourself, Master Werner. You know Master Blackwell should not be drinking beer while he is healing," she said in German.

"That is where you are wrong. The brew helps." He motioned to Asher. "See? He is up and looking as fit as can be. I wager in a few days he will be as good as new."

His words did not offer Jane comfort. She wrapped an apron around her waist before placing her hands on her hips. "You speak nonsense. Too much activity too early could have him on his back in no time." She turned a stern eye to Asher. "Have you eaten anything this day?"

"*Ja*, I have. Werner has given me some bread and a dried piece of fruit or two." Asher patted his stomach. "I am full."

Werner, not Master Werner! The two were thick as thieves. No good would come from this duo, for sure. "You are full all right. With beer. All the way to the top of your head. Methinks you should have a drink of cool water and then lie down a bit."

Otto chuckled. "Why are you so grumpy, Ella? Come sit with us." He tapped a thin paperbound pamphlet under his fingers. "We were just having a fine discussion about God's grace and Catholic indulgences."

Her insides dropped to the floor. *What was he thinking?* They knew nothing about Asher Blackwell and here Hanenburg's spiritual leader sat discussing matters that were best said with those of like mind. Did he not care for his own safety? "I do not think this is the time or the place to be discussing such things. I think it is time for you to leave. Master Blackwell needs his rest."

"I am not to leave until your aunt returns." He tucked the pamphlet into his doublet but did not move from his chair.

While heat torched every fiber of her being, Jane kept her calm gaze fixed on the good pastor, all the while Asher watched intently. "Ack, Master Werner, I almost forgot, a large branch has fallen near our shed. I believe Hans is helping his father in the fields and will not be coming for a visit this day. Perhaps you could help me move it."

Slowly, Otto rose from his seat. "*Ja*, sure." He smiled at Asher who returned a warm conspiratorial gaze. "We will be right back."

They were barely out the door and by the shed when Jane turned on the preacher. "What are you thinking? Talking about such personal things with Master Blackwell. We know nothing about him."

He blinked and looked about. "Where is this branch you speak of? I did not come out here for a lecture."

"There is no branch. I just want you to use caution when choosing your words around strangers."

Mirth danced in Otto's and lit up his face. "And do you use such caution? I think not."

"I no naught what you speak of," Jane said flippantly.

"*Ja*, you do. You protect him like a mother hen protecting a chick. You are not worried for me, for I stand in the meeting hall every week and profess my Protestant faith freely. You are worried that Asher Blackwell will get caught up with the Champions of Christ and could be harmed again. Admit it. You are a wee bit attracted to him."

The *Doktor* always had a way of seeing things that others did not. She lifted her chin and looked away. "This is foolishness. I care only for his welfare and that of the people of Hanenburg. He is a stranger to us. Once he is able, it would be better for Master Blackwell to leave." Her words soured in her mouth. For if truth be told, she wanted Asher to stay, but she did not want him to be wrapped up in the prince's games.

Wisely, Otto did not try to challenge her pithy attempt to hide the truth. He went right to the heart of the matter. "He has come here to be part of it all."

Jane nodded but added no words. Tears pressed at the backs of her eyelids.

The pastor reached out and lightly touched her hand. "There, there. I wish I could change what is about to happen, but we must remember we are in God's army and we must follow His will."

The preacher's words did not quiet her soul. Instead, her spirit shook with doubt. Should she tell him about the coins? That Asher could be a spy? Surely the *Doktor's* thinking would change. Yet such words could seal Asher's fate, and those who beat him might come back to finish the job.

Once again, she stood in the middle. Were the lives of many worth the one? Her head began to ache. Assuredly, God did not wish to have thousands slaughtered just so she could sit on the throne of England again. Nay, this could not be His will. Tonight, while Hildegard slept, she planned to show Asher the errors of his ways. With a little enlightenment, she was certain she could persuade him to change his course and not join the Champions of Christ.

"Come, come now. Do not look so sad. Everything will work out. You shall see. Blackwell has agreed to come to meeting next Sunday." Otto patted her shoulder.

The words slammed hard into her chest. "The prince will be there. Besides Ash— Master Blackwell is too weak to walk to the meeting house. Please, do not encourage him to go."

"If we are pleading, then please call me Otto." He gave an impish smile, his familiar way of cutting the tension.

"This is no time to play that game. Do not change the subject. Master Blackwell cannot go to the meeting house."

Herr Doktor shrugged. "I am sending Hans with a cart to pick everyone up. Blackwell is looking forward to it."

Jane's hand coiled into a tight fist. She wondered if it was a sin to throttle a man of God.

Asher knew something was amiss when Ella wished to spend the night by the fire because "Master Blackwell looked a little flushed." If he were rosy-cheeked, it was because of the beer Werner had given him, not because he felt ill. However, he went along with the ruse and even groaned a little, not because he felt bad but because he enjoyed having Ella near. He liked watching her work the needle through her mending, kneading dough for bread, and sweeping the cottage while humming a merry tune. Each task she did was taken on not because she had to but because she wanted to. She found joy in what others would think would be mundane.

When Mistress Brandt's snores could be heard from the loft, Ella came over and stood by his bed. "Master Blackwell," she whispered in English, "are you able to walk?"

Asher rolled to his side and lifted himself up on one elbow. "Aye."

She then helped him up and threw a cloak about his shoulders. With quiet steps, they slipped out the door into the moon-filled night. A light faint breeze rose from the south, giving them a promise of the summer to come. The earth beneath his feet was soft and supple. Asher thought of his small patch of land not far from London. How he longed to be there, turning the soil, planting, and bringing forth new life. He inhaled deeply and let out a quiet sigh.

"Are you all right?" she asked as she led him past the shed to a sturdy log in a small clearing.

"I am fine." He sat and raised his eyes to the starry night. "I was just remembering my home. If you would go beyond the torch lights of London, the sky would look just like this."

"So it would."

"Come again?"

He could not make out her features in the night, even so, she turned away. "I mean, I imagine it would. It was the same near Frankfurt."

The ears of a spy told him the slip of her tongue was not by accident, but the magic of the night dulled his senses, and he reached out to take her hand. "Come sit by me."

She ignored his request. In the distance, Matilda gave out a low moo. "She heard us leave and wishes to come with us."

"I have never heard of a cow that would have such keen hearing or such thought. A cow wandering the night would get lost."

"Not Matilda. If she was left out in the pasture day or night, she would wander back home. She may be old, but she is a smart cow. However, her milk becomes less and less every day, and Master Gaerter will not bring one of his bulls to mate with her because of her age."

"What happened to her last calf?"

"Master Gaerter took it. It is his payment for breeding. I meant to ask the prince for a young cow, but he has other things on his mind these days."

No doubt. Planning to overthrow a queen would take precedent to a maid's milking cow. "Then I shall buy you a new one." He knew without seeing that she was smiling and that her eyes were shiny and bright. An undesirable urge to run his finger over her lips and down her soft neck rippled through him. "Come sit by me," he said quietly.

This time she did not hesitate, her thigh brushing against his when she sat down. "I thank you for your generosity, but will not Audrey be jealous? She would not like it that I sit by you or that you are giving me gifts."

He chuckled. He must have mentioned Audrey's name while he fought for his life. A prick of apprehension skidded down his back. What else had he said? He moved closer to her. "A man from England would hardly try to woo a maid with a milking cow. Considered it payment for saving my life. And as for Audrey, my sister has seen me sit next to many a maid."

Her features softened in the moonlight. "A sister. I never thought... I do not need a gift for doing what God would want us to do." She lifted her chin, and a soft glow highlighted a small smile. "If time would stop, I would not be disappointed. For I could gaze into these heavens forever. But that is not why I have brought you out here." She paused for a moment, clearly debating how she should proceed. "I think it is unwise for you to go to the meeting house next Sunday."

He tipped his head to the side, ready to pick up some valuable information. "And why not? I am getting stronger every day, and by week's end, I am sure I will be ready for a little excursion."

He could see her work her lovely jaw, struggling for the correct words to negate his plans. "I shall speak plainly. The prince will be there, and if he sees you walking about and conversing with others, he will come and question you most severely. I am not sure you are strong enough to handle the ordeal."

Asher shifted away. "I am flattered by your concern, but I wish to meet him."

She turned and tilted her head, sending a soft brown curl to her shoulder. "Why? Why would you seek those who wish to cause dissension? Why do you not seek peace instead?"

Oh, indeed that was exactly what he wanted. Peace. But that would not come until one more was killed. "All men seek peace, but peace, at times, must come through trial."

She curled in and wrapped her subtle arms about her knees. A faint breeze whistled through the budding trees. "At one time I thought as you did, but now I am not so sure. One man's peace seems to always cause another man's trial. Men fight and squabble, always seeking to right a wrong. But their right might be someone else's wrong. It is like a mad dog chasing his tail. When he catches it, he yelps out in pain realizing this was not what he wanted anyway."

For a simple peasant girl, she had great insight. Queen Mary could learn much from this maid. The hairs on the back of his neck stood. Indeed, she talked like a woman who had been reared to carry on intellectual debates. But Asher shook the thought away for Ella couldn't be noble. She probably lapped up any words she heard at the castle. "True. Though it does pain me, I must admit, as long as man walks the earth, there will never be peace."

"Then why go on Sunday? Why seek out the prince? Why fight at all?" She reached over and grabbed his hands. Heat ricocheted through his body. "As soon as you are able, leave this place. I am sorry for your loss, but if your brother was alive, what would he tell you? To stay and fight or leave and live?"

The answer was easy. His brother was a man of peace. Yet, as lofty and noble as her words were, his brother still died trying to bring a peaceful solution to a volatile situation. "You are young and have not lived long enough to know the ways of the world. Why, even Christ was killed for speaking words of love and kindness."

Her whole body began to shake. "I know more than you think. The wicked prevail often, and the innocent always suffer."

On this they were in agreement; however, that did not explain why she desperately wanted him to leave. His gut clenched, and his mind doubted her humble status. "What happened to your parents? Why are you not living with them?"

She pulled her hands away, and her head fell to her chest. "My father…both my parents died of the sweating sickness long ago."

She lied, and the answer was staring him right in the face. "They died because of their faith, did they not? That is why you came northward to live with your aunt."

Ella shook her head. "Does it matter?"

"Aye, it does. Just as I seek justice for my brother's death, you seek the same for your parents' death. But instead of wanting revenge, you seek to protect others, even those who mean to harm you." Her purity and selflessness stunned him, and he wanted desperately to have a piece of it.

Like a thief stealing a widow's last loaf of bread, Asher leaned over to kiss her. In those brief seconds when her lips met his, all his anger and resentment subsided. He was wrapped in her loving goodness. As quickly as it had begun, the kiss ended.

She rose and smoothed out her skirt. "I am not that way, Master Blackwell."

He shook his head. "I know. Forgive me. I know not why I did such a thing." He did, but he did not wish to frighten her any more than he had already.

"I think we should return to the cottage. My aunt would be very cross if she found us here in the middle of the night." She held out her hand to help him up.

Her fingers were warm, and he had to fight not to crush her to his cold body. "You are right. I would never want your virtue compromised."

Nothing further was said until they reached the cottage door. She turned to him, her eyes reflecting the moonlight. "Think on my words. Do not go to the meeting house next Sunday. Leave this place."

Oh, how he wished he could. And how he wished he could take her with him.

CHAPTER 14

By the week's end, Asher was strong enough to get up and move around the cottage without someone hovering about. He was more than ready when Hans showed up with the cart to take them to the meeting house. But, alas, his companions were not. Ella moped about as if she were going to a funeral instead of Sunday meeting. Mistress Brandt had a permanent scowl on her face. Constantly, they tried to persuade him not to go. Was their Protestant priest a bore that they did not wish to hear him speak, or did they fear something else? In all the time he had been infiltrating the heretic world, he had never encountered such a lack of enthusiasm.

"Are you sure you wish to come?" Ella asked for the nineteenth time.

"*Ja*, perhaps it will be too much for you. You should start slow with a few walks near the cottage," Mistress Brandt added, putting her cloak around her shoulders. "It is a mite drafty this morn."

Asher managed to dress and put on his boots with no aid, then patiently waited while the others dragged around the cottage like a pair of dying dames. "'Tis time I walked among the living. Instead of wasting away in idleness." His comment was met with grumbles.

Nor did Hans carry any eagerness when asked to help Asher to the cart. There was no mistaking the large German did not like that Asher lived with Mistress Brandt and Ella. If Hans had his way, he would probably finish Asher off for good. But Hans was a dutiful servant and would do anything to stay in the good graces of Ella Brandt. So, he helped Asher to the back of the cart, dumping him on the hard wooden bed like a sack of turnips.

The large meeting house was a flurry of activity when they arrived. Hans hauled Asher from the cart and deposited him on a stool reserved for the old and infirmed. A group of young women immediately enveloped Ella in conversation, and Hans sauntered over to a band of strapping young men. Mistress Brandt sat next to Asher saying not a single word. Nonetheless, Asher could not hide his good mood. Today he would meet every Protestant traitor in the village.

Many villagers hailed others in greeting while a few impatiently mumbled. Asher spotted Karl with a cluster of men huddled in one corner. Slowly their scowling faces shifted to where Asher sat. He smiled and gave them a small salute.

Mistress Brandt leaned over. "Do not encourage them or they might decide to take a few more whacks at your head."

"Would they now? Or perhaps I could persuade them I am a man of like mind and spirit," Asher said without taking his gaze off the band.

"*Pff.*" Mistress Brandt rolled her eyes. "Let me tell you something. It is very hard for a stranger to gain acceptance in Hanenburg if you do not know the right people."

Asher shrugged, letting his gaze roam the room. Most of the villagers stood shoulder to shoulder in front of a wooden dais, where a straight back chair sat off to one side and a rugged wooden podium stood on the left. A few eyes glazed over as if they were steeling themselves for what was to begin.

As if on cue, the crowd parted and a small group of finely dressed men and women entered the hall. Voices dropped to whispers when a tall distinguished man with greying temples and a trimmed goatee strolled to the front of the meeting hall. He took the only seat on the dais and leisurely crossed his legs. The rest of his entourage moved to the right of the hall, while most of the villagers moved to the left. How appropriate—the sheep to the right and the goats to the left.

"That is Prince Nikolaus von Hoffbauer," Mistress Brandt whispered.

Asher stretched his neck as the crowd filled in all the open spaces. So, this was the man who most likely held Lady Jane Grey. Nonchalantly, Asher scanned those who had arrived with him, a few older and middling-year women, but no one young enough to be the Lady Jane. What did he expect? The prince to have her on display for all the world to see. Nay, one look had told Asher this man was no fool. The prince would not reveal his gem until the right time. For all Asher knew, the lady could be controlling the prince. After all, Lady Jane was a learned woman and may have picked up some tactical skills in her secret exile.

The whispers of the crowd faded when a man with a ruddy-red face and wide girth dressed in scholarly robes stepped up behind the podium. By the Holy Cross, it was

Werner! Asher thinned his lips as the man opened with a prayer. He then proceeded to preach to the people, praising Protestant doctrine over the falsehood of the Catholic church. He praised the people of Hanenburg for their enlightenment, which brought positive responses from the crowd.

But while the masses cheered, their patron did not. Prince von Hoffbauer sat quietly stroking his beard. Occasionally, his gaze would shift around the room. Once in a while his regard would rest on Ella. Asher clenched his hands. Perhaps there was more than sewing that she did for the prince. Yet, he did not carry the look of lust in his eyes when he looked upon her. The good prince saved that hungry expression for a lovely middling-year lady wearing a French hood and burgundy gown.

Sneaking about most of his life, Asher had prided himself in the ability to read people's facial and physical expressions. Yet, his mind deceived him now. For the prince gazed upon Ella with a look of satisfaction and...power? Petite Ella stood dutifully, listening to her spiritual leader in her drab brown dress. Her white cap slightly crooked upon her head. What power could be gained from such a tiny dandelion in a room of thorny roses. *But dandelions multiply quickly.*

Asher made a mental shake. His thoughts must still be muddled from the beating he took. The temperature rose and sweat dotted many a forehead. Werner banged his fist on the podium, garnering every wandering eye. On and on his fiery speech went. Speaking of Christian piety and the evils that would tempt a good man.

"I tell you, good people. We must stand together against any tyranny that would dismiss God's grace by the selling of indulgences," Werner shouted, causing many to jump and yell their agreement.

Prince von Hoffbauer just smiled but did not offer up an opinion. Nor did he try to persuade the long-winded preacher to end his speech. At least not until his gaze fell upon Asher. Then as if the prince had more pressing things to do, he uncrossed his legs and cleared his throat. Immediately, Werner brought his rant to an end with one more jab at the Pope.

Prayers were said before the prince rose to his feet. "Many thanks, Master Werner. As always your words have filled us with enlightenment and conviction."

The fraudulent Father blushed and slightly bowed before stepping away from the pulpit. The crowd mumbled a little as the prince moved forward, placing one of his ringed hands into his doublet. He waited patiently until all attention was fixed on him.

"I hope he is not as windy today," grumbled an old woman sitting near Asher. "If I sit here much longer, I will be too stiff to move."

"Hush, *Mutter*. The prince might hear you," scolded her son.

However, the old woman's complaint turned to be unfounded when Prince von Hoffbauer simply thanked the villagers for their tireless service to the town of Hanenburg and to their Christian cause. He glanced Asher's way once more before walking out.

"Now you've done it," mumbled Mistress Brandt.

"Done what?" Asher asked absentmindedly, his gaze shifting to Ella and her sweet smile, which seemed to be attracting a gaggle of young men. Asher frowned. Ella must be more careful or she could find herself in a heap of trouble.

"He has seen you. There will be no protecting you now." Mistress Brandt waved a hand in front of Asher's face. "Do you hear me?"

Asher blushed as if he had been caught in an illicit tryst. "I—I am sorry. What were you saying?"

"The prince. You are the reason he left in a hurry. He saw you. I wager before night falls he will be standing at our door." Mistress Brandt shook her head. "Ella will not be pleased."

"Come again? Why would Ella care?" he asked.

"Are you blind or just daft?" Mistress Brandt scrunched up her nose. "Perhaps both." She rose to her feet. "Well, you can figure that out on your own. Come now. We must be getting you back to the cottage. You will be needing a full meal in your belly before you meet the prince."

At Mistress Brandt's call, Hans came over and helped Asher to the door where Werner stood, thanking all for coming and promising next week would be just as inspiring. The moment Werner spotted Asher he excused himself from the line of villagers. "Blackwell, a word please."

Hans and Asher paused as the older man caught up. "Interesting sermon, Father Werner."

"Ack. That is not what you call a Protestant man of God." Werner laughed. "We are just pastors of Christ's flock."

Asher grunted. "And when were you going to tell me this interesting piece of information?"

"Even though the Treaty of Augsburg has given Prince von Hoffbauer the right to choose which religion to follow in this territory, many would still destroy our freedoms. It is prudence that forbids us to speak publicly about our beliefs."

"Is it?" Asher cocked an eyebrow. "Or is it because you do not trust me?"

"If that were the case, then I would not have encouraged Mistress Brandt and Ella to bring you here. *Nein*, it is not me that you need to convince, but the prince."

"So I have been told. Excuse me, I am tired."

Werner motioned to Hans to take Asher back to the cart.

Inwardly, he could not be more pleased. It seemed the prince would come quickly. Soon Asher's plans would be set into motion. His stomach growled. He smiled. But first he would have a good meal.

To Asher's disappointment, the prince did not show up that eve. Nor did he do so the next day. The man must be a fool to leave a possible spy with two helpless women. Or more to the truth, he did not care what would happen to the peasant women. Nobles. They were the same in all countries—prideful and selfish.

On the third day after Werner's sermon, Asher awoke to an empty house. He rose from the pallet and peeked out the window. There he found Mistress Brandt and Ella deep in conversation near the shed. No doubt, their conversation was about him. Ella wrung her hands, casting pleading eyes at her aunt. By contrast, Mistress Brandt folded her arms across her chest and stared straight ahead. He concluded Ella wanted him to stay at the cottage longer, while Mistress Brandt wanted to send him back to the prince or the Growl Bear.

He stepped into the doorway. *"Guten Morgen."*

Quickly Ella rushed to his side. "How fare you this morning?" she said in English. "You look a little pale."

He knew he did not, but he could not cause her stress. "I am a mite tired."

"You look fine to me." Mistress Brandt strode to his side and placed a hand on his forehead. "Cool as this spring day. Ella thinks you are doing too much. We were just discussing—"

"Could that not wait until later. We do not want to be late." She turned to Asher with a breathtaking smile. "Mistress Gunther has offered to buy Matilda's fresh milk this morn. It seems a whole slew of her relations showed up yesterday, and she needs more milk and bread to fill their bellies."

Mistress Brandt flipped up her hands. *"Ack, ja,* you are right. She said something about getting there early before the brood awoke."

Without a word, Ella rushed inside the cottage and began packing a bag with cheese and bread.

Mistress Brandt raced to the shed and picked up a few buckets of milk and tied them to a carrying pole. "Will you be okay here by yourself?"

Asher nodded and thought it would be a good time to see just how much he could do without Hans dragging him around. Perhaps he could take a walk or pitch some hay into Matilda's stall if he were strong enough.

"Master Werner will be coming by later, in case you need anything," Mistress Brandt said, before shouting past him, "Come on, Ella. If we are late, her family will beg us to break our fast with them, and I wish to go to the village and buy some grain from the miller."

Ella scurried to the door and blushed before stepping over the threshold. "Please rest some. It would be folly to rush your recovery." She pursed her lips before heading toward her aunt.

Ah, how he would like to taste those lips again. With chastisement, Asher corrected his thoughts. He must keep his mind on the task before him. Too many weeks had passed already, and no doubt, Queen Mary was suffering all sorts of maladies because of his lack of communication and progress.

The pair hurried down the road, chattering away. Asher watched until they were far from his sight before he slipped through the cottage entry. He washed a hand over his face and then began to mentally tick off what he must do to see if he were fit to carry out his mission. First, he would break his fast, and then he would go out to the shed and check on Matilda and the chickens. He spotted a hunk of bread and cheese that were left on the table, probably for him. Like a man who had not eaten for a week, he devoured both, then he went to the shed. Matilda greeted him with a low moo. She may be old and tired, but she still seemed to have a good appetite.

"What shall we do today, old girl?" Asher said, patting her side.

The cow snorted, leaving out a fine spray of moisture.

"To the pasture it is."

He led Matilda to the same clearing where he had sat with Ella. The bright morning sent the birds to chirping, and a small field mouse scurried under the greening brush while a hawk watched with a careful eye. Asher set the cow loose. She lumbered away to a fresh patch of grass.

"Do not wander far for I do not wish to chase you." Matilda turned and gave out another snort before lowering her head to her feast.

The day proved to be a beauty. The warmth of the sun helped ease his tight shoulders and brighten his mood. He inhaled the fresh air deeply. How he could get used to this life. Far from London's stench and far from Queen Mary's grasp. If he did not have to worry about his parents' and sister's welfare, he would stay here and perhaps raise a family with the pretty Ella Brandt. Asher laughed. "Like that would even be possible," he said to Matilda, who answered him by giving her backside.

The cow had more intelligence than he did. Sweet shy Ella deserved better than him. She needed a man who could match her wit, appreciate her gentleness, and fulfill her every whim. But where in Hanenburg would she find such a man? Certainly not the dull-headed Hans Mueller or Karl who waylaid him. Werner was a pleasant fellow, but clearly too old and too devoted to his heretic cause. "Where, Ella? Where can we find the right man for you?"

This query caught Matilda's attention, and she let out a low moo.

"Oh, so you know?" Asher asked.

The cow answered by swatting a fly with her tail.

Asher laughed again and then sat down in the pasture. "All right. I shall leave the matchmaking to you. When you find him make sure to let me know—run right up to him and lick his face. I am sure that will get Ella's attention, hey?"

Pulling up a healthy clump of grass, Matilda ignored his request.

He sighed and lay down, placing his hands behind his head. Aye, this was the life he wanted. A small cottage, a lazy cow, and a good wife. 'Twas those thoughts that filled his dreams when he closed his eyes.

The sun was more than halfway through the sky when Asher awoke. He sat up with a start and did not see Matilda anywhere. By the holy saints, he lost the beast. "Matilda," he shouted, coming to his feet. He pricked his ears but heard nothing. He called out again and thought he heard a faint moo in the direction of the cottage. Perhaps she had wandered back to the shed. Did not Ella say Matilda was known to wander home?

Asher rushed back and was not only greeted by Matilda but by a fine black Friesian horse and Werner's donkey. Male voices could be heard in the cottage. A slight thrill raced up Asher's spine. So, Werner had brought along a visitor. But who in these parts would own such a beautiful piece of horseflesh? Only one man.

Before entering the cottage, Asher returned Matilda to her stall. He picked up a thick piece of wood; he had no intentions of being beaten a second time just in case things went badly. With the board tight in his grasp, Asher made his way to the cottage. There sat Werner and a man dressed in a shiny black leather doublet and black breeches. A heavy gold chain graced his neck while a pair of soft leather gloves sat on the table. The grey of his eyes hid his thoughts well, for Asher could not discern if the man would be a friend or a foe. He stretched out his long legs. His boots were polished to a high luster.

"Prince von Hoffbauer I presume," Asher said in German before bowing low.

"You are a very astute young man." The prince stroked his goatee.

"*Nein*, I saw you at the meeting hall last Sunday."

The prince laughed yet did not look amused. "But of course. The question is just who are you? Are you a spy from the south, or perhaps you are here on the orders of the Holy Roman Emperor? Tell me, Master Blackwell," the prince switched to English, "are German and English the only languages you know? For your German is terrible."

"So I have been told." Asher dropped the log he had been holding and raised his hand, bringing his thumb and forefinger close together. "I know a little French."

"A pity. We could use someone in Spain. Do you not agree, Otto?" the prince said in German.

"*Ja*, but I think he will be of use nonetheless." Not surprising, Werner took a slurp from a frothy mug.

"Mmm, I wonder." The prince stroked his goatee again, and Asher made note of the habit. "I understand you come from a farm in England. What was the name of that town again?"

"Outside of Ipswich, Prince," Asher answered in the same language; the interrogation had begun. A game Asher mastered long ago.

"And you have come here to escape religious persecution because you are a Catholic?"

Asher smiled. The prince thought he was cunning. "Nay. Because I am a Protestant."

The questions came fast, sometimes in English and sometimes in German, but none that Asher had not heard before. Did he believe in Latin mass, or should the Church use the language of the people? Can an indulgence forgive a man's sin? Are priests divine? The questions went on and on, but like the devil who knows every piece of scripture, Asher could answer every question like a good Protestant should.

"Remarkable. You know more than I expected. Odd for a farmer, do you not agree?" The prince looked at Werner, who gravely nodded. "Even those who profess to be good Protestants cannot answer half of the questions I have given you."

"My faith is everything to me. If it were not, I would have stayed in England." Spoken like a true reformed zealot. Asher knew he had them when the prince looked away.

"Well, I am satisfied," Werner said.

"Then so am I." The prince motioned to a stool near the table. "Come. Sit."

Asher tamped down his excitement. He complied and folded his hands on the table. Then he waited for the information that would lead him to the Champions of Christ and Lady Jane.

"How are you feeling, Master Blackwell?" the prince asked.

Now that he passed the scrutiny, they were interested in his health? Asher had to hide a smile. It would be his turn to learn from them. "I am fine. I think I am ready to return to the village and see if Master Schmitts still needs another smithy."

"You are not afraid of the men who accosted you?" the prince asked in fluid English.

"I am hoping Master Werner has spread the word that no one has anything to fear from me. I believe these men were members of the Champions of Christ, and I wish to become one of them, but I think Master Werner has told you such or you would not be sitting here."

Werner almost choked on his beer and gave Asher a look of warning. The prince paused the stroking of his goatee and cocked an eyebrow. He cast a glance to Werner. "You were right. He is a bold one." The prince's gaze then flipped back to Asher. "But that is not what we need."

We. There it was, the word that usually proceeded an entry into a secret Protestant world. He had chosen the correct path by being direct. These Germans were not like the English who had to be courted and coddled into giving up their confidences. "Tell me what you need and I will be it."

"See? I told you he was eager. We need a man like him. He took a healthy beating, and he still did not shrink away." Werner leaned over the table. "Let us get on with it."

Get on with it. Oh aye, let us have all the details so I can be finished with this nasty task.

The prince barely moved his hard gaze from Asher. "I have been doing a little exploring while you were recovering. Do you know what I discovered when I sent one of my men to Ipswich?"

Asher could feel the blood drain from his face. Like in a game of chess, he had become the loser. Checked by the knight. This was not a first for Asher either. He held his tongue and looked contrite.

"So, let us try this again. Where are you from, and why should I trust you?"

CHAPTER 15

Asher had only one move. He held up his hands and cast a wary gaze between the men. "Master Werner, please go to my pallet, near the corner closest to the wall you will notice a mound of dirt. Underneath you will find a pouch."

With a nod, the prince gave Werner the approval to go search the area. It did not take long before he threw the pouch onto the table with a definite *thunk*. "Filled with coins, no doubt." Werner returned to his chair and opened the bag and let out a low hiss of air when the German, French, and English coins spilled into his hand. "No farmer would have a purse like this. I am sorry, Prince. I should have let Karl, Wilhelm, and Hans finish the job they started."

"'Tis not what you think. Please hear me out." Asher then spun the same tale he told Ella. "There you have it. I am a thief and a wanted man. But I am a Protestant. What must I do to prove who I am?" Asher waited as both men digested his words. They would either kill him now or give him some vile test.

But the prince did neither. "Well then, Master Blackwell, is that your real name?" the prince asked.

"Aye. I am Asher Blackwell."

The prince reached into his doublet and pulled out Asher's missing dagger, placing it on the table.

"Take it. It is yours, is it not?"

Asher paused. Was this another test? He leaned forward and swiftly picked up the dagger. "My thanks in returning it."

The prince nodded, then casually crossed his legs. The soft tips of his fingers tapped the table. "I think I have a task for you if you think you are up to it."

Ah, here it was, the test to win his trust and the key to their secret world. "Then speak it. For I am growing stronger daily and am eager to prove my worth."

"The task might take all of your strength and none of your strength, but you are in the right place to carry it out. Is that not so, Otto?" The prince's fingers stilled.

"*Ja,*" Werner answered with a lack of eagerness, "but perhaps we should—"

The prince waved his hand, silencing the preacher.

Asher braced himself for the ugly task they would send him on. This was not the first time he had done something he would regret, but it sure better be the last.

The prince leaned back and folded his hands across his lean stomach, a thin smile split his lips. Why was it the wicked who took so much pleasure in watching others squirm? "We would like you to stay here and keep an eye on Maid Brandt."

Did his hearing deceive him? They wanted him to stay here and keep an eye on Ella? Why? Unless she was...he almost shook his head at the absurd thought. Lady Jane Grey would be kept under lock and key, not allowed to go traipsing about the countryside wearing a crooked cap on her pretty head. Nor would Prince von Hoffbauer put such a valuable pawn in Asher's charge. "Here? Would I not be of more service in the village or better yet at the castle?"

The prince laughed. "Nay, certainly not the castle. You are needed here. Ella is not a supporter of the Champions of Christ."

"We fear she may try to leave and tell our enemies some very important information," Werner finished the prince's thought.

Asher's heart jumped. Would Ella do such and sympathize with the Catholics? If so, then perhaps he could encourage her to leave this place...with him. A ridiculous notion. She would never leave her aunt, nor would she go with a man who would help destroy half the men in her village, including their spiritual leader, Otto Werner. Asher clenched his jaw. Nay, she would hate him and rightly so.

He wanted to be honest and tell them to give up their plan. It had already been discovered by their enemies. If he failed to kill Jane Grey and destroy their rebel group, others would follow. But he was not an honest man.

"Hans Mueller would be the sounder choice." Asher shifted a pleading gaze between the men. "He is most attentive to Ella."

"The reason he cannot be the man," the prince answered. "She would turn his head in a second, and before you know it, he would be escorting her to the Pope himself. Nay, you are the best choice. You are already here, and she would suspect nothing. Besides, I think she is quite fond of you." The prince started stroking his goatee again.

This would not do. Asher gritted his teeth to hide a frown. How could he discover Lady Jane's whereabouts being trapped at this cottage? How could he foil the plans of the Champions of Christ from here? "Your plan may sound good, but I am almost certain that Mistress Brandt wants me gone."

"Do not worry about Mistress Brandt." He then turned to Werner. "Bring her to the castle later."

Werner's eye's brightened, and he gave a hearty nod.

Seeing any further attempt to dissuade the prince would only cause more suspicion, Asher began to devise a plan of his own. "All right. I will watch Ella, but I shall go mad here with nothing to do. I would like to go to the village and pick up some supplies."

The prince lifted his eyebrows. "What could you possibly need?"

"Each week's end I see Mistress Brandt and Ella carry heavy sacks and milk buckets to Hanenburg market. I wish to purchase a cart and buy a horse to aid them. In addition, I would like to fix up their shed to accommodate a few more animals and a proper place to house their chickens." He motioned with his chin to the bag of coins on the table. "Surely there is enough there to pay for such things. Take the rest but leave me a few coins for the purchase."

"I told you he was a good man," Werner said, a merry smile on his face once again, though why the so-called "good spiritual leader" had never in the past offered his own donkey to the ladies mystified Asher.

The prince gave out a short sniff before he stood. "All right. If that is your price, then we have a bargain. You stay close to Ella and send word if you see anything suspicious."

"One more thing?" Asher asked. "The ladies need a new milking cow. Surely in your benevolence you can give them one."

"All right. I will get them a new milking cow. I will secure one before the summer is over. Anything else?"

Asher shook his head.

The prince stood without taking a single coin out of the pouch. "Come, Otto let us leave this good man to his rest."

Werner quickly drank the last of his beer before rising from his seat. "I shall see you on the morrow. I will help you pick up the supplies." With that, both men mounted their beasts and headed back to Hanenburg Castle.

Asher rolled his shoulders to release a tight kink. By some miracle, the prince had not killed him, however being stuck at this cottage would not aid his mission. Nonetheless, he would take the gift given him. He had his town visit, and more importantly, he would be taking Ella to the castle every week in a newly purchased cart. While she collected the mending, he would search the castle. Asher picked up his dagger and examined its tip. When he found Lady Jane, this all would be over. *God, lead me to your will. Help me to find the traitor and end these murderous plans.*

CHAPTER 16

Jane woke in the loft, playing the same events in her mind that had disturbed her sleep every single day since she snuck out of the cottage with Asher. *The kiss they shared in the moonlight.* Granted, she knew many injured men in strange places would become grateful to their caregiver and would do such things. The kiss was nothing more than his expression of gratitude—but her heart wanted it to be so much more.

Guilford, her deceased husband, had been sloppy with his kissing. In truth, he was sloppy even in the one time he bedded her. What did she expect? The match was not made in heaven, but by their two fathers. Hatched from the desires of power and greed. Guilford and she were nothing more than pawns in a very deadly game. Often in her youth she fancied herself married to King Edward. They had so much more in common—their love for books and the reformed religion. Oh, how she missed the talks they would have. At one time, even her own parents thought it would be a wise match, but he was betrothed to another. And then he died. Little did she know his death would be the end for her too.

Jane sighed and sat up, watching Hildegard's chest rise and fall with each easy breath. The events of last eve puzzled her even more than the kiss. Hildegard wanted Asher gone and planned to tell him so that eve. Instead, later, Otto Werner had shown up and the pair left for some time. Perchance both had finally taken the first step in courtship. Yet when Hildegard returned, she was in a foul mood. Her words were terse, and she greeted Asher, who had been resting on his pallet, by closing the curtain, shutting him off from the rest of the room.

There was no talk of him leaving as they ate their evening meal. Suddenly Hildegard announced that it would be a good idea for Asher to make a bed for himself in the shed on the morrow. He readily agreed, and that was the end of the discussion. Jane would have her own bed again. The idea was grand, but even in spring, how would Asher fare in the cold shed?

Jane quickly dressed and slipped down the loft ladder. She tiptoed past the closed curtain and quietly added wood to the hearth, stoking the fire with the poker. The flames crackled and glowed to life. Warmth covered the room, chasing away the morning chill. She paused when she heard a stirring behind the curtain. With a groan, Asher's feet hit the floor. His bare toes peeked out of the bottom of the curtain. They were long and lean, but not overly callused. Another giveaway that he was not a man who worked long hours in the fields.

She smiled at the thought, but then her spirit filled with doubt. He arrived in Hanenburg by foot. He had no horse, and if he did, surely someone would have told her. The more she thought on it, the greater her fear grew. A fugitive who had traveled all the way from England to here should have worn-out shoes and weathered feet. Asher had neither. However, he did have a sack of coins. Obviously, he had used his lucre to gain easy travel. There, mystery solved. And yet, she could not tamp down the panic that seized her soul.

He pulled back the curtain. "*Guten Morgen*. Did you have a pleasant rest?" His German was getting better, but she still preferred his rich English accent.

"*Ja*. I slept like a baby cub next to her furry *Mutter*." They both laughed, knowing full well that Hildegard would not appreciate being compared to a bear.

The merriment did not last long as the woman in question could be heard mumbling up above. Asher put a finger to his lips and pointed to the cottage door. In a flash, they stumbled outside, laughing as they made their way to the pasture.

"I must take care of my morning needs," Jane said as warmth flooded her skin.

"*Ja*, me too."

She pointed toward the woods. "You go over there, and I shall walk in the opposite direction. We shall meet here after."

He laughed. "All right, Ella. We shall meet here."

Jane quickly ran away, hoping she could control the pinking of her skin. Later, she returned to the clearing but did not see Asher anywhere. Surely it could not take him this long. Did he decide to return to the cottage?

A splash in the river that ran south of their cottage drew her attention. She should return home. Hildegard would be wondering where they had gone. Considering her grumpy mood last eve, Jane was not ready to start the new day with another lecture. But then again...

As fast as her legs could carry her, Jane raced to the stream. Her feet stalled a good quarter furlong from the water's edge. There she found him. Swimming in the frigid water, droplets gleaming off his bare chest. "Are you mad? Fresh off the sickbed, you should not be bathing."

Asher bobbed up and down in the water. "Have no fear. I feel strong. I will not drown."

Being English, she expected him to have a little more sense. "I speak of the chill. It could seep into your bones and weaken your body."

"You have been living with your aunt too long. That is all nonsense. Come. Join me, the water is fresh. It will invigorate you."

He flipped onto his back, and Jane closed her eyes. "Nay, I will not. I have no desire to feel Aunt Hildegard's switch on my backside." She peeked through her lashes.

"Whatever pleases you. Stay dirty, then." A roar of laughter split the air and then gurgled away as he dunked his head under the water.

Dirty! She was not dirty. Why just yesterday she had washed herself off. Yet, she could not help but take a sniff or two. Nothing, she smelled fine, did she not? "Please come out," she called. "Aunt Hildegard will be wondering where we are."

His head popped above the water. "What did you say?"

"Come out, please." She twisted her hands in her apron.

"All right." He swam toward the shore and started to stand.

Jane gasped, turned away, and covered her eyes. "Do you not care for my virtue?"

His laughed again. "Ah, but I do. Give me but a moment and I will be solemnly dressed just like a monk before vespers. There now. You can look."

A strip of cold fear slid down the middle of her back as she turned to face him once he was dressed. "Those are odd words for a Protestant."

A flicker of shock shot through his merry eyes; his jaw tightened. "You must remember, I was not born a Protestant and sometimes old words come to mind."

Was that true? He had said his whole family had been ruined by the Catholics. And if they were converts, most were zealots and would never speak of a monk unless to detest his heretic ways. "You must be more cautious or others will truly believe you are a spy."

He acted like he did not hear by tilting his head to one side to drain his ear.

Jane found the ruse perplexing. Perhaps his faith leaned toward Luther's teaching instead of Henry VIII's. "Of course, Luther was a monk."

"Aye, and married with a large family." Asher pulled her into his arms and kissed her soundly on the lips.

Her body instantly flamed. She leaned in and took in a little more of the pleasure before her mind caught up with her carnal lust. She pulled back, a soft scent of spring water mixed with his hearty musky scent filled the air. Jane touched her lips before she cried out. If she stayed… Quickly, she ran back to the cottage. His laughter nipped at her heels and sent another tinge of heat through her skin. She arrived home and slammed the door behind her. The sight before her was worse than the one she had fled.

A wooden-faced Hildegard glared at her. "Where have you been?"

At that very moment, the door behind her burst open and a dripping-wet Asher entered.

Hildegard harrumphed. "If you are to stay here, I expect you to keep Ella's virtue in the foremost part of your mind. Now grab your things and take them to the shed. Once you are finished there, you may break your fast. After that, stay out of our way, Ella and I must make a batch of poultice this day."

Asher did what he was told without a word, but the moment Hildegard turned her back, he winked at Jane, sending her heart into a rapped panic. Perhaps having him stay here, even in the shed, was not the wisest decision. Not only would her mind be distracted by the kisses they shared, but now every time she would close her eyes, she would envision him frolicking in the water. May the Lord have mercy on her wayward thoughts and keep her mind on the straight path.

Chapter 17

Asher stuffed his makeshift bed with straw, then searched the small shed where he could hide his coins. The uncomfortable morning at the cottage almost made him laugh out loud. Without a doubt, Prince von Hoffbauer had spoken to Mistress Brandt, for she was as cross as friar with no scripture to read. However, like a good cleric, she would comply with her superior's wishes. Poor Ella was in a muddle, uncertain as to why her aunt had relented. Or, what he wished were true, her mind had drifted to the sensual kiss they had shared at the stream.

Originally, he had pulled her into his arms so she would forget his misspoken words, but he could not deny the fire between them once the kiss started. Where was his caution? He knew better than to let any emotion seep into his soul while he did Queen Mary's bidding. And yet, he could not get the sight of Ella touching her lush, red, thoroughly kissed lips from his mind.

None of it would have happened had he not taunted her innocence. Alas, he could not help himself. All night long he had thought of her and what the prince had said—*We fear she may try to leave and tell our enemies some very important information.* First, Asher's thoughts were on the possibility of taking Ella away from this Protestant mess, but then his mind settled on the prince's words—*tell our enemies.* Tell them what? What would the petite Ella know? Did she see Lady Jane during her castle visits?

Had Ella ever mended any of Lady Jane's clothing? Sorry to say, he had never paid attention to what she was mending. If she did, then she would know exactly where the witch would be hiding. His lips thinned. He had more questions than answers.

Asher raked a hand through his hair before digging a toe in the soft ground at the far corner of the shed. He would bury his coin here later. Matilda let out a low moo. In all the commotion this morn, she had not been milked nor had the chickens' eggs been collected. He looked at Matilda. "I guess these will be my tasks now. We both know Mistress Brandt will not step foot in here as long as I am residing within."

Asher was not put off by either chore. Sooner or later he would leave this place and he too would be living on a small plot of land where he would have a fine cow and chickens. Asher pulled up a stool and patted Matilda's side. The cow mooed, turned her head, and licked Asher square on the face.

"Ack, you silly beast. Save your tongue for the grassy fields or finding Ella's mate." Asher wiped his cheek before sitting on the stool. He whistled as he filled the bucket, the hens merrily clucking along. Deep into his task, he did not notice Ella enter with a large coverlet and a basket in her arms.

"Aunt Hildegard wishes you to have this," Ella said in English, holding out the cover.

"She did, did she?"

Ella looked down and nodded. Her cheeks filling with color.

"Then why did she not bring it out herself?"

Ella shifted her feet and bit her lovely lower lip, clearly trying to come up with the words that would hide her lie. Finally, she just shrugged.

If he stopped his task, he knew he would drag her into his arms again and that would not do, especially with Mistress Brandt a handful of paces away. Asher motioned with his head to the straw-stuffed pallet. "Place it there."

Swiftly she complied before turning to the chickens. "Are you sure you will be comfortable here? Even though the days are getting warmer, the nights are still chilly."

Asher gazed around his new home. A cow, a few chickens, and mice. He had slept in worse places. "I shall be fine."

She nodded again but did not say more. Was her mind on the kiss as well?

Finished with the milking, Asher put his hands on his thighs. "I am sorry for taking advantage of you. At times I can be a cur. I promise it will not happen again."

His words were meant to relieve her, but instead a dark shadow crossed her face.

"Ella? What is it?"

"I—I fear this is not the best place for you either."

Aye. It was not, or perhaps it was... "Ella, what do you fear?"

She picked at the straw on the edge trough, and Asher worried she would not answer. Finally, her jaw eased. "I worry that you are still in danger. You are a foreigner who asks too many questions. But now Hanenburg is crawling with strangers. Perhaps my fears are for naught. Still, Hanenburg is not the quiet sleepy village it used to be. 'Tis not safe anymore."

Asher sucked in his breath. "What do you mean?" *Please, Ella, please. Tell me what you know so I can end this and take you away from this dangerous place.*

But she said nothing.

Asher rose and came to her side, letting his fingers softly trail down her cheek. "Ella, I am one of those strangers. You know I have come here to get involved in the Protestant cause."

Her eyes filled with tears. "I know. But sometimes you do not speak like them. They may harm you again. These men play a treacherous game."

She spoke of his slip of words this morning. Clearly, his kiss had no effect on her for she had not forgotten their talk. Yet she cared what happened to him. What a beautiful gentle soul. A tear slid down her face, and Asher caught it with his finger. "I will be careful. They will not harm me again, once they know I am a friend."

She shook her head and stepped away. "Do not use that word so lightly. Friends can turn on you faster than your enemies. Life only gives us a few true friends. Friends who should be protected at all costs."

By the holy virgin, he had never imagined. She did know where Lady Jane was, and somehow, they had developed a friendship? The bottom of his stomach opened up and sucked in his heart. Ella would hate him after he... By all that was holy, he did not want to hurt her. He did not want to hurt anybody anymore. But his family was depending on him.

Suddenly he knew the truth. When this was done and he returned to England, there would never be any peace for him. Ella's sad eyes would haunt him forever, just like all the others he had exposed for their wayward beliefs. There was no mercy for a man like him. He would be tortured by his thoughts for the rest of his life, and then he would be tortured in the flames of hell. He deserved both.

Indulging in his pity was short-lived as the braying of a donkey filled the air. "Master Werner is here," Ella said. Wiping the tears from her face, she pushed past Asher, leaving the empty basket at his feet.

Asher quickly filled the basket with eggs and grabbed the pail of milk from beneath Matilda. "I will come for more later," he said to the cow before he stepped out of the shed.

"*Guten Morgen*, Master Werner. What brings you by so early?" Ella asked, trying to sound cheerful. "Will you break your fast with us?"

The barrel-chested man slipped off the donkey's back, tying his reins to a nearby tree. "*Ja,* sure." He barely looked in Asher's direction as he followed Jane into the cottage.

"Master Werner," Mistress Brandt said in a too formal manner.

As if he lived here, the Protestant priest took his usual seat at the table. "'Tis nice to see you too," he said warmly.

Asher placed the basket of eggs on the table along with the bucket of milk.

Mistress Brandt frowned and turned away. Her actions did not seem to bother Werner for he dipped a cup into the milk and took a long drink. He wiped his mouth afterward. "Ah, Matilda gives the best milk."

The rest of the meal was spent with pleasant small talk until Mistress Brandt asked the important question. "Why are you here?"

Werner sat back in his chair and smiled. "Why, I have come to take Master Blackwell to town."

Asher nodded, and he gently lowered his cup to the table.

Ella's eyes widened with fear, and Asher quelled the idea of taking her into his arms to calm her.

"What does he need in the village?" Mistress Brandt narrowed her gaze, shifting it between the pair.

"*Ja,* why does he need to leave?" Ella asked, her voice filled with concern.

Asher raised both of his hands. "I need to buy a few supplies." His words were met with a look of shock from Mistress Brandt and a sigh of relief from Ella.

"Would you like to come with us?" he asked Ella.

Asher's heart swelled when she lit up brighter than any candle burning in a church.

"*Nein.* She is needed here. This is the day we make our poultice." Mistress Brandt extinguished the fragile flame of hope.

Asher opened his mouth, ready to give argument, but then he stopped. Truth be told, Ella probably would be safer here. He could not traipse about town digging out information and keep an eye on her as well.

"Then, we shall see you later." A look of appreciation skipped across Mistress Brandt's face. Or perhaps it had just been his willful imagination. "Are you ready, Werner?"

The wayward priest shoveled another mouthful of food into his mouth before he stood. "*Ja!*"

Ella had not lied. Hanenburg was teeming with strangers. Most were fighting men. Even a simpleton would know this was the makings of an army. Asher's mouth went dry. His injuries had lost him valuable time. He should have been looking for Lady Jane and foiling the plans of the Champions of Christ instead of lying on a pallet gazing at the sweet Ella Brandt. The faster this army grew, the harder it would be to squelch this rebellion. Now more than ever he had to find Lady Jane. Once she was dead and the news spread far and wide, these men would shuffle back to their homes and perhaps return to the true faith.

Werner dismounted his donkey and handed the reins to Asher. "Tie up the beast at the stable before you make your purchases. I will meet you later."

Asher watched Werner amble over to a group of straggly strangers. A few words were spoken before the group disappeared between two buildings. Asher wanted to follow, but he would be spotted with a donkey trailing behind him. Probably the reason Werner had handed him the reins in the first place.

With that option closed, Asher went to the stable, purchased a good workhorse, and left both the donkey and horse there until later. He then went to buy a cart before going to see Schmitts, the blacksmith. Devastating heat and the loud ring of hammers filled the air when Asher entered the shop. A sweaty lad stoked the fire while

Schmitts and another man forged the metal. Swords, maces, and battle-axes hung from the rafters. The makings for a deadly army.

"By the Lord's goodness, I never thought I would see you again," the blacksmith cried. "We could use your help. Are you well enough to handle a hammer?"

Asher ran a hand across the back of his neck. "I am sorry, but I have not come for work. I am here to purchase a hammer and a good ax."

The blacksmith frowned as he smashed and molded a piece of hot metal. "I will give you double what I paid you before. You can always chop trees when the war is over."

Asher's gut took a twist. War fever was indeed running high in Hanenburg. "I have another task that must be taken care of before I could help you or wield a sword."

"Like you would even know how to wield such a weapon." Master Schmitts's hammer slammed the metal again.

Truer words had never been spoken. Asher spent most of his time sneaking about and when necessary using his dagger. "All the more reason for me to be chopping trees instead of men."

The smithy wiped his brow and then motioned to the back of the shop. "Out back, I have an old mallet, but not an ax. I have none to spare."

Asher opened his pouch and pulled out a couple of coins. "Are you sure you do not have an extra ax?"

A brightness entered Schmitts's eyes before his hammer came down hard on the metal. "Take whichever you want."

With a purse filled with coins, it did not take Asher long to acquire all of his supplies. Nor did it take him long to secure a safe place for his purchases until it was time to leave. Somewhere, Karl Krumler lurked these streets. This time Asher would make sure he would get the information he needed or he would pummel it out of the snake.

A tip of a dagger in his back made Asher freeze. "What ye been up to, Master Hayes?"

The English voice was familiar though not well liked. Asher swung about to stare into the icy blue eyes of Randell Benton. His dirty brown hair hung like strings around his face. The man not only stunk, he was a stench that permeated the streets of London. Another of Queen Mary's spies, willing to do any disgusting task. All this Asher could accept since he was not a saint either, but Benton enjoyed inflicting pain. He relished in each killing. Torture exhilarated him. He would rather fillet a human being than a fish. If he were here, that meant the queen was growing impatient.

"Master Benton, what an unpleasant surprise. I would ask what brings you to this humble hamlet but let us not stand on formality. I know why you are here."

Benton lowered his weapon. "The queen has an itch under her skirts wondering what has been going on here."

Crude, but Asher expected nothing less from the man. "I had a small interruption, being almost beaten to death."

"Aye, I heard. I also heard ye are staying on von Hoffbauer's land."

"I am not within the castle walls if that is what you are thinking. I am staying in a cottage not far from the castle. But worry not, I have recovered and I do have a way of entry into the castle."

"Ye think the missy is there?" A glow flamed in Benton's eyes. Already the man was thinking of slowly slicing Lady Jane.

"I am sure of it. But I will take care of the problem. You can return to England and assure our queen that things will be over very soon." Lady Jane would die by his hand, not by this monster's, and Asher would make the death as painless as possible.

"Nay. I am to stay here and encourage ye to complete yer task." Benton tapped his dagger in the palm of his hand.

Asher fisted his hands. How grand it would be to smash this cur in the face. "I need only a sennight and all this will be over."

"I hope ye are right. Because the way this bunch looks right now, they might march just for the sake of cracking a bunch of heads."

"Then perhaps you should join them."

Benton's lips twitched. "Watch what ye say, Hayes. Or ye might find a blade in yer own back."

"Try it." Asher stepped closer, and his voice pitched lower. "In fact, do it now."

Contemplation filled Benton's eyes before he stretched the distance between them. "Just get the deed done. Quick." He then took off and blended into the mass of mercenaries.

Asher scanned the square. One thing the lout was right about. If Lady Jane was not dead soon, there would be a trail of blood all the way from Hanenburg to London. The thought left a foul taste in Asher's mouth. He licked his lips and walked to the Growl Bear. Where better to meet members of the Champions of Christ.

Hearty voices and laughter rang out of the inn. The smell of roast pork made Asher's mouth water while he tried to find an empty spot.

Liesel Sommer waved to him and pointed to a small table next to the hearth. "'Tis good to see you up and about."

"I am happy about it myself." Asher sat as Liesel put a tankard of beer in front of him. He handed her extra coin. "This is for the charity you extended me the first night I came to Hanenburg."

She blushed, looked around the inn, then casually scooped the coins into her hand. "'Twas not my doing. Are you hungry?"

"*Ja,* a plate of your pork would be much appreciated."

She nodded before her smile faded. "I do not have a single room for you." She paused. "But if you like, you could have a space on the floor in the back."

Asher took a long pull of his beer. "Ah, that is good. My thanks for the offer, but I will not need it."

Liesel waited for more explanation that Asher did not offer. The woman then retreated before returning with a heaping plate of pork and onions. "If you want anything else, just give a yell."

He had eaten only a few mouthfuls when the door burst open and in sauntered Karl with another man. Neither seemed surprised to see Asher. They strolled to his table and took a seat. "You come back for more?" Karl dug a dirty hand into Asher's food.

"*Nein,* but you already know that. I am certain Master Werner has spoken to you and the rest of your *friends*?" Asher let his hands drop to the dagger that rested against his thigh.

Karl smacked his lips and pushed the plate of pork toward his friend. "*Ja*. But that does not mean I care for you. In truth, I do not like any of *you*." The last comment was made with a wave at all the men in the room.

"Blame Prince von Hoffbauer, not me, for the others. He put the call out for fighting men."

"You are to come with us." Karl leaned over the table while his friend stood.

Nonchalantly, Asher sat back in his chair. "I am not a fool to fall for the same trick twice."

Karl put a hand across his heart. "I promise not to hurt you."

The other man tried to step behind Asher's chair, but Asher was quicker. He shot to his feet and brought his dagger to the man's throat. The room stilled. "I will go with you, but I will keep my blade where it is."

Another old man in the back of the inn started to laugh. "About time somebody put a knife to Wilhelm's neck. Keep an eye on him, sir. He's a mean one." The room rung out with guffaws and taunts.

Even Karl seemed to be amused by his friend's predicament. "Not many get the jump on Wilhelm. Come along, then."

Asher followed Karl out of the inn but kept his weapon at Wilhelm's throat. They had not gone far when Karl slipped into the weaver's shop, heading to a room in the back. He cracked open the door, releasing the smell of sweat and stale beer. At least ten men sat around a rickety table while another five leaned against drab wooden walls. It took a moment for Asher's eyes to adjust to the muted light.

"Now that is not necessary, Blackwell. We are all friends here." Werner sat at the head of the table with his arms folded about his large belly. "Come, have a seat." A man vacated a chair, pushing it toward Asher.

Removing the blade from Wilhelm's neck, Asher sat down, his back to the door. "I assume this is the band known as the Champions of Christ?"

"Some of us, but not all," Werner said.

Indeed. Where was Prince von Hoffbauer and the infamous Lady Jane Grey? Nonetheless, Asher was pleased. He had been brought into the fold. "Then I am hoping my presence here means I am to be trusted?"

"But of course." Werner smiled, while a few of the other men frowned and grumbled. "I have told the men that the prince trusts you and that you are performing a most valuable service."

"I do not think watch—"

"No need to go into details. We all do our part." Werner's censure brought the whole room to silence.

A smart idea. If only a few knew what the others were doing, then there would be less chance of failure. Unfortunately, the prince had trusted the wrong man. For now, Asher would play the dutiful member until he found his true quarry.

He eased back into his chair. "Then what shall we talk about?"

"We just wanted you to know how sorry we were for what happened earlier and that it will not happen again. Right?" Werner stared at Karl and Wilhelm until they both bowed their heads and nodded. "We all have to keep a sharp eye. There are so many strangers in Hanenburg that we do not know whom we can trust. Best to get them out of town and to a place where they can begin their training. When the time comes, we need to fight like a warrior army, not a bunch of hay farmers. Now leave us. I wish to speak to Master Blackwell in private."

No one moved for a moment until Werner cleared his throat. Grumbling again, they brushed past the table, making their way for the door. When the last man had left, Werner turned his attentions back to Asher. "I brought you here so they knew who not to trifle with in the future and for you to give them wide berth. From now on I want you to come to market day with Hildegard and Ella, to keep them safe. I fear the prince did not think that so many would heed his call to join the cause."

"Then you best round them up and get them to your camp, Father Werner."

"Ack, there you go again. I am no priest. I am just the spiritual shepherd here. Please call me Otto."

Asher slowly shook his head. "Nay, you will always be Werner to me."

"Fair enough. And you shall always be Blackwell to me. Now then, let us go to the Growl Bear and have a beer." As Werner rose, Asher grabbed the man's arm.

"I think not. We must talk. I want you to know I will protect Ella and Hildegard with my life. They are good women—"

"That is good to hear." Werner sat back down.

"But I need to know everything. Where is the army camped, and what other nobles besides the prince are involved in this?"

Werner wrinkled his brow and leaned toward Asher. "And why do you need to know this? How will this serve you in protecting the ladies? 'Tis best that you know as little as possible. Think on this, if the disciples knew that Christ was to die, would they have followed him?"

"He did tell them, but they did not understand."

"Exactly." Werner's warm breath drifted over Asher's chin. "If they would have understood, they would have tried to save Jesus from his grizzly crucifixion, and then where would we all be? Wallowing in our sins with no way out."

Asher almost stated that they still wallowed in sin. For where was God's love and mercy in watching men kill each other? "How am I to trust anyone when I do not know what is going on?"

Werner rose from his seat. "I would have thought you knew the answer to that one by now. Trust no one and treat all as if they mean to do you harm."

"Those are not words of encouragement from a shepherd of God." Asher rose and followed Werner to the door.

"Perhaps not, but they are prudent words at a very dangerous time."

With an army being formed and men like Benton roaming the streets, these were perilous times indeed. Asher rolled his shoulders and resisted the urge to shake his head. All this danger could end with the blood of one life. Only this time it was not the blood of Christ that would save the world, but the blood of one lone woman… Lady Jane Grey Dudley.

CHAPTER 18

At the Growl Bear Asher thought the enticement of beer might loosen Werner's lips. However, the preacher guarded his words like a maid guarding her virtue. Surprisingly, he had only one beer and could not be coaxed into another. "You had best get back, no telling what those two women might be up to."

"I believe they are making poultice to sell later this week in the market square. What is there to worry about? Come, have one more beer."

Werner pushed away from the table. "*Nein*. We must be getting back."

The laidback Werner had changed into a careful, shrewd man. Or perhaps he had been that way all along and Asher had never noticed. No matter, it was a long ride back to the cottage, especially with a cart laden with goods. Surely Werner would open up on the road.

The sun glowed bright orange in the western sky before the cottage lay before them. All the way, Werner talked about the weather, the purchased items, even how he had come to own his donkey, but he refused to speak about the Champions of Christ and where the army was located.

At the cottage, they found Hans standing with his own ax amidst a heap of firewood, sweat pouring from his brow. He took one look at Asher and immediately frowned.

"Ah, Hans, I am so glad you were here to keep an eye on the ladies," Werner called.

"*Ja.* Ella enjoys my help." Hans threw the ax over his shoulder and glared at Asher.

"I am sure she does." Werner maneuvered the donkey toward Hans. "Would you mind helping Master Blackwell with the supplies?"

Without waiting for an answer, Werner dismounted and secured the beast before entering the cottage.

"Go on inside, Hans. I will take care of the wares." Asher jumped from the cart and began unhitching the horse.

Hans walked over and looked inside the cart. "What is all this?"

"I thought the ladies might like a cart and horse to take their goods to market. The hammer, ax, and other supplies will be used in expanding the shed to accommodate the horse, and other things."

Hans shook his head as he rummaged through the back of the cart. "Mistress Brandt and Ella do not need an ax. I chop their firewood. You wasted their money."

Asher smiled. "An ax can be used for other things beside chopping wood, and I purchased everything, not the ladies."

Hans lifted his eyebrows. "You bought all this for them? Why?"

Asher said nothing but led the horse into the shed and tied him a good fifteen hands away from Matilda. The cow looked at her new companion with a wary eye. "Be not afraid, Matilda. Goliath is not here to take your place. Are you?" The horse let out a nicker as Asher scratched his neck. Her replacement would come later when the prince came through with the other cow.

Hans poked his head into the shed. "Why are you still here? You look well enough to leave. I can look after the women. They do not need you."

"That may be so, but I have been asked by Prince von Hoffbauer to stay."

The bag of supplies in Hans's arms hit the ground with a thud. "Why would he do such a thing? I am supposed to watch them."

"Not true. Your task was to beat me senseless, and mine is to protect these fine women."

Color flew up Hans's neck. "We did not know who you were. Rarely do we have strangers show up in Hanenburg that do not have relatives here. I am not proud of what I did. I was just doing what I was told to do, and Wilhelm got carried away."

Asher thought about the man. He came from the same stock as Benton. Some men just enjoyed inflicting pain on others. "All is in the past. Let us not discuss it further. We are on the same side now. I have just come from a meeting." Asher kept his voice low and added a hint of intrigue.

"*Ja.* I knew they were going to let you in. I thought you would stay in town until Mistress Brandt told me otherwise. I just did not know why."

Mistress Brandt! Asher would have thought it would be Ella, hoping to get rid of the big blond once and for all. Truth be told, Mistress Brandt did not want either of them hanging around Ella. The protective hen watching her chick. Still, if Mistress Brandt had a choice, she would have chosen Hans as protector.

A niggle of unrest settled in Asher's gut. Something was not right, but he could not fathom what caused his turmoil. "You can put the other supplies over there." Asher pointed to the opposite wall.

With a long face, Hans picked up the bag and dumped it on Asher's bed. "It looks like you are planning to stay here a long time."

"On the contrary, I am not sure I will be able to finish the tasks I am going to start. If I do not, promise me you will?"

Puzzlement crossed Hans's face "What are you planning to do?"

"I plan to make this shed sturdier and a little larger so it can house Goliath, Matilda, and a new cow the prince will be giving the ladies. Then I plan to make a separate home for the chickens."

"Where did you get all the coin to buy these things? When you arrived, Mistress Sommer told me you did not even have enough to pay for a night at the Growl Bear and had to go to work for Master Schmitts."

Asher winked. "I lied. I stole the coin from a very evil man." He then picked up a small sack. "This flour goes in the cottage."

"Does Mistress Brandt and Master Werner know you have such coin?" Hans dutifully opened his arms and took the smaller sack.

"Of course, they do. But my sin had been forgiven once Master Werner knew what I planned to do with the money. So now that everything has been purchased, we have much to do."

Hans did not even look at the sack in his arms. "What do you mean, *we*?"

"I mean when you are not working on your father's farm, I want you to come by and help me with the shed. I am certain you are capable of such a task, and I know Ella would be most pleased when all is finished."

Hans blushed. "Why? Why are you being so kind to me? Especially after what I did to you."

"Because our Savior said to do unto others as you would have them do unto you." Asher then came to Hans's side and slapped him on the back. "Besides, if something happens to me, I want to make sure Mistress Brandt and Ella will be taken care of. Promise me."

The big blond nodded and thankfully did not say another word.

Jane could not put her finger on it, but something had definitely changed between Asher and Hans over the past few days. Hans used to come to the cottage to see her, now he came to be with Asher. When the pair announced that they were going to fix the shed, Hildegard had been quite upset. She even threw them out of the cottage and then gave Otto Werner a good tongue lashing for taking Asher to town in the first place. Still, even she seemed pleased when the old shed took on a new look. Now, Hildegard would daily recite a verbal list of chores Asher and Hans could do once the shed was done.

But Jane had noticed something else that no one else did. At times, when she looked out the window, it was only Hans cutting and hammering the logs into place.

Asher was nowhere to be found. When she questioned Hans about Asher's disappearance, the blond would just shrug and say Asher was looking for good trees to cut down. At first, she accepted the answer, but then she began to keep track of the time he was gone. Often, he left at noontime and did not show up until the sun was almost set with a few tree branches in hand. Asher was not a sluggard, for when he was here, he accomplished twice as much as Hans did. Nay, there was something else going on.

When the shed was completed, Hans had to return to his father's fields and Asher started fixing the loose shutters on the cottage. Hildegard was so pleased she began to give him extra helpings of turnips and kraut during mealtime. There was no more talk of Asher leaving. In fact, Hildegard started singing of the man's virtues and what a fine husband he would make for a maid someday. However, she was prudent enough never to leave Jane alone with him.

The truth be told, she was never alone. If Asher was not there, then Hans, Otto Werner, or Hildegard were present. At times, Jane felt like she was a prisoner in her own home. Perhaps it was the fear of war that kept them all close. One could not walk down a single street in Hanenburg and not hear whisperings of the fight to come. If she did not leave soon, then all would be lost. Every time she brought up leaving to Hildegard, the older woman would brush her concerns away. Her words were always the same. "There is time. The army is far from ready. The prince does not have enough men." They may have time, but Mrs. Ellen did not.

Jane jammed the prince's mending into a sack. Their weekly visits had become tense, and she feared soon he would expose her to the Champions of Christ and the whole village as well. When that happened, she would never get away. Her hands stilled on the bag; her fate was sealed already. As long as Asher lived here, she could not leave. He would immediately tell Otto who would alert the Champions of Christ. Unless she came up with a plan. She shook her head. "It would not work."

"What would not work?"

Her heart sped up when she turned to find Asher standing in the doorway. "'Tis nothing. I was just talking to God."

He chuckled and leaned against the doorframe. "Is not God capable of doing anything?" His smooth English words awoke her senses.

"Aye, but sometimes I do not think he is listening," she answered in the same language.

"I know what you mean, I have felt the same way many a time." He then paused and looked around the cottage. "Where is your aunt?"

"She took the horse and cart and went to visit Mistress Meyer and others. She will not be back until late."

"Really? That clearly is proof that God exists. For it is a miracle she has left us alone together. Praise the saints."

The smooth tone of his voice sent a shiver down her spine, and a warmth grew in her belly. If his words ignited her body, what would his caresses do? She dropped her eyes to her toes at such a primal thought. Best to think of what he said and not his hands. She could not figure those out either. He said he was a Protestant, and yet once again, he spoke like a Catholic, calling on saints. She knew it was out of habit, but if he did not stop...

"Sir, you must—"

"Asher. Say my name, sweet Ella. Do not stand on formality when we are alone."

Her throat went dry. "Asher," she whispered.

He took a step forward, then stopped. His hands curled and uncurled at his sides. His hard chest rose and fell. He fought to protect her virtue, and all she wanted to do was throw it away.

Jane picked up the bundle of mending and closed the distance. "Thank you for your chivalry," she whispered, her lips close to his cheek. Before he could stop her, she rushed out of the cottage and began her short walk to the castle. If she stayed, she knew what would happen.

"I am sorry," he called from the door, but she did not look back. She could not or he would see the desire in her eyes. And then he was right next to her, keeping up with her hardy pace. "I just wanted...us to be friends."

Friends. Had that not already been established? *A kiss here, a kiss there.* To him all this was nothing more than a game of friendship, but to her it was so much more. What would he say if he knew he could make her stomach a messy mass with just his charming smile? Or how his voice, in any language, heated her to the core? *Heaven help her!* She had been a married woman. She had shared the marriage bed, albeit only once, but she had never felt such a driving desire. If she stayed on this path, it would only lead to destruction. Hers, she could take, but not Asher's.

Oh, how she wanted him to leave before he found out the truth. She could not bear to see his face once he knew she was Lady Jane Grey. Then all would change. Would he act like a dutiful subject? How she would loathe that. Right now, they were equals and she wanted it to remain so. She wanted the easy banter. She wanted his light teasing. She wanted his...nay, she would not think it. There was no future in thinking about what could never be.

Jane lifted her chin and picked up her pace. "Of course, we are friends," she said lightly with a heavy heart. "Now go back and finish whatever it is you are working on."

He was silent for a moment as if pondering some grave words. "Good. I am glad we find favor with one another, but I shall not turn back."

"Why ever not?" She kept her eyes straight ahead.

"You should not be out without protection."

She stopped. "Protection!" Her heart tumbled. Did he know who she was?

"Aye, there are many disagreeable men lurking about these days. I shall go to the castle with you." He started walking, but she did not.

"The prince will not meet with you."

Asher paused and turned to look back. "I am not interested in meeting the prince. I am interested in walking along with the beautiful Ella Brandt."

Oh, he was a charmer. He reminded her a little of the men at court who were always trying to woo some maid. "Then if you wish to waste your day, come along, but let us talk about other things."

"Such as?"

"Protestant beliefs or scripture." Such topics surely would not arouse the carnal spirit.

"All right. Should we talk about the beauty of priest vestments or the loveliness of Rome?"

"You sound as if you agree with both? I dare say you sound more Catholic every day!"

He flashed her a dashing smile. "On the contrary, I was just thinking how your beauty rivals both."

Oh, he was a dangerous man. May God help preserve her heart.

CHAPTER 19

The rest of their short journey was spent in simple pleasantries and a small amount of talk about Christian beliefs and doctrine. Though Ella clearly wanted to keep the topic on thus, Asher enjoyed watching her blush when he shifted the conversation to her beauty and wit. How he wanted to pull the cap from her head and let the sun shine on her unusual golden-brown hair. But Ella was ever modest and kept her head covered most of the time. She was such a timid bud of a flower just waiting to bloom.

What the women at court could learn from such a gentle soul. Apprehension tingled down his neck. Why would his mind put Ella at court? Those women would devour her. Nay, his thoughts played a mean trick. Better the flower remained here—safe. Again, his mind conjured up a picture of Ella in royal robes. The vision froze him to the core. He blinked his eyes to dispel the foolish notion.

Once through the castle gate, they were separated. Ella was taken to the great hall, while Asher meandered around the bailey. When those about lost interest in him, he began to search in earnest. There had to be a way to slip away to the living compartments. Lady Jane must reside there. His heart kicked up a pace as he squeezed the dagger at his side. He would be quick, a fast slice at the throat and this foolish campaign of the prince's would be over.

Asher found a door that led to the kitchen. A few servants lifted a brow, and a rotund man lifted a large butcher knife. "Get out of here, thief."

With a hasty bow, Asher skidded around the man and ended up in the hall. He assumed he would run into Ella and possibly the prince, but neither were about. In truth, few were in residence. An old man slept by the door while a maid swept out the hearth. Taking advantage of the situation, Asher smiled and deftly slipped up the stone stairs. A large, ornately carved wooden door stood to his right, probably leading to the prince's chamber. There were several more doors, one of which had to lead to Lady Jane's room.

He had to choose carefully. If he picked the wardrobe, he would probably find himself face-to-face with Ella. That would not do. A niggle of apprehension skidded down his back. What if Ella was with Lady Jane? Then what would he do? His mind quickly hatched a plan. He would give a few apologies, suffer Ella's scolding on the journey home, and then, later this eve, return to finish the job. 'Twould be easy now that he had the lay of the castle.

Asher leaned his ear against a different door, thinking for sure it had to be the lady's chamber. Still, he heard nothing. Slowly, he lifted the latch. Heavy curtains covered the window, blocking out the day's sunlight. A musty smell permeated the air. The walls were painted with faded green vines and multicolored blooms. A lovely carved bed sat against a wall, and a dusty leather chair sat next to a hearth filled with cobwebs. This could not be Lady Jane's room for it had not been used for some time. He turned to leave and then paused. Yet, this should have been her room, for clearly it was meant for the lady of the keep.

He stepped back into the hall. Where could she be? Could the prince have given her his room or changed the wardrobe into her chamber? There was only one way to know for sure. Asher stilled his breath and listened against another door. Nothing. He tried the latch, but it was locked. Again, not surprising if the room was indeed the wardrobe. Certainly, Prince von Hoffbauer had many valuables he wished to protect. One, in particular. Asher fished his dagger out of his doublet and worked the latch. The door popped open.

The wardrobe was just that. Filled with trunks, jewels, clothing, coins, and—Asher took a sniff—spices. The room had not been changed into a lady's chamber. That left one other room, Prince von Hoffbauer's. Would he give Lady Jane his room? If so, then where was he residing? Asher leaned an ear against the door that connected the wardrobe to the prince's chamber. He heard voices. Indeed, one of those belonged to the prince. The other was higher, a woman's?

A clearing of the throat drew Asher's attention toward the hall. There stood Werner, his eyes full of glee. For a man of wide girth, he had light feet. "Are you hearing anything of interest?"

Asher put a finger to his lips before exiting the room, closing the door behind him. He pulled Werner to the steps and did not stop until they had left the hall. "I know I should not have been up there, but when I did not find Ella in the hall... I was wondering."

Werner started laughing. "You thought the prince and Ella might be having a liaison? Oh, I am so glad I stopped you before you did something foolish. They are not. In fact, I am sure if you opened the door you would have found the prince's steward and possibly more within. It is usual practice that the prince tries on the shirts Ella mends before she leaves. I can assure you she is never alone with the prince." He looked away when he made the last comment. Perhaps to hide a lie.

"And you come here often enough to know this?" Asher asked.

Hesitation filled Werner's face before he quickly smoothed it away. "But of course. The prince has some of the best beer around." He grabbed Asher's arm and started leading him to the buttery. "Come, let us have a little. It will be some time before Ella is finished."

"How long could it take to try on a few shirts?"

Though Werner chuckled again, the older man's body tensed. Heaven forbid the prince was taking advantage of Ella. She had said they lived in the prince's cottage because of his gracious mercy. Asher started heading back to the hall. Being a prince did not give him the right to abuse Ella.

"Where are you going?" Werner called. "The buttery is this way."

Ella rushed out of the hall with a large bundle in her arms just as Asher was making his way up the hall stairs. He grabbed her by the upper arms. Her rosy cheeks and shortness of breath made Asher see red. "Are you all right? What did the prince do to you? If he touched you—" His last words came out in a shout.

"What are you suggesting?" she asked in a low voice, the color draining from her cheeks.

"I—you were alone with him," Asher sputtered.

She stepped away from his grasp. "Do you think that little of me? Has anyone told you such, or are these thoughts the makings of your own mind?"

Her angry words sapped up his anger. 'Twas true. He had jumped to a conclusion that was less than respectful. Werner had told him the truth, and yet he refused to believe. What was happening to him? In the past he had always taken his time and weighed out each situation. Now, he rushed ahead and lashed out with rash conclusions.

Asher looked about. Werner stood near the bottom step shaking his head. Many others had paused their tasks to watch the conversation unfold. If any heard a word, Ella's reputation could be destroyed. Not because what he said was true, but by what his mind had conjured up. He stepped back and bowed. "Forgive me."

She threw the bundle of mending into his arms and then marched to the castle gate with her head held high. Even though the sun shone brightly above them, it would be a frosty walk back to the cottage.

The beautiful afternoon and sweet spring air hung like ash in Jane's mind. Asher followed along apologizing profusely. Without question, he took her tense nature as a product of his ill behavior earlier. Little did he know she had almost dismissed his words immediately. She had more pressing problems to think about.

According to the prince, his army would soon join with Lord Kraus's and Lord Reinhardt's men. Other principalities would then give their support once they knew Jane stood at the head of the prince's army. No matter how many men the prince could muster, the army was doomed to fail.

Spain and the Netherlands would side with England, and what would France do? Remain silent? The prince hinted to a secret contract with the French. But would they side with a simple German prince with a large ego? Jane could not believe a Catholic country would throw in their lot with Prince von Hoffbauer. However, the French did not care for the Habsburg Empire and its vast control in Europe. Many believed that King Philip, Queen Mary's husband, wanted war with the French. And what of his uncle? Would Ferdinand remain silent? Of course not. He would fight Prince von Hoffbauer, and it would be the people of Hanenburg and the northern German principalities that would suffer.

Then there was Scotland. Many claimed the country leaned toward Protestantism even though they had strong Catholic roots. Would they defy Queen Mary? Prince von Hoffbauer believed the people of England would rise up against her.

If Queen Mary did lose her crown, Princess Elizabeth would be named Queen of England. What was the prince really after? Did he truly believe the English would choose Lady Jane Grey Dudley over Princess Elizabeth? Foolishness!

The prince sought power for himself. Jane tightened her jaw. Did he believe he could control her like her father and Lord Northumberland had in the past? Nay, she would never be that timid child again.

Time was running out. She had to leave now. Jane glanced at the crestfallen man walking next to her. Could she trust him? An English merchant would know the fastest and easiest route back to England. But would he help her?

Asher had made it plain he had come to Hanenburg to be part of the Champions of Christ. Without batting an eyelid, he would probably run to the prince with her plan of escape. Where did he go when Hans was busy working on the shed? There were many things she did not understand. If Asher wanted to be part of the rebellion, why did he stay at the cottage? Why was he not with the prince's army? Perhaps that is where he went during the day, but then why did not Hans go with him?

Jane slowed her steps and put a hand to her head. All these thoughts baffled her brain.

"Please do not stress so. If you wish, I will go back and confess my failures to all and sing highly of your virtue." The tender concern that wrinkled Asher's brow almost brought tears to her eyes.

"Nay, what is done is done. Let us not worry about it." She licked her lips, a plan forming in her mind. "I am wondering, when do you plan on leaving the cottage? Are you going to be part of the prince's grand army?"

His dark repentant eyes became hooded. "Why? Do you wish me to leave? I thought you would want to instruct me more on how to act and sound like a true Protestant."

The sides of her mouth quirked upward. "But you are a good Protestant."

"True, but I need to sound like one when I meet our future queen, Lady Jane."

His words were meant to tease, but her stomach flopped like a dying fish. Did he already suspect her identity? "What makes you think you would meet her? You are but a commoner like me."

"But you do know her, do you not?" The merriment left his eyes, and his tone became sober.

Indeed, he fished for the truth. She dropped her gaze to the dirt and started walking again. "How would I know her? How do we even know she is alive? Just because the prince has said she lives does not make it so. All this could be a lie so the prince can mass a large army." Her words rushed out so fast even she did not believe their worth.

"Ella." He moved close and softly touched her arm. His warm breath teased her neck. "It is not only the prince's mending that you do, is it? No man would have that many clothes to mend each week."

It took a moment for Jane to sort out his words. He had apologized for jumping to the wrong conclusion about her virtue. He did not figure out who she was, he believed she mended Lady Jane's clothing. A bubble of laughter escaped her throat as the fear in her stomach eased. Jane took the bundle from his hands and emptied it onto the ground. "Look, do you see any gowns or woman's shifts?"

Asher bent down and held up a tunic. "This might be…"

She grabbed it from his hand and held it up to her body. "I may be petite, but Lady Jane would have to be larger and taller than you in order for this to be hers." Jane bent down next to him and picked up a pair of breeches. "Maybe these are hers. Perhaps that is how she is hiding, as a man!" She thought her words would make him chuckle and bring a smile to his face, but they did not.

His frown deepened as if he were contemplating the possibility. "Perchance my thoughts are indeed foolish."

"Sometimes I do mend women's clothes—his servants' clothes. The prince does not want them looking shabby. Nor does he want them distracted from their regular duties by spending time stitching up their clothing." Jane cocked her head to the side. "The prince can be generous at times." That ended the conversation on the subject, but the glint in Asher's eyes betrayed his mind that still harbored the thought. She bent over and began shoving the mending back into the bag. "Best we get back to the cottage. I am sure Aunt Hildegard will be home shortly."

Their fingers touched when they reached for the same pair of breeches. Neither pulled away. Slowly his fingers slid upward as his thumb rested in her palm. Her breath froze in her lungs when he leaned inward and captured her lips. The kiss was tender, soft and welcoming. Glorious like a prayer given to the Lord most high. Her belly flamed at the sacrilegious thought, but the warmth in her heart spoke of purity and love.

He groaned and brushed a hand through her hair, unsettling her cap. He deepened the kiss. "Ella," he whispered when their lips separated. Waves of desire rolled through her. She threw her arms around his neck, pulling him closer. His lips took away all her worries, all her fears. With him she was needed and wanted, not for power, not for wealth, not for position. He just wanted her. And she wanted him.

"My sweet, sweet Ella. You torment me so," he cried out as his hands encircled her waist.

Reality slammed into her mind and awoke her wayward thoughts. She was not his sweet Ella. Not now, not ever. Jane opened her eyes and pulled away. Her cap lay next to the bundle, but Asher stilled her hands when she reached for it.

"Leave it off," he said. "Why do you want to hide your beautiful locks under a dowdy cloth?"

Because the roots might show another color—brighter, redder. She grabbed for the cap anyway, securing it to her head. "If you have not noticed, most women in Hanenburg cover their heads."

He sighed. "Not all. Mistress Sommer does not."

A light prick of jealousy annoyed Jane. She jumped to her feet and smoothed out her skirt. "Well, I am not Mistress Sommer. I do not tease men into doing things."

He did not move. Instead, he smiled and picked up an old stick, twirling it in his hands. "Doing what things? Like kissing men on the path?"

Jane's whole body erupted with heat. "I was not the one who started this game. You kissed me first."

Asher stood, dropped the stick, and pulled her into his arms again. "You cannot deny the attraction we have." He stroked his forefinger down the side of her face. "Do not fight it."

She pulled away and fisted her hands at her sides. "And what good is that attraction if you continue on this fool's mission. If you join the rebellion, you could get killed. And for what? So the prince can put a puppet on the English throne and control her like her parents did? Perhaps she does not want any of this. Perhaps she wants to be left alone. To live a humble life like you and me." Jane bit her tongue at the force of her words. What had she done? Asher was an astute man. Surely, he would see the truth.

His gaze narrowed, and he tilted his head. "Do you believe this because you know or because you wish to protect those you love?"

She should say both and confess all. But she could not. For all his words of adoration, Asher might still betray her. Where did he go when he slipped away? To the village for libation, to see Mistress Sommer, or did he practice with the prince's secret army? If the prince found out she planned to leave, her days of freedom would be over. Nay, she would not say anything until she knew for sure she could trust Asher.

"I do not want to see Master Werner, Aunt Hildegard, Hans, or you suffer. War is never a good thing. Surely there must be another way. Can we not tolerate each other's beliefs? The Treaty of Augsburg was supposed to do just that, and yet here we are, on the verge of war." Tears pricked her eyes, and she lowered her gaze to hide them.

He took one step forward and raised her chin. "You have seen so much death, have you not? Your parents, others? I promise you. There will be no war. This will end here."

The tightness of his features frightened Jane for a moment, but then he gave her a tender kiss meant to comfort, and her fears dissolved away.

He broke the kiss, took her hand, and led her down the road back to the cottage. "You will see, Ella. Everything will be all right."

Oh, how she wished he could make it thus. She squeezed his hand and prayed he was the man she hoped him to be. This eve would be her proof.

CHAPTER 20

Asher did not want to admit it, but Ella's mood on the path frightened him. Something happened at the castle. It was still unclear if Ella really knew Lady Jane or if the talk of the coming campaign had prompted old memories of her parents' death. Being the sympathetic sort, Ella may have transposed her feelings as being the same as Lady Jane's. Asher shook his head. As if Lady Jane could be as noble as his common maid.

His common maid. Aye, every day he began to think more and more of Ella as his. Granted, she was a Protestant, but not a very strong one if her words could be taken as truth. Had she not professed she wanted all to live in harmony with the Catholics? With a little instruction, he was certain she could become a good Catholic. His mind was made up. Once this business was over, he would take Ella as his wife. Together they would raise chickens and hoe their small plot of land. They would raise English-German babies and would happily live out their days—if Queen Mary would let him.

There was the curdled milk. As long as he lived in England, he would always be at the queen's call. But Ella and he could not stay here. Certainly not after he killed

Lady Jane. Nay, that would never work. He would puzzle out the problem later.

When they returned to the cottage, they found Hans sleeping next to the woodpile. "I shall go and get him a coverlet," Ella said.

Asher stayed her retreat. "Nay, he will be up soon. Go about your chores. I will take care of Hans."

The big blond wheezed like an old man and mumbled like a babe. A pleasurable dream brought a smile to his lips. "Ah, El...la." Hans's words brought a swift kick to his thigh from Asher's boot. Hans opened his groggy, dark-rimmed eyes.

"If you wish to sleep, stay home," Asher barked.

Hans washed a hand across his smooth face. "Ack, that I could. If I stay home, my *Vater* would put my back to the plow. I cannot march all night and work all day without some rest."

March all night. What did he speak of? Last night, Asher had met Benton at the soldiers' camp east of Hanenburg. If you wanted to call it a camp. There were perhaps a hundred men, and they were ill prepared. According to Benton, there was little going on. Even he could not bring himself to kill a single soul as none in camp were worth the effort. Yet, Hans claimed to be up all night marching and drilling. Come to think of it, Asher never saw Hans at the camp.

"Come then. Take my hand and go rest in my bed." Asher helped Hans to his feet before leading him to the shed.

Inside, the big German fell on Asher's pallet, putting his arm over his eyes. "My thanks."

Asher nodded. "One more thing before you rest. Do you march far from the east camp?"

"Eh? East camp. That is naught but a ruse to deceive the spies or those we do not trust. The prince is a cautious man. Besides, he can smell a traitor before they even open their mouths."

"Not always."

Hans peeked out from under his arm. "You were our only mistake. Though Karl still thinks you cannot be trusted."

Clearly the prince did too for Asher did not have knowledge of the true camp. That would explain why he was assigned to watch Ella. 'Twas all a ruse to keep him far away. Old hatred brewed in Asher's gut. Did the prince use Ella as a pawn who could be so easily discarded? The man deserved a dagger in the heart as much as Lady Jane. "I would like to go with you this eve. If that would be all right?"

"What about keeping an eye on the women?"

"You know as well as I that there is nothing to protect here. Mistress Brandt would take her thin blade to anyone who would tip an eye at Ella."

"*Ja,* for sure. You can come, but if the prince spots you, I will not come to your defense."

Asher had no intention of seeing the prince, at least not until the task was completed—search the camp for a maid that might be dressed as a lad. If Lady Jane hid among the ranks, he would find her and finish her off. Then, he and Ella could leave this place.

After the evening meal, Asher and Hans retreated to the shed and waited for the ladies to retire. When all looked quiet, the pair slipped out and headed across the clearing to the west. They walked on until the moon shone high in the sky. Often Asher had to remind Hans to step softly, to which the blond would boom, "Why? We do not take the road. Our men have secured this area; none get through who do not know the call."

His total trust in the ability of others made Hans a very foolish man. Any good soldier, villain, or spy would be able to slip through a defense. Those that believed they were mighty were the easiest to dupe. Experience had taught Asher that the quiet and the patient were usually the ones to fear. For they would weigh out their options before they would crush and destroy.

Asher kept looking over his shoulder and surveying the landscape. With all the noise Hans was making, anyone could follow them. If this was how the man approached the camp nightly, then for sure it had been infiltrated with Queen Mary's spies. Ella was right, this campaign, these men, were all doomed. Now more than ever, Asher felt an obligation to end this mess.

Finally, Hans lifted his head and let out a piercing hawk like cry. He was answered in kind. "Come, it is safe now."

They slipped into a thicket, and indeed there were men armed with bows spread along the edge of the clearing, at least a good quarter furlong apart. Under the cloak of darkness, this line could easily be penetrable. Another sign of weakness.

Making it through, they came upon another larger clearing, protected by forest and brush on all sides. Asher's mouth went dry. Here stood a vast number of pavilions and modest tents. Men by the thousands mulled about like ants on a dusty field. Lances, longbows, battle-axes, nailed clubs, and maces rested near an armory tent. Men practiced by torchlight. If this army was a secret, it would not be for long. How the prince had mustered so many men was a miracle. But whether they could sustain the long trek to England was another matter, or did the prince plan to march south first, conquering the rest of the German nation?

Hans tapped Asher's shoulder. "Come on. My commander does not like it if I am late." They hurried into the camp to where Hans picked up a strong battle-ax. "The prince lets everyone have the weapon of their choice. He has provided all. He says we will be invincible if we are strong and fight as one."

Asher gave a slow nod. "Then go along. I will follow later after I have chosen my weapon." Hans took off toward a group of men while Asher slipped between two pavilions. It would take him months to uncover Lady Jane in this mass of men. However, when in doubt, think like your enemy. Only a foolhardy person would hide a woman as a lad among a bunch of rowdy men. Therefore, Lady Jane was not dressed as a lad, unless she was supposed to be serving a noble. Even then her safety would not be guaranteed.

Would the prince trust another noble to guard his prize? Probably not. Then she would be hidden and protected by someone who knew not what he had. As much as he hated to admit it, Asher would need Benton's help. The villain would relish in the game of seeking out the lady and slicing a few throats along the way. 'Twould not be easy reining in the man. If they were discovered, a trail of blood would flow from here to England.

Tonight, he would search as many pavilions as he could. Especially those where soldiers stood guard. On the morrow, he would enlist Benton's help. Perhaps by week's end the task would be done. The plan was sound, simple, and stealth. Yet, Asher could not shake a foreboding that niggled at his mind.

And for good reason, his ears pricked as he heard voices that were not German. He turned, and a coldness swept through him. The French were part of this army.

Jane followed the pair for a distance and then stopped. She knew where they went. The prince had boasted of his vast army. That had been a fortnight ago. Now it was ten times larger.

Asher was deep into this rebellion and would not aid her. She would have to make the journey to England alone, with the help of God. Jane returned to the cottage and started to make a mental note of all the things she would need. How far would she get on foot carrying a large sack of provisions? She had to take Goliath. Guilt infused her body. Hildegard would once again have to walk to market day. Jane sighed. Yet there was no other way. Even with the beast and a few provisions, she would not get far. She needed coin in order to get to England. Hildegard had little. That left only one option—Asher's coin pouch. Jane's insides became queasy. Stealing was a sin, but so was letting thousands die needlessly. Asher would be gone for a few more hours; she doubted he would take a bag full of money into a camp of greedy men.

Quietly, she slipped into the dark shed. The door creaked open, and the pounding of her heart filled her ears. She jumped when Matilda let out a snort. "Hush, girl. 'Tis only I." With a pat on the neck, Matilda settled down. Goliath did not even look her way. 'Twas a good thing Asher and Hans had made a separate chicken coop or the hens would surely give up her whereabouts.

Her gaze scanned the shed. Where could his hiding place be? She carefully felt beneath his straw pallet. Nothing. In Matilda's stall, Goliath's stall, in the feed bin, milking buckets, and the rafters above her head, she found nothing. Could he truly have been so unwise to take it with him? Perhaps he did. She had been raised with privilege where she wanted for naught, but what of Asher? A bag full of coins would be precious to him.

A merchant's son would have more than a peasant, but he would be shrewd with his money anyway. Where would a shrewd man hide his coin? As if by divine power, her gaze drifted to the back of the shed. The ground was soft all around, old empty grain and flour sacks lay about, distracting one's eye. One corner remained empty, the ground well packed. Of course, he would hide it in plain sight. She dug with her hands, her fingertips becoming encrusted with moist dirt. Less than a hand below the surface, she found the pouch.

A scrape outside made her pause. She tried to focus her hearing above the loud beat of her heart. Again, she heard it. Had Asher returned? She closed her eyes and cleared her mind. Listen. The night wind howled, followed by the harsh scrape. Jane filled her lungs with a cleansing breath. "A tree branch scrapes against the shed. 'Tis nothing, Jane, get ahold of yourself."

Quickly she opened the pouch. Coins spilled into her hand. There were many English and French coins, but only a few were German. If she took one of each, would he miss them? No matter. She needed them. The plan in her mind was set. Next Sunday, she would go to the meeting hall with Hildegard, then feign off ill, returning to the cottage. She would collect her provisions and take Goliath. No one would know she was gone until later in the day.

Jane tucked the coins into her bodice and returned the pouch to its hiding place. Carefully walking backward, she smoothed out the ground with her hands. Finally, she sneaked out into the night and back to the cottage. Once inside she quickly undressed, lying down on her pallet. She clutched the coins and lifted her eyes to the loft above. "Please, Lord, forgive me for this theft. And, if possible, make restitution for me by being bountiful to Asher and Hildegard. All praise and glory are yours. Amen."

Guilt still hung heavy upon Jane the next morn. Like a true thief, she hid the coins in a small purse tied to the inside of her skirt. Over and over she stroked the spot where the coins lay, trying to smooth the guilt that weighed her down.

She could not even look at Hildegard the next morn when she descended from the loft, but the older woman was quick to Jane's habits and did not mix words. "What ails you this morn?"

"Nothing," Jane said rapidly, turning to smooth out the lumps in her pallet.

"Uh-huh." Hildegard picked up a basket and held it out to Jane. "Then perhaps you can fetch us some eggs?"

Jane could feel her face flame, giving Hildegard a piece of valuable information. With a thump, Jane sat down on her bed.

"Ah, as I thought. Your worry has to do with Master Blackwell." Hildegard dropped the basket on the table and sat on a stool. "Out with it or I will have to guess, and I am sure you are not ready to hear my thinking."

Jane dropped her eyes to the floor as a calamity of feelings pressed against her heart. "I—I wish to leave now. I do not wish to march in front of the prince's army. I do not wish to be Queen of England. I do not even know if Mrs. Ellen is still alive. You promised me we would leave, and then you turned cool on the subject. I need to know why."

Hildegard leaned back and began to tap her fingertips on the table. She licked her lips and then shook her head. "I know that is what you want, child. And I so wish I could give it to you, but I cannot."

Jane rushed to her side and fell to her knees. "Why will you not leave with me? We could be gone this very eve while Asher goes to practice and drill with the prince's army."

As if she had been stabbed, Hildegard's face turned white and her eyes bulged. "What do you mean he is practicing with the army?"

"I saw him leave with Hans last night, and I followed them at a far distance, but I knew where they went. Hans bragged often that he marches with the rebel army at night. Do you not see that would be a perfect time to leave? No one would miss us until the morn, and even then, if Asher slept late—"

Hildegard looked out the window. "Blessed! Is the sun already that high in the sky? I have to go see Mistress Meyer." Hildegard stood and wrapped her cloak around her shoulders. "We shall talk about this later this eve."

Jane's hope fell. Hildegard would not leave with her. Ever. She rose to her feet. "Do you not want to break your fast first?"

"*Nein*. You stay put." Hildegard pointed a finger toward Jane. "No talk of leaving until I get back." With a definite thump, the door closed—Hildegard was gone.

Jane stood in the middle of the cottage and went over their conversation. What sent Hildegard off in a hurry? She had all but confessed that she did not want to leave and seemed ready to state why, but then suddenly she was up and out the door. The morn had barely broken upon the sky. Jane's fingers trailed along the rough edges of the basket. Their talk had begun and ended with Asher.

That was it! Hildegard was upset that Asher was training with the army. Why should that bother her? Asher had made it plain he had come here to join the rebellion. That he trained should have produced a shrug not a panic.

A sharp splinter pierced Jane's finger. Blood oozed from the tiny cut as she pushed the wood from her skin. Like this nagging piece of wood, Asher always turned Hildegard's face sour. She wanted him gone, and then suddenly she was fine with his presence. She warned Jane never to be alone with him, and then she left them alone. An all-too familiar curl of uneasiness crept into Jane's stomach. 'Twas like being back in England where she could trust no one—except Mrs. Ellen.

But Hildegard was not Mrs. Ellen who had wiped her tears and listened to Jane's sorrows from little on. Jane's heart cracked. Had she made a mistake in thinking Hildegard could be like Mrs. Ellen? Jane's breath came short and fast. Why had she not seen the truth? Hildegard lived on the prince's property. Hildegard had offered

Jane's mending services to the prince. Hildegard was the prince's eyes and Jane's jailer.

With sweaty fingers, Jane clutched the coins in her skirt. She could not stay here. Not one moment longer. But she did not wish to wake Asher, and she certainly would if she tried to take Goliath from his stall.

Another plan hatched in her mind. She would go to town and buy a horse. To quell suspicion, she would lie and say Aunt Hildegard wanted another beast of burden. Upon returning, Jane would pack her few belongings. Hopefully Asher would sleep late since he had been gone most of the night. If all went as planned, she would be long gone before anyone would be alarmed.

Heavenly Father, give me swift feet and a safe journey. And please, please detain Hildegard until I am far away and make Asher's slumber deep.

Chapter 21

The slam of the cottage door brought Asher to full consciousness. The night had been long and unsuccessful. He had searched a good many tents and had found nothing. Not a female in sight, nor a lad that was not such. To make matters worse, upon his return he realized someone had been through his things—his pouch was three coins light. He spent the rest of the night trying to discern who would take only a few coins and leave the rest behind?

He thought he had his culprit when he saw Mistress Brandt rush away this morn. Quickly he donned his breeches, tunic, and doublet, planning to give pursuit, but the door opened again. This time Ella exited. She paced back and forth, looking at the shed as if she were debating some great problem. Then she scurried off as well.

Where would she be going this early? Without hesitation, he followed at a safe distance. He expected her to head to the castle, but she turned toward the village and made a straight path for the stables. A twinge of elation twisted in his chest. The prince had been right. Ella did indeed plan to flee and no doubt planned to use his coin to purchase a sturdy mount.

Were both women in this together, or did Ella act alone? Asher hung back and leaned against a building, waiting to see Ella's purchase. He looked up at the rising sun, not a cloud in the sky. It would be a fine day, excellent for travel, but if she departed by noontime, he feared she would be discovered before the eve set in. He smiled. They would have to have a talk before she attempted such a journey.

"What ye be watching, Master Hayes?" The gravelly English voice of Benton dampened his joyful mood.

Asher turned, blocking the man's view of the stables. "I have been looking for you. I have some information I think would be of interest."

Benton lifted his eyebrows. "Ye do? And what would that be?"

Asher casually lifted his hand, curled his fingers in, and looked at his nails. "I fear these people do not trust you."

"Hey? What do you speak of? Trust. I am in their bloody army."

"Nay, you are in the army they wish you to be in. The true army is west of here, not east, and has more men than you can fathom. I wager you are never alone in the eastern camp, are you? Have you made a close friend or two who seem to stick by your side most of the time?"

"Aye. There is Karl and Wilhelm. When I came, they immediately befriended me. They seemed like a good pair."

Of course, Benton would think they were good. Karl and Wilhelm were just like Benton, beat a man close to death and ask questions later. Either way, the pair knew Benton was a spy. Asher scanned the village square. If they saw him with Benton, there could be trouble. "Listen to me. Lose the pair, head west out of town. I am sure you can figure out a way to get into the camp without being caught."

"Aye, it will be easy," Benton said, scratching his beard.

"Look for Lady Jane and do not draw attention to yourself. No unnecessary killing. Do you hear me?"

"I hear ye," Benton growled.

"I will meet you in a small clearing east of the camp. It is easy to find. Wait for my signal, three sharp screeches like an owl."

"I know the signal. I ain't stupid."

The comment was debatable, but Asher was running out of time. He spotted Ella leaving the stable with a fine grey mare. Not even with his own haggling skills could he have made such a bargain. Admiration exploded in his chest. He turned his attention back to Benton. "I have to go. Remember, later, meet me in the clearing."

Benton headed out of town, and Asher looked about before he stepped out into the square. He followed Ella without raising suspicion. Before she got to the cottage, she tied the mare to a tree, out of sight. Indeed, she was taking every precaution. She tiptoed past the shed.

Now, would she wait for Mistress Brandt to join her, or would she leave on her own? Either way, Asher planned to stop her. He paused briefly at the mare's side. The horse had good flanks and excellent bone structure. The muscles and weight seemed to be balanced well. Aye, this was a fine animal, and Ella could travel far and fast on such a mount.

Another question popped into his mind. Outside of town, she mounted the horse and rode as if it was second nature. Where did she learn such a skill? There were so many things he did not know about Ella, nor did he have the time to learn them. But once Lady Jane was dead and the army dispersed, he would have a chance to focus his attention on Ella.

A warm sweat beaded upon the back of his neck as he made his way to the cottage. With a quick knock, he entered. As suspected, a sack lay on the table along with a few gowns, a white cap, and a practical pair of hose. A sensible pair of boots stood on a stool.

His mouth quirked upward when he saw a few books in her hands. Alas, she could not be thinking right, for what would she do with books she could not read? "Ella, what are you doing?"

The books in her hand dropped to the table with a heavy thud. "I—I am cleaning."

He stepped into the cottage. "Are you?"

She nodded, pushing the books under the sack. "I am gathering items for the poor." She nodded again as if doing so could make her lie truth.

"You are giving all your clothes to the poor?"

Her cheeks colored. "These are not *all* my clothes. I—I have others."

He held up a pretty green gown with the simple laced collar. "You are giving this to the poor? Is this not your best gown? And Werner's books too?"

Every bit of exposed skin on her body turned purple. She grabbed the dress from his hands and jammed it into the sack. She tilted her head to the side and pursed her lips. "I have many beautiful gowns, and what makes you think these are Master Werner's books? They could be mine."

It took all of Asher's strength not to laugh out loud. Instead, he took a deep breath and smiled. "Ella, most cannot read. I know you are trying to flee from the prince. Please do not worry so, I am here to help you."

Her hands stilled, and she fixed her gaze on the sack. "I do not know what you speak of."

Asher took a step closer. "Do you know why I am still here and not living in the village?"

She lifted her shoulders but not her gaze. "Because I wanted you here and Aunt Hildegard allowed you to stay."

He pressed even closer. "Nay. The prince asked me to keep an eye on you because he feared you might betray him and Lady Jane to the Catholics, King Philip, and Queen Mary of England."

"What?" Her chin rose as shock rode across her face. "That is nonsense."

"Nay, it is not. 'Tis obvious you do not approve of the rebellion. You do not like the Champions of Christ. You think you can stop them if you share your knowledge with Queen Mary."

Ella sat down, dropping her chin to her chest. "Then you know." Heavy defeat filled her voice.

He knelt down and placed a hand gently on hers. "You know where the prince is hiding Lady Jane, and if you tell the Catholics where she is, we can stop this war before it has begun. But you do not have to run away to do so. I can help you."

She lifted her chin and knitted her brows. "Nay, you are confused. That is not why I am running. There is nothing you could do that would help me."

Asher placed his fingertips on her lips. "Aye, I can. I can kill Lady Jane, and then we can leave together."

She pulled back, her face paled, and her lips trembled. "What? You want to kill—"

"You have been right about me all along. I am a Catholic. A spy sent by Queen Mary to kill Lady Jane Grey Dudley. If I find her, then this can all end."

Ella rose and stumbled backward. Tears spilled across her cheeks. "But you said your brother was killed by the Catholics."

The confusion and pain she felt punched at Asher's soul. He wanted to take her into his arms and comfort her. To let her know all would be fine if she trusted him. "My brother was a priest, and he was killed by Protestants not Catholics in Wyatt's Rebellion."

Soot blackened the bottom of her skirt as she retreated onto the cold hearth's stones. "You are an assassin," she screeched.

A knave could have handled this better. Now, she feared him. How could he make her see she had nothing to worry about? He would never harm her. He held up his hands. "Listen to me, Ella. I do not usually go around killing people. I have no desire to harm anyone, but Queen Mary has threatened my family. If I do not kill Lady Jane, my family will never get out of prison. My sister may suffer a far worse fate. I do not wish to see her used in an ill way. Surely you can understand this? I am not a monster. I will not harm you."

The tears on her face dried, and a wariness replaced the terror in her eyes. He saw her hand wrap around an iron poker. "Why would Queen Mary choose you, a merchant, and not someone of a worthier stature?"

Asher cleared the thick lies from his throat and let the truth ring free. "My name is Asher Hayes. I was indeed born to a merchant, a Catholic merchant, who lost almost everything under King Edward's reign. By fortune, I heard of the king's death before most. I am the man who warned Queen Mary of Lord Northumberland's and Lady Jane Grey's treachery."

Jane's face paled all the more, and she all but crawled into the hearth. "I am sure you were rewarded handsomely for your efforts." Her voice was frosty. The eerie detachment in her eyes rolled a chill down the back of his spine.

Asher swallowed hard. "The queen knighted me and employed me to round up Protestants, but I swear to you, I did not kill them." He stepped closer, and she raised the poker to his chest.

"Oh, you are so noble, forcing others to do the killing!"

"I am a lout. I will not deny it. I wish I could erase the blood from my hands. But no matter how hard I try to change, the queen will not let me. All I want is the simple life. I thought maybe with you—"

"With me," Ella shouted. "I am a Protestant and proud to be such."

"But you said you do not condone the rebellion? Are not the Protestants just as bloodthirsty? I am here to end this once and for all. To save both Catholic and Protestant lives. Once you are away from these people, a beacon of light will shine upon you, and I know you will return to the true faith."

She pushed the poker against his doublet. He did not try to disarm her, for if she wished to strike him, stab him, so be it. He was far from a saint and deserved punishment.

"Ahh," she cried before throwing the poker across the room. "Get out. You are all thickheaded. Do you believe

God wants us to kill each other in His name? Who is right in this, the Catholics or the Protestants? Whoever sheds the most blood? Whoever wipes the other out? Whoever holds the power? I tell you, neither are right. All are wrong. God's name should never be used for bloodshed. Never!"

Ella crumpled to the ground; her cries clawed at Asher's heart. He took her into his arms and kissed the top of her head. "I will make this right. I swear, Ella. I will protect you."

With both hands, she pushed him away and let out a maniacal laugh. "You are going to protect me? You do not know what you are saying. Get out. Leave me be."

Asher knew he would get nowhere with her in this state. He stood and offered his hand. "Come. I think you need to rest a bit."

She looked at his outstretched hand as if it were a viper. "I do not need your help."

He took a deep breath. "Please. Lie down for a bit. You had a shock."

Her head bobbled to the left and then to the right. "Perhaps you are right. I need a little rest." She ignored his offered hand and stumbled to the pallet, throwing an arm across her eyes. "Leave."

Asher stared at her for a while until her chest rose and fell evenly. He went to the door and then looked at her sleeping form over his shoulder. "I swear," he whispered. "I will make this right. I swear on my life, we will seek harmony together—when this is all over."

Quietly he shut the door. Tonight, this would all end.

CHAPTER 22

Panic seeped through every part of Jane's body when she awoke to the heat of the day. She flew off her pallet and looked out the window. The sun had already started its slow descent in the west. Her plans had all gone awry. Without warning, her earlier conversation with Asher flooded her memory and sluiced open her soul. He was a Catholic who had come to kill her. His soft words of caring and protection would vanish once he discovered her true identity.

Perhaps she should seek him out and let him end her life. For in truth, it would cease the war, or would it? The prince was hell-bent on shedding blood. Could she bargain with Asher? Her life, if he would go and plead for Mrs. Ellen's release. Would he do it? When had a Catholic ever come to the defense of a Protestant? By his own admission, he had arrested many. Nay, he would not think twice of a poor Protestant woman burning at the stake.

Quickly Jane shoved the rest of her clothing and a few loaves of bread and a bit of cheese into her sack. She cringed when she took the few coins Hildegard had saved in the broken milk pitcher. Would God forgive someone who purposely stole twice? She raised her eyes. "Know that I do this out of desperation." Only time would tell if God would be merciful.

Jane peeked outside but did not see Asher anywhere. Perhaps he went to find Hildegard, or he could be in the shed where his coin bag could still be hidden. Jane fingered the coins in her hand. If she found the bag, she could return these to Hildegard's pitcher and add a few extra for good measure. Surely his coin was given to him to carry out her murder.

He had played her false with words of longing and passionate kisses. She had been nothing to him but a means to an end. A tool to be used and discarded once its service was rendered. How could she not see him for who he was, an opportunist, a man willing to crush all who got in his way. She had spent her whole life with his type, yet her eyes and mind had been clouded because of…love?

Her body froze as the thought took root. Had she given her heart to him? What would she know of love, never having felt its touch before? She had never received love from her parents and certainly not from any at court. The closest she had come to parental love had been from her dear Mrs. Ellen whose life was now in danger. As far as companions or friends, she had none.

Jane rubbed her temples. Maybe a love between a man and a woman was just a word. She had been married, lain with a man, and yet, not once, did her heart or body stir with even the slightest inkling of that dearest emotion. Her knowledge of love stemmed from what she had learned through scripture. What had been written in Corinthians—*Love is patient, love is kind. It does not envy, it does not boast, it is never proud. It is not self-*

seeking, it is not easily angered, it keeps no record of wrongs. Love does not delight in evil but rejoices with truth. It always protects, always trusts, always hopes, always perseveres.

Love never fails.

And yet it had failed her. Heavy tears fogged her vision and slid down her face. All her life she had sought love by being humble, quiet, and submissive. The only time she thought of boasting about her faith was before her neck was supposed to meet the ax. And what happened? She wound up in a different country and another died for her.

A loud bray drew her attention to the window. Truly the Almighty did not want her to leave, for there, dismounting his donkey, was Otto Werner. Quickly she hid her bag under the table and smoothed out her skirt. She plastered a fake smile on her face before he gave a hearty knock on the door.

"Herein," she called before straightening her cap.

"*Hallo,* Ella. How are you this fine afternoon?" Though he spoke to her, his gaze shifted around the entire cottage.

"Why, I am well. What brings you this way? Aunt Hildegard is at Mistress Meyer's."

"And Master Blackwell, he is not about? I checked in the shed, but I did not see him."

Relief pushed away a little of her tension. Asher was gone, and if she could get rid of the preacher, then she would still have plenty of time to make good on her escape. Jane shrugged. "I know not where he went."

"Then he is not here." Relief crossed Otto's face before he took a seat at the table. "I thought perhaps I saw you buy a horse today. Did something happen to Goliath? There is a mare in his stall."

Heaven help her. She could not move a stone's throw without someone knowing about it. Clearly, Asher found the mare in the forest and put him in the shed, but where did he go on Goliath? Fear crept up her spine as the pastor's gaze never wavered from her face. "Master Blackwell thought we needed an extra horse, so he gave me coin to buy one." Jane went to the cupboard and pulled out a mug. "Would you like a beer?"

He rubbed his scruffy jaw. "*Nein*. I cannot believe he would not purchase the beast himself. For a man is a better judge of horse flesh than a young woman."

An argument brewed on her lips, but now was not the time to affirm a woman's judgment was just as good as a man's. Instead, she held her opinion, placing the empty mug on the table.

"In town, I saw Asher watch you from afar." Otto stretched out his legs, and his foot kicked the sack, and a round of cheese rolled out. "What is this?" He reached under the table and pulled out the sack. When she did not answer, he looked inside. "Jane? What is going on here?"

There was no other escape but through the truth. "I am leaving. Asher Blackwell is not who you think he is."

"*Ja*, he is an English spy. He says his name is Blackwell, but I think that is another false name."

A bubble of anger spewed from her belly. "You knew all this and you did not warn me?"

Now it was preacher's turn to raise his shoulders. "I wanted to, but the prince insisted on hiding the truth from you. He found great mirth in the fact that the one person Asher searched for was hidden right under his very nose.

A dangerous game, for sure. Hildegard and I tried to sway the prince to a different thinking, but he would not have it."

Jane slammed her hands on the table. "He was sent to kill Lady Jane Grey. Did you know that?"

Otto turned white and shot to his feet. "*Nein,* I did not. The prince said he had secured information that Blackwell was harmless. That he was sent to seek out and find Lady Jane, but then to report her whereabouts back to Queen Mary. Come, I must take you to the castle immediately. This has turned sour."

Jane crossed her arms and shook her head. "I am not going anywhere with you, but I am going back to England to throw myself on the mercy of Queen Mary. Hopefully she will spare the life of my dear nurse, Mrs. Ellen. You know, I have never had any desire to be Queen of England. Not when Lord Northumberland forced the crown upon me and not now when Prince von Hoffbauer wishes to do the same."

"But all Christendom depends on you." Otto pointed his beefy finger and her. "You cannot run away. Not with a murderer on the loose and God's mighty army ready to march."

"God's mighty army? Do you hear your own words? God does not want war. He wants us to give Him praise and glory. He wants us to honor Him by loving one another. You have even preached on such words. 'Love thine enemy.'"

Otto took his seat with a thump.

Jane fell to her knees before him, grabbing his forearms. "You have let the prince's ambition cloud your good thinking. Please, let me go. This is the only way to save many lives. I know deep down you do not want bloodshed. The Peace of Augsburg was accomplished by healthy debate. Surely this is just the beginning of Catholics and Protestants living in peace."

"Debate had nothing to do with it. That treaty was made with the Lutherans only because Emperor Charles V knew he could not hold onto his empire and soon his brother Ferdinand would control the German principalities, which has come to pass." The preacher pulled his arms away. "Prince von Hoffbauer smells the destruction of the Habsburg Empire. The French are eager to help him. They would rather see you on the throne of England than Queen Mary or Princess Elizabeth."

Jane clenched her jaw. "So I have been told by Prince von Hoffbauer. But I am not that weak girl who falsely accepted the crown years ago. I am much stronger now and have my own mind."

He smiled at her. "*Ja,* you do. But I am afraid we cannot turn away from this course of action. You must come with me. Perhaps you can plead your case to the prince one more time."

She had been doing so ever since she learned his awful plan. Nay, she would no longer hide. It was time to return to her true home and accept her fate. Jane stood and picked up the empty mug, returning it to the cupboard. Her hand slid to a sturdy metal pot. "All right. I will come. I see you will not be swayed."

Otto stood and picked up her sack. "This will all work out. I will get the mare." He turned and threw the sack over his shoulder. Before he could make it to the door, Jane rushed up behind him and cracked him in the head with the pot. He crumpled to the floor.

With her breath coming fast, she grabbed the sack and rushed out of the cottage. She untied the pastor's donkey and gave him a good swat on his behind. The animal took off with a hearty bray. She then rushed into the shed and led the mare out into the yard. With one fluid motion Jane mounted the animal, fixing her gaze northward. With a swift kick, the mare took off toward the northern coast— to England.

Jane pushed on, fearing the prince and Otto would soon overpower her. But when darkness came and no pursuit followed, she wondered if she had fooled them by heading north instead of east. She took a deep breath and tried to focus on her escape route, but the niggle of Corinthians' scriptural words would not let go.

Love protects.

Was that not what she was about to do by returning to England? Would she not be protecting all who foolishly believed a mighty army could change a country's heart? What man had ever given up their country's beliefs by force? Outwardly perhaps, but never inwardly. A man could not be forced to believe in something they would not willingly give their heart to.

Love perseveres.

Would not her physical sacrifice to Queen Mary preserve Mrs. Ellen's life and those of others? Surely the queen did not really want to kill a woman who had dedicated her life to serving others? Surely, she did not want war. The queen had shown mercy once. Surely, she would again.

Love hopes.

Jane's insides turned cold. All her life she had clung to hope. She hoped her parents would love her. She hoped Queen Mary would forgive her. She hoped Asher would... Tears returned to her eyes and streamed down her cheeks. Nay, love did not protect. Love did not persevere. And love certainly did not hope. Love was cruel, malicious, and painful. It muddled the mind and mauled the heart. It was selfish, proud, and greedy.

A heavy wind whistled through the trees. A loud clap of thunder brightened the sky. Heavy droplets of rain broke from the heavens and sluiced down Jane's cheeks, hiding her remorse. For a long while she sat there letting the rain and wind try to wash away her anger. But it could not.

Lifting her gaze to the dark mass of clouds above her, Jane gritted her teeth. She knew the truth now, and God could not hide it from her anymore. "There is no kindness and goodness in this world. I shall never trust a soul again. For love really does not exist!"

CHAPTER 23

Chilled to the bone, Jane stopped at an inn well north of Hanenburg. She planned to travel much farther this eve, however, the heavy downpour and the multitude of lightning strikes left her with little choice. She hoped the weather would stop the prince from his pursuit as well.

With the mare placed in a local stable, Jane inquired about a room. The owner, a round-faced older woman, scolded her for traveling alone and then immediately took her to a room near the back of the inn.

"I will watch out for you this eve. But on the morrow, I suggest you return to where you have come. Nothing back there could be as bad as what lies ahead of you." The innkeeper handed Jane a tallow. "Think on my words."

Jane thanked the woman and promised to take her words to heart. Yet, Jane knew keeping them in her heart or setting them free to the wind would not change her course. She would return to England and plead for Mrs. Ellen's freedom. Once granted, Jane would happily lay down her life for her past crimes—all would be as it should have been two years ago. With a heavy sigh, Jane stripped off her wet clothes and hung them up to dry before she crawled under the coarse coverlet. If God allowed it, soon she would be singing with the angels.

Her sleep did not come easy. Most of the night she tossed and turned and dreamed of a band of dragons chasing her around a deep dark forest. Fire billowed from their nostrils and burned everything in sight. She ran and ran and knocked on every door she came to, but each time she was turned away.

Suddenly loud voices filled the air, breaking into Jane's fitful slumber. "I'll get the magistrate, I will. You have no right to go in there," the innkeeper shouted.

"I can assure you, Mistress. The woman does know me." A loud pound on the door caused Jane to clutch the coverlet and wrap it around her body. "Open the door, Jane. I know you are in there. 'Twas easy to track the horse from the cottage to the local stable. Open the door, we must speak. Something has happened." Besides the use of her true name, the harshness in Otto Werner's voice propelled her to the door.

"I will not go back," she shouted through the door. "You cannot make me. I refuse to be a part of this debacle anymore. Tell the prince to release his army."

"Hans is dead."

Her stomach dropped. Jane opened the door.

Otto's tear-streaked face greeted her, and she knew his words were true.

"How? When?" The crack of her voice sounded foreign to her ears.

"He was found early this morn in the clearing near the west army. Stabbed through the heart." Otto took his cap from his head and rotated it between his fingers. "They found Asher Blackwell over his body."

A rush of screams roared around her before she realized they were her own. As if she had been pierced by the same knife that killed Hans, her heart tore in her chest. "Asher killed Hans? Why?"

"I do not believe he is the killer. Blackwell was the one who alerted us. He was screaming for help, but nonetheless the prince has arrested him, and I fear there will be a swift trial."

Part of her wanted to shut the door and let Asher get what he deserved, but another part of her knew that Otto spoke the truth. If Asher had not killed Hans, then the killer was still loose. But who? The prince? But why would he do such a thing? He did not need to create a crime to arrest Asher. Being a spy for Queen Mary would be enough proof to hang him. Nay, someone else fashioned this mess. But who and why?

She bit her bottom lip. "Give me but a moment to dress and then I will return with you."

All the way back to Hanenburg, Jane pondered what had happened, and still she could not come up with an answer. Hans could not figure out a simple ploy let alone her identity or that of Asher's. What benefit would there be in Hans's death?

The village square was a buzzing hornet's nest when they returned. A trail of villagers stretched from its center all the way to Hanenburg Castle. Shouts of blood and justice filled the air and curled Jane's stomach. One look at her riding on the mare's back settled the masses.

"That be Hans's betrothed," she heard one man say. Nothing could be further from the truth, but those same words could very well help convict Asher, who many saw as an intruder in their orderly life.

Within the castle bailey lay Hans and another stranger. Both killed with a blade to the chest. On the hall steps stood Prince von Hoffbauer dressed in his finery; next to him stood a bloody and beaten Asher. His eyes were puffy and blackened. Crusts of blood spotted his face and his body. From head to toe he was covered in grime and mud from being dragged through the streets.

Cloaked in black, the magistrate stood on the opposite side, a bloody knife in his hand. The grim look on his face spoke volumes—Asher did not have a prayer.

Dismounting her horse, Jane made her way to where the bodies lay. A sharp twist flooded her chest when she gazed upon Hans's pale lifeless face. This is what happened when you followed a group such as the Champions of Christ. For all their boasting, they did not heed the words of Jesus. Christ was a man of peace and would not condone what happened here.

Jane straightened her shoulders and looked to the magistrate and then to the prince. "Tell me the truth. What happened?" A hush fell over the crowd at the force of her words.

Prince von Hoffbauer cleared his throat and pointed to the body of the stranger. "This man Benton is a known spy for the Queen of England. On more than one occasion, Asher Blackwell has been seen consorting with the deceased man."

A cool chill swept down Jane's back. How convenient. Hans's death at the hands of a traitor would fuel the masses into an unholy anger. The mob would ignite the army, and they would be a force to be reckoned with all the way to England.

"It is believed both of them planned to foil our great army by killing the true English queen, Lady Jane Grey." The prince's words sent the crowd into another fevered uproar. The magistrate called for silence, but the crowd did not honor his pleas.

"Hans figured out their diabolical plot and killed Benton in a struggle. When Blackwell discovered the death, he sought out Hans and stabbed him through the heart," the prince shouted. The mob lurched forward, ready to carry out their own justice.

Fearing the worst, Jane dropped to her knees between the two bodies and wailed. The voices of the mob dimmed. She clutched her chest, glancing between the two dead men. She had patched up many a stab wound since coming to Hanenburg. Hans was indeed killed by the knife the magistrate held, but the wound in Benton's chest was not large and could not have been made by the same blade. Only a small trail of blood coated the man's shirt. This wound was made by a sleeker knife, one used to gut fish, an action Hans did often. The prince's story was plausible.

However, the blade the magistrate held was not Asher's. If he were so enraged, would he not use his own dagger to do the deed? Jane's head ached with doubt and wariness. Whatever the truth, she could not let Asher die.

"He did not kill Hans. He could not." She stood. "Asher was with me most of last eve." The crowd gasped and murmured.

Otto stepped forward and started to bluster. "That is not true. She was at an inn, north of here."

"He was found over Hans's body near the army camp. Surely you are confused." The prince's feigned tender gaze spoke of caution, but Jane could not let the man she loved die.

Love. Heaven help her, she loved the man sworn to kill her.

"*Nein*, I am not. We were both in the clearing where Hans's body was found. We were planning to leave Hanenburg." She lowered her gaze and willed tears to spring up in her eyes. "Master Blackwell... Asher wanted to retrieve some of his belongings, which he left in camp the night before. We went to the clearing, and that is when we stumbled upon Hans's body and called for help. Asher told me to leave and we would meet later at the inn where Master Werner tracked me down."

The pastor dropped his head to his chin for he could not prove her words false.

The mob erupted, this time calling her lewd names while others professed her to be a liar. The magistrate roared, and the crowd ceased instantly, waiting to hear the end of the tragedy. "Will you swear to this?"

A look of warning flickered in the prince's eyes and traveled to his closed fist. She squared her shoulders and lifted her chin. "I do not need to swear, but I will if you wish it. That blade you hold is not Asher's dagger. To that I will swear."

Shouts filled the air, and the prince's guard had to hold the mob back.

"Ella, do not protect me." They were the first words Asher had uttered.

The prince seized on this moment. "Indeed. He cannot harm you. Let him receive the punishment he deserves."

If the mob knew who she truly was, no army would prevent them from engulfing her. Jane removed the cap from her head, letting the warm sun beat on her fading hair roots. She threw back her shoulders like the regal queen she used to be. "What I have said is true. I have been led through the nose too many times. No more. I decide my fate and no other! Asher Blackwell is innocent."

'Twas then she felt the pull of Asher's stare. Jane's words had betrayed her.

His flinty gaze spoke volumes. Finally, he knew Lady Jane Grey stood before him.

CHAPTER 24

"Release him," shouted the magistrate. Like a pack of hungry wolves, the mob surged forward, ready to devour whomever stood in their path.

Within moments, Otto Werner was at Jane's side. "Come. You must leave. 'Tis not safe for man or beast, now that the crowd has been riled up. I shall meet you at the cottage later." Immediately, she was handed over to Wilhelm. "Make sure she stays safe. I will follow once I have retrieved Sir Blackwell."

Sir Blackwell. Well at least that part was truth. The man was indeed knighted, though Blackwell was not his real name. Both of them had weaved false tales. Oh, how better it would have been if they could have lived the lie, forsaking the truth. But God and His judgment is never denied. One cannot hide in a world of his own creation, for it is full of valleys that lead to the devil's pit. Only in God's light can one find redemption. Today, her judgment would come, and if God was truly merciful, He would forgive her sins.

Numbness settled over her body; how she arrived at the cottage was nothing more than a blur. The certainty of her death would come once Asher returned. A cold dagger could not be any sharper than the frozen chill in his eyes the moment he realized her true identity. Because she had cheated death long ago, God had deemed to use her love to kill her once and for all. So be it. She would happily die by his hand.

But she needed him to return to England and plea for the release of Mrs. Ellen.

Jane stumbled into the cottage and at first thought her distraught heart was playing a trick on her. Hildegard sat at the table, her hand resting on her deep furrowed brow. Her apron covered with a large stain of blood.

"Oh, thank God, you have been found." Hildegard's dark shadowed gaze slid from Jane's face to Wilhelm's. "Leave us." Upon her command, Wilhelm carefully shut the door on his way out. "Is he dead?" she choked out.

"If by he you mean Asher Blackwell, then *nein*. He still lives." Jane's broken heart split once again as she waved to the bloody apron. "Tell me, what is your hand in all this?"

Hildegard's jaw sagged as she shook her head. "This is all my fault. I knew this would come to no good. And so it has." She dropped her head into her hands. "I am so sorry, child. I thought it was the right thing to do."

A coldness swept through Jane; betrayal had become a familiar friend. "What have you done?"

"We knew all along that Asher was a spy, but we did not know he had found the real army."

"By we, I assume you mean the prince and the Champions of Christ?"

Hildegard nodded. "*Ja*. My coming to Hanenburg was not by accident. My dear departed husband and daughter did not die of the sweating sickness. They were killed by the Habsburgs in Frankfurt. My family's only crime was their refusal to crawl on their knees to the cross on Good Friday." She beat her hands against her chest. "I then came here. The prince and I created the Champions of Christ. My anger and grief colored my vision, and I wanted to punish every Catholic as my dear Gustaf and Heidi had been punished."

"Two wrongs never make a right." Though she tried, Jane could not find pity for Hildegard even if her crime was justified. "You killed the man who killed Hans, did you not?"

"I did not mean for any of it to happen. After I left you, I went to find Hans. He did not deny taking Asher to the camp, and truly I could not fault him, he did not know Asher's true identity."

"So, you told Hans that Asher was really Asher Blackwell, a spy."

Hildegard shook her head. "Not Blackwell. Hayes. The man's name is Asher Hayes." She looked up and glared at Jane. "We too have spies in England, but that is not what I told Hans. I said Asher and you were going to run away together. I cannot tell you how much that enraged Hans. I then left him in the clearing and hid in the brush, knowing Hans would probably beat Asher to a pulp once again."

Though Hildegard's tale was frightening, there was some consolation knowing that finally Asher had been honest about his true identity. "Did you know Asher wanted to kill me?"

Hildegard clutched her throat. "Nay. If we had, he would have suffered more than just a beating. Otto never would have brought him to our door. Nor did I ever believe the prince would find the arrangement perfect once he found out. Having Asher around was like having a wolf in a hen house. I knew no good would come from it.

"As he got better, anyone with eyes could see Hayes was enraptured by you. The prince found great humor in that. I thought it was foolish and dangerous. That is why the prince ordered Otto to stay close to you, though he did not know how dangerous Asher could be. But as time went on, I saw the truth. Hayes was besotted. The truth was blind to him because of love."

"You speak nonsense. He has never made a profession of love." Jane looked away.

Hildegard grunted. "You two are a perfect pair of fools, dancing around each other like shy children. Neither knowing the other's love."

Jane snapped her gaze back to Hildegard's dark eyes. "There is no love between us!"

"No?" Hildegard cocked an eyebrow and licked her lips before wagging a finger. "You and I have been together long enough. Do not try to hide your feelings from me. I see how you look at him."

"What I feel or not does not give you the right to send an innocent man to his death."

"*Ja,* in this we are in agreement. Hans waited in the clearing, but Asher did not come right away. Instead that other man, Benton, came along. He too was a spy, and for once in his sad thick head Hans had put the pieces together and figured out Benton and Hayes were working together against the prince's great rebellion. Hans pulled his knife, but Benton was faster.

"The scum ran off. By the time I got to Hans, he was dead. Lying there in a pool of blood just like my husband

and my sweet Heidi. The devil took hold of me, and I could not quench my anger. I did not rest until I found the tent where the villain was hiding. I stabbed him with my thin knife. When I left, shouts were coming from the clearing. I knew Hans's body had been found. I should have told all what had happened, but the rage had left me once I killed Benton and fear swept my soul."

A foul taste crept into Jane's mouth. The story was so similar to her own. "So, you just let Asher take the blame for your crime."

"That was not my intent. I went to the prince and confessed, but he saw the disaster as a great opportunity to whip up support for the rebellion and get rid of Hayes. I am surprised you are standing here. I thought the prince would have taken the opportunity to expose your identity and then immediately take you into his custody."

He would have, but Jane had turned the prince's great moment into her shame. "I professed publicly Asher and I were together in the clearing and he could not have killed Hans. I told all that we had been together and that we were going to run away."

Hildegard's shoulders drooped even farther. "Oh, child, what have you done? The prince might just kill you both."

"Maybe so, but you must do something for me before this happens."

"If you mean confess my sins, I promise I shall do so now. Publicly." Hildegard stood as Jane reached out and stayed the older woman's steps.

"*Nein*. Not yet. I want you to help me leave before Master Werner returns with Asher. I believe he has figured out who I am and may indeed kill me."

"Heavens." Tears sprung in Hildegard's eyes. "I do not think he could harm you. Nonetheless, I want no more bloodshed. I have had my fill."

The words had barely left her lips when a commotion could be heard outside the cottage. Fear and acceptance mingled throughout Jane's body—a deep familiar voice called out to Wilhelm.

Asher was here.

"Quick, hide behind me. I shall take care of the cur." Hildegard picked up a blunt knife from the table.

Gently, Jane placed her hand over the blade. "*Nein.* This ends here. In my sack there is my prayer book. I instructed Mrs. Ellen to give it to Queen Mary after my execution, but instead I found it next to me when I woke up on a ship. If the prince and the magistrate let you go, promise me you will go to England and give the book to Queen Mary. If you can, beg for Mrs. Ellen's life. Promise me you will do this."

A flood of tears fell from Hildegard's eyes. She nodded. "I promise. I am so sorry. My grief and selfishness have led to your demise. Forgive me."

Jane's own throat clogged with tears. "We have all made mistakes. Worry not over this. I cheated the executioner once, now all will be made right this day."

At that very moment, the door swung back on its hinges. In strode Asher like a demon of the devil. A dagger in his right hand.

CHAPTER 25

A sher knocked out Wilhelm and took his dagger. He then stormed into the cottage where the two tearful women huddled together on the dirt floor. The pathetic sight drew little sympathy from him. Let them weep and wail, they had sealed their fate the moment they started weaving a tapestry of lies. He should cut them both down before they could utter another wicked word.

"Hold there," Werner shouted from behind. "You do not know the truth of everything."

Asher squeezed the knife handle. "Do you not see? These two have used you and your perfect idealism to produce evil. There will be no debate between Catholics and Protestants. The Almighty's return will happen before there is peace between the religions. God will cast all into the fire."

Werner maneuvered his way between Asher and the women. "Would a God of love truly burn us all?"

Oh, how Asher hoped so. Right now, hell's fire would be a welcome gift to the pain that clawed at his chest. An anguishing growl escaped his throat as his grip on the blade tightened.

"Give me the dagger. You do not want to do this." Werner held out his hand.

Asher's hand shook. He should just kill them all. Then he would let Wilhelm finish him off. Once Queen Mary found out what happened, would she honor their agreement? Would she free his family? Without him to hold her accountable, she probably would let them rot in debtors' prison.

Asher gritted his teeth and drove the dagger into the wood of the table. "I wish to speak to Lady Jane alone."

Werner shook his head. "*Nein.*"

Lady Jane rose to her feet and placed a hand on Werner's shoulder. "'Tis all right."

"*Nein.* He means you harm."

A weak, pathetic smile spread on her face. "Perchance. But if I come to ill, then it is God's will. Please leave and take Hildegard with you."

"I refuse," Mistress Brandt shouted, rising to her feet. "I shall stay."

Lady Jane turned toward the older woman. "You must go. Remember what you have promised me." A fresh set of tears rolled down the older woman's face before she nodded. She hugged Lady Jane and then made her way to the door. "May God have mercy on your soul."

Mistress Brandt probably ran to the prince, whom Asher expected to show up forthwith. He narrowed his gaze. "Leave, Werner. My quarrel is not with you, even though you chose to deceive me too. I know you are a man of conscience, and I pray that someday that conscience will lead you back to the True Church."

"I will not leave until you promise me you will not hurt my lady." Werner pushed Lady Jane behind him.

Asher motioned to his dagger stuck in the table. "There, take my weapon."

Werner did not move. "That is not enough. You could kill her with your bare hands. Give me your oath, you will not harm her."

Asher laughed. "Think on how I have made my living? Does my word stand for anything?"

Werner puffed out his chest. "It would to me. Give me your word that you will not harm the lady and I will leave."

The man was so admirable and so misguided. No one would take the word of a villain who snuck around in the shadows and gained success off the misfortunes of others. Asher shook his head. "You are a fool. Nonetheless, I give you my word. I will not touch her while we speak." But when the words were done...

A moment of doubt crossed Werner's face, but then he gave a quick nod before pulling the dagger from the table. "You have only a few moments. Then you must leave. For I am sure the prince will follow as soon as he can."

When Werner left the cottage, nothing stood between Asher and the witch. He curled his hands into fists. Why had he made such a promise? With a quick snap of her neck, this all could end. Instead, she stood with her head held high like a warrior ready to do battle. Nay, like a beautiful queen who could sneak into his head and heart and destroy his soul.

"I am sure my words of caring and devotion must have given you a good laugh, Mistress Ella." He held up his hand when she opened her mouth. "Ah, I must correct my speech. Lady Jane, false queen." He then further mocked her by bowing deeply. "Forgive me."

She gave him her back. "Stop this. I did not enjoy deceiving you any more than you did me."

Rage rolled between his shoulders and twisted in his gut. He fought the urge to tug on her dyed hair. His desire for her had blinded him from the obvious. "Do not play the victim with me, madam. How you must have laughed when I asked you to leave with me. Tell me, what did you relish the most? Being coy with me or letting another unfortunate woman die in your place?"

She spun about. "I did not leave England on my own accord. I was prepared to die for my deeds, but John Feckenham and Queen Mary deemed to change the plan. Not I. Mrs. Ellen gave me a draught to ease my nerves, and the next thing I remembered was the foul smell of a ship's hull. The thought of another woman taking the punishment for my sins haunts me daily."

Her fierce words spoke of truth. "But why would you not return when Queen Mary started the slaughter of Protestants? Hundreds died professing you as a martyr. They stupidly believed they would follow you into the Kingdom of God."

Her petite shoulders shook, and she dropped her head to her hands. "My whole life has been nothing but folly." She raised her tear-streaked face. "Believe me when I say I never wanted any of this. I never wanted to be queen. I never wanted to flee England. I never wanted to be a martyr for the Protestant faith. I never wanted to be the head of some great rebellion. All I ever wanted was to live a quiet life—alone with my books and educational pursuits."

Now all was beginning to make sense. The books she had been stuffing into her sack earlier were hers. Her ability to flawlessly speak other languages. Her small stature and bold words. Her false name, Ella taken from

Ellen, the nurse Queen Mary held in her jail. Everything bespoke this was Lady Jane Grey. Anyone could see the truth. But not him. Not this besotted fool. His mind blinded him while the truth shone like a bright burning star. *A man only sees what he wants to see.*

Nay, 'twas not his mind that blinded him, but his heart. Asher's stomach flipped and made his knees weak. By the Holy Mother, how had this happened? He had been struck by the one emotion he never wanted—love. He who had guarded his heart and foolishly mocked those who had suffered such a fate. He who had always been cautious had broken his own rule.

The revelation unsettled him. He wanted to strangle her for stealing his heart. Asher grabbed her by the upper arms. "What have you done to me?" His lips captured hers, hard, unyielding. The salt of her tears burned his throat. A true tragedy—he could not kill her, nor could he let her live. He broke the kiss and placed his forehead against hers. "What shall I do with you?"

With a light touch she placed her tender fingers on his cheek. "You are going to take me back to England so I can plead for Mrs. Ellen's life. My life for hers and your family. I think the queen may like the bargain."

Indeed, she would. But he did not.

"She did not ask me to bring you back alive. The queen only wants your head." Her shoulders constricted under his grasp as her eyes clouded with grief. The worry did not ease the pain in his chest.

"Then you must do as she asks. I have but one favor, plea for Mrs. Ellen's life. Beg the queen to stop all this bloodshed for it solves nothing but only incites hatred."

A soft cry left her lips when he squeezed her shoulders. "Aye, I should kill you. It is the remedy for many things, but not all." He almost laughed as her brow wrinkled while she pondered his words. Could she not see that love and hate were two sides on the same coin?

"What will it not cure? The prince would quickly lose his army once all hear of my death. Queen Mary's rage might also subside once she knows I am no longer a threat. My death might be the catalyst for peace."

Unable to speak the truth, Asher tried another tactic. "My dear lady, I have sworn an oath. If I kill you now, Werner will not hesitate and do likewise to me. And I would greatly like to draw breath for a few more years."

A deep pout settled on her beautiful lips and Asher wanted to kiss it away. Aye, he wished he could kiss Lady Jane Grey into oblivion and replace that awful woman with his sweet country girl, Ella Brandt. The thought greatly warmed him, but reality chilled his weary bones.

"Then I shall tell Master Werner this is my choice too. I will make him promise not to hurt you but to aid you on your journey back to England." She tried to pull away, but Asher held her fast.

He meant to argue that Werner was a pawn of the prince, but then Asher paused, a new idea forming in his thick brain. "Aye, bring him in."

A brief look of sadness and disappointment flickered in her eyes before she quickly masked the emotions. She tipped her chin upward, an act he was rapidly realizing she did to gain courage. "All right." She cleared her throat. "Master Werner, could you come in please?"

The man was through the entry before any could draw another breath. "I am here."

Her throat visibly constricted as she swallowed before she opened her mouth. "I want you—"

"To help us stall the prince." Asher reached out and took Jane by the elbow. "Lady Jane wishes to return to England and plead her case. I vow to help her arrive there safely."

"That is not what you said," she cried.

Asher held her fast as she struggled, yet again, to free herself from his grasp. "You said the queen wanted my head and you feared Master Werner would kill you if you took it."

Werner slowly raised the dagger in his hand as Asher continued to struggle with Lady Jane. "Now would be a good time to make Werner see killing me would indeed be a foolish thing."

Lady Jane stilled. Her eyes grew wide as if she had just figured out Werner's intentions. "Stop," she shouted, holding out a hand. "Do not kill him. I forbid it."

Spoken like a true queen.

Werner let his hand drop to his side, but he did not release the dagger. "He means to harm you. I have been thinking. You are right. God does not want bloodshed but for us to glorify his name, be we Protestants or Catholics. I hoped to let Asher go, but now I see he cannot be trusted."

"Nonetheless, I agree to his terms. My life for the safety of many." Her gaze softened on the older man. "You know this is right. We cannot let the prince march on England."

Werner's head slumped to his chest. "*Ja*, but I cannot let this man kill you. I had hoped when he saw you that maybe—"

"I would give my oath to protect her all the way to England," Asher pronounced, letting go of her elbow.

She stumbled away. "Your oath to protect me? How foo—"

"I accept. You have my word. I shall protect you with my life." He bowed and waved a hand. "There you have heard it, Werner. If I break my vow, may God strike me dead where I stand."

A huge smile rose like a sunrise on Werner's face. "*Ja,* I have heard it, and I will hold you to it." He dropped the blade to the floor and reached out, pulling Asher into his arms. "I knew I was right about you," he whispered in Asher's ear, before releasing him.

Indeed. Asher grimaced. No matter how much he wished it were false, anyone with eyes could see the deposed queen had wounded and demanded payment for his heart. If he did not get control his feelings, Lady Jane could wind up very dead. How he meant to save her once they arrived in England, he did not have a clue. Nor was he sure he wanted to save her. But surely God would give him the answer, one way or another.

"Quick," boomed Werner. "You must go." The older man ushered them both out of the door. "Take the mare and Wilhelm's mount."

Wilhelm rose to his feet, rubbing his head. "Mine! I ought to have killed you when I had the chance."

"Cease this," Werner roared. "There will be no more talk of killing! You hold your peace. You will come with Mistress Brandt and me. We will go see the prince and set this wrong to right."

Mistress Brandt nodded, then stepped toward Lady Jane, handing her the prayer book. "Here, girl. Give this to the queen yourself." The pair hugged before Mistress Brandt raised her gaze to Asher. "May God protect both of you."

"We cannot waste any more time." Werner pushed Asher and Lady Jane to their horses. "Wilhelm, you go and round up the rest of the Champions of Christ and have them go to the weaver's shop. I shall meet them there as soon as I can."

Wilhelm spat on the ground and frowned at Werner. "Seems a shame to give up on the plan." Wilhelm motioned to Asher and Lady Jane. "We could kill this lying scum and help the dear lady regain her crown. Seems best for all."

Werner tipped his head to the side and placed a hand on Wilhelm's shoulder. "We have not been placed on this earth to do what is best for us but what is best for God. Our Lord and Savior condoned the shedding of His blood, not that of others. Though the Catholic religion is full of folly, dethroning Queen Mary will not change men's hearts. Only God can do that, and hopefully through honest debate and discussion, this will come to pass."

"You are a dreamer, but I shall do as you ask because you are a man of God, and if God thinks this is a better plan, then I will follow it." Wilhelm mounted Werner's mule and took off down the road.

Nettles of apprehension swept through Asher's gut. He turned to Jane. "Come. We dare not tarry."

Werner nodded. "*Ja*, this still may go badly. Ah, wait." He ran back into the cottage and came out with the dagger. "I believe this is yours. I shall pray daily that God grants you a safe journey."

Asher took the blade and placed it into his doublet. "My thanks. If all Protestants were like you, then peace would truly reign. May God bless and protect you."

Werner's eyes glistened. "Take care of her."

With a nod, Asher took off with Lady Jane at his side, and Otto Werner's words bore into his soul. *Take care of her.* Oh, that he could. Oh, that he wanted to. Asher prayed that in the long journey ahead of them God would reveal His desires. For right now, Asher did not know what to do. His gaze locked briefly with the woman next to him. To be certain, from this day forth their lives would be bound—at least until they reached England.

CHAPTER 26

Her backside bruised from hours of riding did not deter Jane from praying. The Lord had somehow managed to grant her exactly what she wanted—well, most of what she wanted. She had dreamed of riding away from Hanenburg with Asher at her side, but those fanciful thoughts had never included a trip back to England. But alas, this journey was indeed the only solution to a terrible problem.

The sun had long since set before they stopped at an inn on the outskirts of a small eastern German town. The plan was to make it to Calais and then to England. If all went well, they would be there in early summer.

The inn seemed mostly deserted, yet they waited in the shadows of a copse of trees without approaching the establishment. A brisk wind ruffled Jane's skirts and gave her the courage to speak to Asher who had remained mostly silent since leaving the cottage. "Do we plan to stay here, or should we look for another place? There are lights in yonder village."

He did not look her way or give any indication that he had heard her words. She opened her mouth once again, but before she could speak...

"Say not another word, madam," he whispered.

"Well, I do not know why we sit here and do noth—"

"We wait to see if what lies before us is a trap or safe haven. And when I deem it to be safe, I will secure a room."

"Are you not worried someone might abscond with me while you make your query?" Even in the darkness of night, she could tell he wore a deep scowl.

"Do not jest. You may not enjoy my company, but I am the only one who will hold your virtue intact. Being a past queen will not protect you from any black hearts who may reside within."

"If you remember, I was alone last eve in such an establishment and no ill befell me."

"You were only several furlongs from Hanenburg in safe countryside. We have ridden three times the distance, and I assure you, whoever lives within this establishment will not hold you in high esteem." He dismounted his horse and handed her his reins. "Stay here and make not a sound. If I do not appear in good time, then go to town and scream at the top of your lungs for the magistrate. It will not change my fate, but you will be safe. At least until the prince comes."

His words offered little comfort. "Do take every precaution," she called in a forceful whisper.

His answer was a finger to his lips before he disappeared into the inn.

And then she waited and waited and waited some more. She perked her ears as if in doing so she would be able to hear through the inn's wooden walls and paned glass windows. Instead, her focus gained her nothing but the hoot of an owl, a nicker of a horse, and a cry of a... *Dear me, what beast howled like that?*

When all seemed lost and she was ready to make way to the town, the door to the inn burst open and Asher's long, familiar strides gave her relief. "Where have you been?" she scolded a little louder than a whisper.

"I have been drinking with a fellow by the name of Bartholomew."

"You were drinking while I sat here chilled to the bone and worrying over your demise?"

He tipped his head upward, and she was able to see his ever-permanent frown. "'Tis a mild spring night and I was not gone long." He took the reins of his horse and mounted the beast.

"I was making ready to leave," she snapped.

He looked her way, bafflement wrinkling his brow. "You were going to town already?"

She gave a firm nod and wished she were close enough to give his head a good cuff. "I have just said so."

"Perhaps next time you should wait a little longer." He rode forward. "We are going to Bartholomew's farm. He is letting us spend a night in his stable." Asher coughed. "He thinks you are my sister."

"Is the inn filled?"

"Nay, there is not a soul within other than the innkeeper and, of course, Bartholomew."

"Well then, why are we not staying there?" she asked, irritated that she would have to spend the night on stiff straw in a cold barn instead of on a fluffy bed by a warm fire. "And why your sister? Could you not have told him I was your wife?"

"An inn would be the first place any of the prince's men would look. To your second question, if I said you were my wife, he would expect us to be friendly with one another. It will not take him long to figure out we are not on good terms. I would rather he think it is because we have a sibling disagreement than to think our marriage is weak."

"That is foolish nonsense. In fact, making me your sister might embolden the man to make advances." Jane worried her lower lip. This eve could go badly.

"Exactly, that is why he will take the chance to put us up. Plus, I gave him a nice sum." His lips tipped upward. "Have no fear, if he does try to have his way with you, I shall prevent him. If I can hear him. If I am not sleeping too soundly."

He meant to raise her ire. She gritted her teeth, trying not to fall for his bait. Though he had agreed to take her on this journey, his animosity toward her was evident. She had deceived him, but then he had done the same to her. If they did not come to some agreement, they would never make it to Calais, let alone England.

Once inside the stable, Asher handed her a horse blanket. "Here. This may ward off some of the damp air."

Jane nodded her thanks.

"I am sure you are hungry. I will go and see if I can persuade Bartholomew into giving us a few scraps of meat and bread." Asher turned to the doorway.

His small kindness emboldened her. "Please wait. I know you have put your life into great jeopardy by helping me. Even if this plan does not come to fruition, know that I am grateful."

A cloud of darkness descended on his face. "Do not offer your goodwill, for I do not know even after giving Werner my pledge that I will be able to uphold my end of the bargain. Today we are safe, but we do not know what the morrow will bring. Best you send your prayers to God, for He is the only one who can make this right."

While Asher slipped out of the stable, Jane folded her hands and did what he suggested. *Dear God, you are wiser than any living being. I come to you not for my own sake for I am ready to meet you in your heavenly kingdom. But my petition comes for the health and safety of my friend, Mrs. Ellen. She suffers much on my account. The same can be said for Asher. Guard and protect them. Give them long and productive lives. If it be your will, answer my simple plea. In your son's name, who gave his life for a miserable sinner like me. Amen.*

Not a horse neighed or a chicken clucked as Jane sat in the quiet of the barn. A soft wind blew in through the cracked wooden walls and wrapped her in a soothing peace. More so than ever she needed to be still and listen for God's answer, for surely He had not forgotten her and those she loved.

The bright and breezy days that followed almost gave Jane the sense that all would be well. Their travel had been easy thus far, with no signs of the prince or his army. Perhaps Otto Werner and Hildegard had been able to persuade him to give up his plan. Her hopes blew away as quickly as they came. Nay, he would not. Though Prince von Hoffbauer said he formed the army for his Protestant faith, there was another seed that grew more deeply within him. His hatred for the Habsburgs. He wanted all of them far from German soil. The prince would not be satisfied until he had crippled the Habsburg Empire for good.

"As if that would change anything," Jane mused out loud.

"Hey? Did you say something?" Asher asked as he rode next to her.

"*Nein,* it is not important," she answered in German.

He gave her a quizzical look but did not question her further. "If all goes well, we will be in Calais this eve and on a ship to England on the morrow. Perhaps you should work on using your French or English tongue a little more."

Before they left Hanenburg, she loved speaking English with Asher. But the farther they got away from her German home, the more she wished to speak that language and English less. "You think we shall secure passage that quickly?"

Asher sighed when he heard her German words. "My lady, there is not a man or woman on earth that has not been tempted and persuaded by the magic of the coin," he answered in English. "Aye, we will find passage, and even faster if we travel as English and not as Germans."

Jane's grip on her reins tightened as the insides of her stomach became a muddy mass. "All right, we shall travel as English." His face shone bright at her English speech. "Shall I use my real name?"

A shadow descended over his features. "I think not. We shall travel as a couple. I your husband and you my wife. You shall use Lady Ella Hayes."

A satisfying warmth spread through her body and unsettled her immensely. 'Twas wrong and foolhardy to find such pleasure in a title that should cause her woe.

"Worry not, it is only for a little while. I assure you I would never lay claim to you."

Clearly, he had misinterpreted her silence. "I am not worried over a silly name. A name means nothing." But that was not true.

"A name means everything," he said quietly.

There then their minds were on the same track. Her name and heritage would soon lead her to death. So be it. "Let us speak of something else."

Suddenly Asher sat up straight and scanned the thicket of trees around them. "My lady, we must—"

Seconds later, they were surrounded by a band of men wearing the prince's colors. Their swords drawn. Archers peeked out from behind bushes. All had their weapons centered on Asher. The clomp of a horse's hooves drew Jane's gaze.

"Your little adventure is over, my dear. If you do not yield, I will have to kill Sir Hayes where he stands." The prince met Asher's frown with a brilliant smile. "How funny it is that you would choose to run away with the very man who had come to kill you."

Jane lifted her chin. "Better to die by his hands than to be used as a pawn by yours."

"A pawn! I seek to put you on the throne of England where you shall rule a kingdom." The prince placed his hand on his heart and lifted his eyes upward in feigned hurt.

"I do not wish to be queen. Can you not see that my death is the only way to have peace? Stop this. Do not march on England. You will not win. The Habsburgs and Queen Mary will organize a great army. You will be crushed."

Prince von Hoffbauer's face twisted into a hideous mask. "It is they who will be crushed. I will not rest until the German principalities are free of Habsburg control. You will lead me to the prize that will make that happen."

Lead him to the prize. Whatever did he mean? "You might as well kill me now, for I will not help you."

A slow slippery smile spread across the prince's face. "Take Sir Hayes back to the house we just passed and throw him into the barn. Guard him well." He then turned his attention back to her. "Oh, my dear, you will do exactly what I want or I will kill Hayes and your dear Mrs. Ellen." He pulled out a wheel-lock pistol and pointed it at her chest.

Her stomach dropped at the crazed look in his eyes. "Perhaps we should talk further."

"Indeed." A gust of cool wind rolled heavy clouds over the sun. The prince smiled.

Jane wrapped her cloak tight about her as she followed the prince. Sooner or later, Asher's life would be lost whether she helped the prince or not. She looked up to the foreboding sky. *Please God, truly you do not wish to see all this bloodshed. Send us a warrior angel to spare Asher and all who would die in such a needless war. As always, not my will, but thine's be done.*

A drop of rain fell from the sky and hit her cheek. Jane could only hope that meant God cried with her and not against her.

By the time they reached the farmhouse, rain poured from the skies. A band of at least twenty men, all members of the Champions of Christ, stood by the barn. More probably within. Even as cunning as he was, there would be no escape for Asher. Somehow, she would have to convince the prince to let Asher go. But how? The hard lines on the prince's face spoke volumes. He would not relent.

Jane removed her cloak and was surprised to find Otto Werner residing within, but no one else. "So, you still do this man's bidding? I thought you had a change of heart?" She then turned and narrowed her gaze on the prince. "And what did you do with the good people who lived here?"

The prince laughed. "Do not think me so sinister. I gave them a healthy sum. More than they would have made from a season of crops. They are at an inn and will live handsomely for a few days. As for Master Werner, well, he has much to atone for. Is that not right, Otto?"

The preacher dropped his head like a beaten horse and would not look at Jane. "*Ja,* is so."

A plate of cheese and dried meats sat on a wooden table with fresh milk. "Come, have something to eat. Surely it has been a while since you have broken your fast?"

True. Asher and she had been living off the land and only went toward a village if the weather was intolerable. They had been so close. If she closed her eyes and took a deep breath, she could almost smell the sea air. Regrettably, all their caution had been for naught. "I am not hungry," she said as her stomach growled.

"Please sit." The prince pulled out a chair next to Otto Werner. "I was delighted to hear that Hayes did not finish you off. It will be so much easier this way."

She plunked down and folded her arms across her chest. "I know not what you mean. Easier. You knew all along that Sir Hayes was sent to kill me?"

The prince laughed and poured a glass of milk and pushed it toward Jane. "But of course. I also knew the fool would not kill you, so taken by your charms. Your protector and your killer all rolled together. The thought of it gave me much mirth."

"He could have killed me, then what of your plans?"

"Oh, Jane, with or without you my army marches. If Hayes had killed you, your dead body would have incited the masses against that evil Queen Mary. Though I am so pleased you are not dead. This way it is so much better."

"I will not be queen. I will refuse the crown. If you want to rule England, you should be courting Princess Elizabeth."

"You are such a silly girl. I care not if you become Queen of England. I only care if those Habsburg beasts Philip and Ferdinand believe you want to be."

What turn of events was this? "I do not understand. I thought you wanted me to sit on the throne? If not, then why am I so important to you?"

Laughter bubbled from the prince's throat again as he leaned an arm against the hearth "'Tis all quite simple. Ferdinand, though tolerated by the Germans, is not one of us. Spanish blood flows through his veins. The French king, Henry II, is not fond of Protestants, indeed he hates them. However, he fears the Habsburg Empire more and wishes to crush it for good. The French have been fighting against the Habsburgs in Italy for years. Henry believes Philip will move more forces northward to England, leaving Italy weak and defenseless once and for all. With the French help, we will take Calais and then all of England. The French have given their word not to resist or fight against me."

"But there are others that will come to Queen Mary's defense."

"Philip, who most English hate, is not like his father. The Habsburg Empire hangs on by a thread. I will walk into England and capture Queen Mary."

The dawning of his intent settled heavy on Jane's shoulders. "You wish to hold her for ransom, and I am just a pawn, a catalyst to use to incite the English people."

The prince pushed off the hearth and leaned over the table. "Jane. Think on that. Would I want the English people to start sympathizing with a queen they hate? *Nein*. I want her dead and her sister as well. I only need you to take the blame."

"I do not understand." Jane's head swam with his words.

The prince snickered. "It is all planned. Princess Elizabeth will die soon after Queen Mary is dead. It will be easy to make the English believe you ordered this out of your desire to regain the throne. I dare say, you will not be queen for even nine days this time."

"If Queen Mary, Elizabeth, and I am dead, then Mary of Scots, who is engaged to the Dauphin of France, Francis II, will be queen."

"*Ja*. France will have control of England and Scotland. Together we will crush the Habsburgs. King Henry will secure Calais for France, plus the disputed lands in southern France and northern Italy. I will have control of a new united German nation."

A chill slithered down her spine. "What makes you think the French will let you have control? You are a Protestant."

The prince smiled wickedly. "Once England is in Henry's control, Philip will head for Spain or Flanders. Henry will set his sights there while I will return home. It could be years before the French even think about the Protestant Germans."

This was madness. Did he really believe Ferdinand and Philip would give up their empire so easily? Now more than ever Jane wanted this to end before all of Europe was bathed in blood. This plan could not go farther. She looked at Otto. "Why do you still stand by him? This has nothing to do with furthering God's glory, only Prince von Hoffbauer's lust for land and power. You know this is foolish and yet you follow him."

The pastor shook his head while the prince roared with laughter. "Tell her, Otto. Tell her what is at stake here."

The worn-out spiritual leader lifted his eyes. "I am sorry, Jane. He has Hildegard rotting in a cell in Hanenburg. If I do not stand in front of this army as their spiritual guide, he will kill her. I cannot let that happen."

What happened to his strong resolve to stand against the prince and stand up for God? Was she surrounded by weak men?

The prince must have taken her lack of enthusiasm as a sign of defeat for he smacked his hands together and began pacing the room. "Since the weather has turned foul, we will stay here for the night. On the morrow we will head south and meet my army. Eat and rest, my dear. For the future will indeed be an exhilarating ride."

Heaven help them all. If God did not intervene soon, many souls would be standing at Saint Peter's gate very soon.

CHAPTER 27

The man would not cease his prattle. As the evening wore on, Prince Nikolaus von Hoffbauer began to fill his cup with wine, raving about what he would do once he had unified all the Germans. His crazed speech even sent Otto outside for a short spell. Unfortunately, the prince would not allow her the same reprieve. She was forced to sit and listen until she was the one going mad.

"I shall be a mighty king, and all within the realm will marvel at my intelligence."

Most will doubt that you have a mind at all. Jane closed her eyes and wished she could close her ears. She folded her arms on the table and dropped her head.

"Ah, you are tired. Your travels have been exhausting. But cheer up, soon it will all be over and God will have mercy on your soul." He tapped Jane's back. "Come. There is a soft bed where you may rest."

Jane rose from her seat and made her way to the pallet. She doubted sleep would come, but at least she could close her eyes, and hopefully, with no one to talk to, the prince would close his mouth. Quiet reigned until Otto returned. Then the prince began again with visions of his glory. Jane stifled a groan and rolled onto her side away from the intruding voice.

Hours dragged on, and finally even Otto begged off and went to lie on the floor. Soon there were soft snores, and Jane began to assess her chances of escape. Guards stood outside the door and at the barn. If she could get her hands on the prince's wheel-lock pistol, then perhaps she could hold it to his head and bargain her way out of this mess. But how far would she get? To the barn? Down the road?

Thwack!

The loud sound drew her to a sitting position, and there stood Otto Werner with a pot in hand and a crumpled prince lying over the table.

"What are you…"

The preacher held a finger to his lips before gently placing the pot on the table. He rummaged in his doublet and pulled out a long piece of rope. "Here now, help me tie him up. Rip off a piece of that coverlet to stuff in his mouth."

Jane tore a strip from the coverlet and jammed it into the prince's mouth while Otto secured the rope. "You realize there is no way out of here. It is impossible," she said.

"Perhaps not. I have already taken care of the guards at the door. All I need to do is get Hayes and we will be off."

"What do you mean taken care of the guards? And as far as getting Asher, why, there at least twenty men around that barn." Jane checked the knots on the prince's chest.

"I am not proud of it, but I lured the two men from the house to the forest with a small bit of drink. They did not know, but they drank one of Hildegard's draughts. They're tied to a tree, sleeping like babes. Their mouths stuffed just like the prince here."

A tightness gripped Jane's chest. "But what of Hildegard? She will be killed for sure now."

"*Ja*, but both of us are ready to pay for our many sins." He then fished a hand into the prince's doublet and pulled out a bag of gold coins and took the pistol off the table. "Here, take the bag for the journey." He then stuffed the pistol into his doublet. "Now listen. I will go to the barn and tell the men that the prince has ordered me to kill Hayes. I have known these men for a long time, they will not gainsay me. I will take him out on horseback. Deep into the woods.

"Be ready. I will come back for you once Hayes is secured. We will only have two horses, but that will have to do."

With that, he was gone and Jane was left to think and stare at the slumbering form of the prince. She picked up the pot and sat behind him. Just in case he would need another good whack.

After what seemed like an eternity, the door opened and Otto rushed in. "All good here?"

"*Ja*, the prince seems to be in a heavy sleep." Jane stood and placed the pot back on the table.

"Get your cloak on. We must go." He picked up the pot and whacked the prince one more time in the head. "For good measure."

They snuck out and headed for the northern forest. Past a dense thicket, Asher waited with both mounts. Jane rushed to him and fell into his arms, tears pooling at the corners of her eyes. "I am so glad you are safe."

"You can thank this silver-tongued fellow," Asher said, pointing to Otto. "I thought he truly meant to end my life. The way he and the guards tied me to the horse. I expected a knife between my shoulder blades at any moment."

"Come, come. No talk of that. We must get you out of here. The guard will become suspicious soon enough." The preacher took the reins of one of the horses.

Asher mounted and then leaned over, offering a hand to Jane. "You will ride with me."

"*Nein.* She will take this one. The two of you will cover more ground on your own mounts."

A sick cold dread rolled down Jane's spine as his words took meaning.

Asher shook his head. "You cannot stay. They will kill you."

A merry smile split the older man's face. "Perhaps or perhaps not. Either way, this is my choice to make, and it is a sound one. Now make haste."

Jane shook her head. "Master Werner please—"

"Otto. I think it is time to call me Otto."

He continued the same name game as always. His smile tugged at her heart. She placed a hand on his cheek. "All right. Thank you. I shall never forget you, Otto."

He took her hand in his own. "Go with God and may He bless you always." Otto paused, his voice clogged with tears. "Now, let us get you on this horse."

A moment later she sat on the grey mare's back, waving to her friend. "Godspeed, Otto."

He only nodded, and then Asher and she took off toward Calais with heavy hearts and the prince's heavy coin purse.

A trail of unspoken words followed them from Calais all the way to England. Asher's polite decorum drove Jane mad. He did not bring up their time together in Hanenburg. He did not mention their religious differences or the fate she would face. To all who had contact with them, he looked like the devoted husband. Even on the ship, he slept outside her door, telling all who ventured by that his wife had bouts of seasickness.

They arrived on the English coast late under a heavy bed of fog. She followed him to an inn where no self-respecting Protestant would be found. An older man with shaggy grey hair and a slight limp led them to a small room.

"Where you been, Master Hayes? Did you know your family has been sitting in prison?" the man asked as he held out his hand.

Asher flipped him a coin, and the man lifted his eyebrows. "I know, Samuel. My hope is they will be released soon."

"If you have more of these, they could be out by morn." Samuel held up the coin to the candlelight.

Asher's lips thinned. "I wish it were that simple. Tell me, what is the news?"

Samuel looked at Jane with a wary eye. "After you are settled, meet me downstairs."

With a nod, Asher opened the door to the modest room as the man headed for the stairs. A weak fire stood in a small hearth. He closed the door and leaned against the frame. "I know it is not much, but it is safe, my lady."

She spun about. "Please, I cannot take one more utterance of 'my lady.' Your politeness makes me want to pull out my hair."

"How should I act? This road we follow is not easy." His features remained unmoved, but his voice had deepened.

"True, but we must discuss what is to happen. For on the morrow I shall meet Queen Mary." Jane searched his eyes, hoping there would be one ounce of remorse or a glimpse of feeling they once had shared. But her search was met with the raise of his hand.

"Hold there. We are not going to the queen without some thought or plan."

"A plan. You have not spoken a word of such before, and now, when the end is in sight, you wish to plan?" Jane made her way to the bed and sat. Her shoulders slumped. "The only plan I wish to make is that you will plead for the release of Mrs. Ellen when the queen releases your family. Promise me this, and as for the rest of 'your plan,' I do not care."

"Listen to me, Jane. That you are in England and alive will vex the queen greatly. We must approach her with great caution. It is not only you or me who may suffer her wrath. She could easily execute my family, your Mrs. Ellen, and half the Protestants still living in London. I am sure that is not what you want."

It was the first time he had ever used her real name without her title. She had always dreamed he would whisper her name with love and adoration, not cold and matter-of-factly. Jane sighed. "Nay, it is not. What then is your plan?"

He put his hand on the door latch. "I need to talk to Samuel. In the meantime, I think you should try and get some rest. If we meet the queen or not, tomorrow will still be an interesting day."

Then he was gone. And Jane was alone, once again, in England.

CHAPTER 28

In the early hours of the morn, Asher raised the latch on the small chamber door. He had learned much. Word of the prince's army had reached many ears in London, and Queen Mary was not happy. The butchery of Protestants had not lessened since Asher had left the country. According to Samuel, the queen was on a rampage, desperately trying to weed out any spies in the city. All feared the worst of her tyranny was yet to come.

To quell the masses, Mary had set a celebration of sorts in which she planned to ride through the streets of London in hopes to gain the people's support as she had done when she first arrived to take the crown from then Queen Jane. Many of Queen Mary's advisors were calling it a folly and were desperately trying to dissuade her. Zealot Protestants were delighted and saw this as their chance to get rid of the queen and her bloody practices once and for all.

Asher did not know how he felt.

If Queen Mary died, Princess Elizabeth would rise to the throne. A firm Protestant. Von Hoffbauer and the French planned to kill her too, blaming Jane. One thing was certain as he entered the room, Jane was in danger, and he did not want to see her die.

Her selfless words floated in his mind. *God wants us to glorify him and not ourselves.* What man or woman of her station would heed such words? The streets stunk of the heretic pyres. Certainly, even Queen Mary could see this was no way to honor God.

Jane slept like an angel. So peaceful, so innocent dressed in her simple peasant garb, her golden-red hair roots showing in the candlelight. She was either a lamb for the slaughter or a lion sent to tear all apart. What was he to do with her? How could this petite, beautiful young woman be a threat to anyone? Yet she was and would always be as long as she lived.

A plan began to form in his mind, but in order for him to carry it out, he must make sure she stayed far away from any celebrations this day. He cleared his throat, and Jane's eyelids popped open.

"Is it day already?" she asked, giving a yawn.

"Soon," he said wearily.

"I fear I have not had a restful night." She rolled to sit up, her delicate bare feet touching the floor.

"Jane, you must leave. This place is not safe for you."

A weak smile settled on her lips and tore at his soul. "Is there a place anywhere in the world that would be safe for me?"

Asher brushed a hand through his hair. "There is to be a celebration of sorts, and Queen Mary plans to present herself in the streets to the people."

Jane frowned. "That is not prudent. Why would she do such? There are those who would like to see her dead."

"Indeed, and that is why you must not be anywhere near the procession. If she is killed and it is found that you are in London, many may think you had a hand in her murder. There could be riots. Not only Catholic and Protestant blood would flow, but the blood of the old and innocent as well."

Jane's face fell. "True." She slipped her feet into her slippers and quickly plaited her hair. "Then we must ensure that Queen Mary lives."

"Aye, but not *we*, me. Samuel thinks you are my cousin come to help free my family. I want you to go with him to my home in the countryside." He then held out a bag of coins. "If this goes badly and Mary is killed, I want you to leave England immediately. Try to disappear once again. But promise me you will not return to Hanenburg or anywhere in the German Kingdom. It is not safe for you there anymore."

"No country is safe for me. Though I do not want the crown, I will not leave. If we are not successful in saving Mary's life, then at least I can declare in favor of Elizabeth. Perhaps my words alone could save the princess's life."

A pain split through his chest at her wide and earnest eyes and her naïve thoughts. He reached for her cold petite hand. "Jane, do you not see? If Princess Elizabeth survives, she may fear you too."

Jane lifted her noble chin. "I know that, but I am prepared to accept any fate God has for me."

Perhaps she was, but Asher was not. He pulled her into his arms, her chest close to his. "Know that I do this for your own good," he whispered, right before he slid his dagger from its sheath and used the hilt to knock her out.

The rumble of the cart brought Jane back to her senses. A heavy piece of rope dug into her wrist and a rough strip of cloth silenced her tongue. A large tarp lay over her. *Not again*. Why was it that every time she wanted to do the right thing someone always changed her course? She wrestled against the restraints but did not gain her release. She huffed and grunted and moaned, but not a soul could hear her muffled cries. After what seemed like ages, the cart stopped.

Samuel came around to the back and lifted up the heavy tarp. "Ah, you are awake."

She glared at him and shoved a foot at his chest when he reached for her ankle.

"Now, now. I know you are not happy, but your cousin is doing the right thing by you. He does not want you to get mixed up in what is going to happen. Best you just relax at his home for a while. And when it is all over, God willing, he will meet you here."

Jane relaxed her body, for in all honesty, how was she to escape if she could not even get out of this cart? Again, Samuel reached in and helped her up. To her left she was surprised to find a neat little cottage with a new thatched roof. Her heart softened a bit when she noticed a modest field that had been turned for the plow and then forgotten. Could this truly have been Asher's home?

"I can tell you like the place. Master Hayes did not have much time here before he left."

Master Hayes, not Sir Hayes. Oh, Asher did indeed live a private life. She wondered what Samuel would say if he knew just what the good Master Hayes had been up to lately. If she could get this gag from her mouth, she just might tell Samuel the truth.

When Samuel opened the door, a great deal of Jane's anger fled. This quaint cottage was not much bigger than her home back in Hanenburg, though it was clearly meant to house more than one person. Long benches sat on either side of a rectangle table. A large wooden cupboard stood next to an arched brick hearth. A doorway to the rear of the cottage lead to another room. There was also a ladder that led to a large loft. There was even rectangular pane glass in the windows. Asher had taken great care putting this place together. Even though the home looked fresh, a musty smell had settled in. No one had dwelled here for a long time, if ever.

Samuel ushered her to the bench. "I am going to remove your gag. You can holler if you want. Master Hayes likes his privacy. This place is far enough from London, and those who live near mind their own affairs." He then held a blade to her chest as he used his other grubby hand to remove the rag. "There now." He settled on the other side of the bench, holding his dagger steady.

Jane licked her dry lips and wiggled her toes in her slippers, a plan of escape coming to her mind. "Water, please."

"I figured you would ask for that." He rose and with his free hand pulled out another long piece of rope. "I got some in the cart, but first..." With surprising speed, Samuel threw the rope around her midsection and swiftly tied her to the bench. "We cannot have you running off, now can we?"

Clearly not. For an innkeeper, Samuel was quite astute. He walked to the door and returned before Jane had even tried to break her restraints. A different approach would have to be taken if she ever planned to get out of here.

He chuckled as he poured some water into a cup, holding it out to her lips. "You just sit tight, Mistress Ella, and all will be fine. I have seen Master Hayes in a barrel of fish like this before."

The cool water slid down her chin and the front of her gown, but some did make it into her mouth, quenching her parched throat. "Then you really know what Master Hayes does?"

"I have known for years, he snuck about doing things others would not, and best you do not ask too many questions. The less you know the better off you are." He rose and went to the cupboards. "Not surprising. Empty. I got some bread and salted meat in the cart. Are you hungry?"

Jane's gaze slid to the side room. Perhaps she could get away from Samuel's keen eyes. "Nay, but I do have a terrible headache. Might I lie down a bit?"

Samuel scratched his straggly beard. "Guess there would be no harm in that, as long as the door remains open."

As quickly as he had tied her to the bench, he untied the knots and led her to the side chamber. There, Jane had another surprise. A sturdy four-poster bed complete with curtains sat in the middle of the small room. A small trundle bed lay below it. Jane's heart began to beat wildly. A solid wooden chest was nestled below a narrow window—that was her escape.

As if reading her thoughts, he whispered near her ear, "Think not about it, mistress. I will have my eyes on you." Samuel then shoved her toward the bed. He held the long rope in his hands, debating on how he might tie her up.

"Do not worry. I will not leave. My head aches so, I can barely see straight."

A look of worry entered Samuel's eyes. "He cracked you that hard, did he?" Again, Samuel scrubbed a hand over his beard. "All right, but I will not untie your hands." He dropped the long rope at the foot of the bed. "Last thing I need is for you to whack me a good one with one of the pots when I am not looking."

"You have naught to fear. All I wish to do is rest." Jane lay down on the bed and closed her eyes.

Samuel's even breath filled her ears as he stood next to the bed. Had coming into this room been a mistake? Was Samuel a villain who enjoyed harming women? Finally, he huffed and she heard his retreating footsteps.

Hours seemed to pass. Through her eyelashes, Jane looked toward the window. The sun was high in the sky. How long before Queen Mary made her procession in the streets of London?

Her patience was finally rewarded when Samuel rose from his seat and left the cottage. She knew she did not have much time. Quickly she sat up and slipped out of the room. Near the hearth she gained her reward. A knife lay next to a cook pot. Jane curled her bound hands around the blade and then raced back to the bed. Less than a heartbeat later, Samuel walked back into the cottage.

Jane squeezed her eyes shut and rolled quietly to her side away from the door, hiding the knife beneath her body. She threw up a prayer when she heard Samuel approach the room. He stopped at the doorway, and Jane could feel his stare in the middle of her back. He mumbled once before withdrawing to the other room.

Carefully, Jane slid the knife against the rope binding her hands. Perspiration dripped into her eyes as she worked to keep an even breath. She bit her lower lip; the rope broke. Her hands were free, but how would she gain her freedom with her jailer so close by?

Think, Jane, think. She rolled over onto her back and held her hands against her chest as if they were still bound. "Ahh," she groaned, peeking out of her lashes.

"Hey?" Samuel swung his legs away from the bench and stood. "Are you all right?" He came toward the chamber when she did not answer. "I say, are you all right?"

Now he stood above the bed, and Jane let her eyes flutter. "Oh please. My feet, I forgot to take my slippers off, and they ache terribly. Can you remove them for me?"

Samuel's face flamed as if she had asked him to do some intimate task. "I, ah. I…" His gaze fixed on her feet. Just as Samuel bent to remove her slippers, Jane sat up and held the knife to his neck.

"Now then, I think you will oblige me and pick up the rope next to the bed."

CHAPTER 29

Sweat dripped down Asher's back as a heavy set of clouds descended on the city. A foul stench of unwashed bodies filled the moist air. Perhaps if it rained, the queen would give up on this farce and be content to stay in her palace. Yet no such word had come, so all stood shoulder to shoulder and waited, grumbling. Asher scanned the crowd for those who meant the queen harm, but he had been gone so long he could not discern friend from foe. Very little enthusiasm emanated from the people. Most were probably paid to give their praise.

Asher lifted his chin to remain focused, his mind often drifting away to Jane. No matter the outcome, she had no future. He had played every scenario out over and over in his mind. If Mary lived, she would want Jane's head. If Mary died and Princess Elizabeth became queen, she too would want Jane's head to quell any future thought of rebellion. If both queen and princess died, Jane would be blamed. If it had not been for his family and Mrs. Ellen, he would have taken Jane and run away to the Far East or the new world where few ventured.

Neither Jane nor he could sacrifice their loved ones nor did they wish to see their country destroyed over one man's ambition. So then here he stood with no plan at all but to do the right thing and save Queen Mary.

Shouts up the road signaled that the queen had started her procession. Asher pushed through the crowd trying to get as close to her litter as possible. He planned to follow along with a few other faithful Catholics, hoping to ward off any trouble before it started. He had barely moved from his spot when a sharp prick poked his back.

"You will not be stopping this today. Drop the blade," the familiar German words curled into Asher's ears.

The dagger rolled from his fingers as he looked out of the corner of his eye at Karl. "I thought perhaps you had a change of heart like Werner and Wilhelm."

"See, that is where you are wrong. I never took my orders from them. Only from the prince. He was the one who ordered you to be beaten to a pulp. Mistress Brandt was nothing more than a go-between. I left for England the day your Benton skewered Hans."

"This will not work. They will kill you before you leave the street."

Karl laughed, and his foul breath almost made Asher gag. "I think not. You, Lady Jane's lover, are going to take the blame. I will see to that. Others will be taking care of the Princess Elizabeth."

"This is madness." Asher darted his gaze left and right and noticed that all the men he had come with had disappeared. "The princess is well guarded."

"*Ja*, by our men." Karl jabbed Asher in the back. "Get moving."

"Stop this. Think of how much bloodshed there will be."

"Think I care? I am German, and if this gets the Habsburgs off our necks, then I am all for it."

The crowd cheered as the queen's litter moved closer. She waved to her subjects with a brilliant smile on her face. Asher spotted an archer peering out of a second-story window and another man with a sword drawn. Something had to be done or all would be lost. With all his might, Asher snapped his head backward, connecting with Karl's nose.

"Ow," Karl wailed, the knife falling from his fingers. Asher lunged for the blade and then quickly rushed the man with the sword. An arrow whizzed past Asher's ear, heading toward the litter. *Too late.*

Out of nowhere, a peasant girl leaped onto the litter, taking the arrow meant for the queen.

Asher's stomach curled inward, and bile rose in his throat. He reached the litter just as Queen Mary rolled the girl off her lap and gasped, her gaze locking on Asher's. "Saints have mercy."

There, with blood oozing out of her shoulder, lay a very pale Jane.

Dressed in a fine red brocade gown, Queen Mary's skirt rustled against her chamber floor as she paced back and forth. She had brought Jane, who the masses called the godly peasant girl, back to Whitehall where she now lay upon the queen's bed. The arrow, though deep, had been removed from Jane's shoulder, and all expected her to recover as long as the wound did not fester with infection.

Mary dismissed her physicians and glared at Asher, who sat on a stool holding Jane's hand. "Give me one good reason why I should not call for dirt from the hearth or grime from the streets to be ground up and put into her wound."

Asher raised his red-rimmed eyes to his queen. "Because she saved your life."

A slow hiss of air left Mary's lips. "And well she should. I saved hers once before. None of this would have happened had she not scampered off to that godforsaken country. If she would have stayed with the nuns—"

"She never would have become a good Catholic." He turned his attention back to Jane, and a smidgen of hope filled his soul when a healthy color started to spread through her cheeks.

"At least we would not be on the verge of war."

"We have Karl and the rest of his men. Thankfully, Princess Elizbeth is unharmed too."

Mary wrinkled her nose in disdain. "We are most fortunate."

"Soon you will have the proof you need to uncover Prince von Hoffbauer's plot. You know as well as I do the French and others will deny supporting him since you are still firmly in place as Queen of England."

"Yea, well, what shall *we* do with her?" Mary asked, stopping by the foot of the bed.

Asher cocked an eyebrow. "Are you asking me, or are you speaking as a royal?"

"Of course, I am asking you." Mary folded her arms over her chest.

"Then I suggest you make the peasant girl, Ella Brandt, a hero."

"Are you mad? There are those at court who know exactly what Jane looks like." Mary began to pace again,

277

tapping her temples. "What will happen once the people know she saved my life? They might truly revolt. Why, Jane could very well be queen again."

Asher rose and stalled Mary's pacing by taking her hands in his. "Come, sit down. You are not thinking straight."

"And you are?" She pulled her hands from his grasp. "What possessed you to bring a live Jane to England and not just her head?"

He thought to choose his words carefully, but they became unnecessary when Mary answered her own questions.

"Oh, your eyes betray you. Somewhere along the way you forgot your duty to your queen and country. You are enamored with her. I should have you drawn and quartered. How could you choose her over me?" Mary sunk into a gilded chair away from the bed.

Asher came and kneeled before her. "You knew from the onset how I felt about this task. Still, I planned to carry it out."

"Perhaps she is a witch. Something Feckenham and I missed. Perhaps it was she who filled Lord Northumberland's head with thoughts of grandeur and not the other way around. It is quite possible I have had sympathy all this time for one of the devil's own."

Asher shook his head. "You know those words are false. It is not the devil she is full of but the grace of God. More than the grace of God, the spirit of God lives within her. She nursed me, a stranger, back to health, and then when she knew I meant her harm, she sacrificed her own reputation to save my life. Just as she did for you. She saved your life. Jane selflessly took that arrow so you might live. She did not come back to England to rule but to beg for mercy for her nurse, Mrs. Ellen, and for the Protestants you persecute."

"Ah, then perhaps we should anoint her for sainthood."

Asher turned his gaze back to the sleeping angel on the bed. "Aye, if only the Pope would think such."

"Heaven help me. What am I to do with the both of you?" Mary tapped a finger to her lips and went to open the door. "I want Feckenham. Now," she shouted. Footfalls raced down the corridor. She strode back to the bed.

A few heartbeats had passed before a huffing and puffing John Feckenham stood in the doorway. "My Queen, you have need of me?"

"Close the door, John, and come here," Mary ordered.

The chaplain scurried to the bedside and gasped. "Mary, Mother of God," he said, making the sign of the cross over his chest. "'Tis Jane."

"Aye. Come back to be a thorn in my side once again. Tell me, John, do you still have a sharp eye? For I need another to take her place—this time as the queen's savior."

CHAPTER 30

A misty fog settled around her, chilling Jane's cheeks and filling her lungs. A rustle of skirts bespoke of another presence nearby. Had she died? Was she wrong about her beliefs? Was this a Catholic purgatory? A guttural sound filled the air.

A rough cloth brushed her face. "There, there, child. Do not moan so. Mrs. Ellen is here to take care of you."

Jane fought through the fog and grabbed at the hand that held the cloth. Her eyes fluttered open, and a bright light chased away the clouds. A face loomed above her and began to take shape. Tender, soft brown eyes cradled by smiling wrinkles. Dusty grey brows leading to a high forehead. "Mrs. Ellen?"

"Yes, child. It is your Mrs. Ellen. Worry not, we are together once again."

Jane closed her eyes. A peaceful bliss rolled through her being. Indeed, her worries were over. By God's great glory she had made it to heaven. A prick of anguish dissipated her tranquility. Mrs. Ellen was in heaven too—Mrs. Ellen must be dead.

Neither had made it to the pearly gates. As the days rolled by, Jane realized she was not in heaven but in a smaller room near the queen's chamber at Whitehall. Mrs. Ellen had been freed and was allowed to attend to her. Even the dream she had about awaking in Queen Mary's bed a fortnight ago had been true.

And, of course, so were the queen's first words. "Do not get comfortable, for you will not be staying in this bed for long."

Indeed. As soon as she was stable, Jane and her few clothes and books were ushered to this small room where she saw no one except Mrs. Ellen and Chaplain John Feckenham. Just like before her almost execution. And just like before, Mrs. Ellen fussed over Jane's needs and Feckenham spoke of doctrine and beliefs. But Jane no longer had the zeal to defend Protestantism or rail against Catholicism. The only thing she could profess was the love and will of God, for there was her peace no matter her fate.

She expected to see the good chaplain when the door opened this morn, but his tall form did not stand in the doorway. Instead, there in all her royal glory stood Mary dressed in a blue and gold brocade gown. Her French hood was trimmed with pearls. A large golden crucifix hung around her neck, and every finger displayed a jeweled ring. If she meant to impress her noble stature through her dress, then she had failed, for Jane still preferred the simple garb of a peasant woman.

Jane rose from her seat and curtsied. "Your Majesty, I am honored by your presence."

Mary strolled into the room and then looked behind her. She directed her cool gaze at Mrs. Ellen. "Leave us."

Her majesty did not have to ask twice for Mrs. Ellen curtsied two more times before exiting the room, offering a last look of sympathy to Jane.

The queen did not give a greeting but dragged her speculative gaze over Jane's form. With a dismissive grunt, she called over her shoulder, "You may enter now."

"Asher," Jane cried when he walked into the room. She rushed forward, but Mary paused Jane's steps by the raising one hand.

"Stay where you are. Before there are any reunions, we must talk." Mary sat in a chair opposite the one Jane had vacated. Asher stood sentinel behind the queen. His face blank; his gaze fixed straight ahead.

"Asher," Jane whispered one more time.

His only response had been to put his hand on the back of Mary's chair. Jane bit her lip to stifle a cry. Did he not feel anything for her? He must, for Mrs. Ellen was free. What then? What thought traveled his mind now? He was back in England. Had all that had passed between them been forgotten? The rip in Jane's heart was great but expected. They had no future; she would focus on the past when they would sit in the pasture. When they shared laughter and a few kisses.

"Sit down, girl. England cannot wait for you to come to your senses," Mary snapped.

Jane shuffled back to her seat and sat, folding her hands in her lap, trying to steady the fast beating of her sad heart. "Forgive me, Your Majesty."

"It seems that every time we meet I am forgiving you for some disastrous deed. What am I to do with you?"

A dullness settled into Jane's chest when Asher did not even blink an eye nor offer up a word. She dropped her gaze back to her hands. "I am ready to follow your will."

"Are you? Then I ask you, where do I benefit in letting you live?"

Jane remained silent. They both knew the answer. *She didn't.*

"Do you know my chaplain, John Feckenham, still sings your praises? He claims you are not such a zealot any more for the Protestant faith. Is that true?"

Jane closed her eyes. *Your words, Lord. Not mine. Give me your words.* A rush of peace filled her soul and gave warmth to her broken heart. Jane lifted her chin. "I still profess the reformed faith, but I know God will save all who believe in His Son."

"And what of the practices of the Holy Church? Should they all be abandoned?"

"What practices we do cannot save us, but neither do they condemn us. For God loves all and wishes us to care and love one another." Jane paused and swallowed hard. "May I ask you a few questions, Your Majesty?"

"Of course, if it will help shed light on your muddled thinking, then by all means, ask."

"Do you believe in God the Father, the creator of the heavens and earth? Do you believe in Jesus Christ as your savior? Do you believe that the Holy Spirit has been sent to us and dwells within us?"

Mary slammed the arms of her chair and rose to her feet. "Of course, I believe in the Father, Son, and Holy Spirit. What an impertinent question to ask!"

"I do too," Jane said quietly. "I do too. And that is all God wants. How can we profess to believe in Him if we curse one another? How can we profess to be His children if we are maiming and killing each other? How can we profess to believe in Him if we do not love our enemies as He has taught us?" Jane slowly stood and pointed to her books. "May I, Your Majesty?"

283

Queen Mary stiffly nodded.

Jane stepped to the book pile and pulled out her worn prayer book. She turned and held it out to the queen. "I asked Mrs. Ellen to give this to you once the ax fell on my neck. She has told me you refused to take it. Since the day you gave it to me, when I was a child, I have read and prayed the prayers. The same prayers I am certain you have prayed. I am sorry for all the pain I have caused you and will gladly die for it, but please know I will always love you as a fellow sister in Christ. I look forward to the day where we will walk together in His presence."

The hard glint in Mary's eye softened, and she glanced at the offered book but did not take it. Instead, she walked to the chamber's small window and raised her gaze upward. "Well then, this is a turn of events. Catholics and Protestants walking arm and arm through the heavenly gates." She walked back and curled her fingers around the hand that held the book. "Then keep it and when you pray to God pray for me also." Quickly Mary turned away to hide the tears that glistened in her eyes.

Oh, how hard her life must be! Jane wanted to hug Mary, but she knew the act would not be accepted. There was only one thing she could do. "You are a kind and gracious woman. Let not others sway your thinking on this."

Time dragged as the queen's shoulders shook slightly. When composed, she turned to look at Asher. "Perhaps there is a future for the two of you after all."

Future? A seed of hope bloomed in Jane's chest. "I—I do not understand."

Queen Mary came to Asher's side. "Sir Asher wishes to take responsibility for you. He believes you are not a harm to me and you would be happy living with him far from English soil."

"Oh, I would, Your Majesty." The seed within Jane began to bud. "I want the quiet life, and I promise never to plague you with my presence again."

"Ah, but you made this promise long ago and here you are."

"But again, it was not of my own will."

"Indeed, but nonetheless, there are no guarantees you will not be standing in my presence a year from now if I let you live."

The small bud of hope within Jane began to die. Queen Mary was just going through a rudimentary exercise.

"So, there is only one solution to keep the wolves from trying to make you queen. You will marry Asher Hayes and move—away. To the Far East. Asher used to be a merchant, certainly he can establish such a trade again." Mary cast a side glance at Asher. "Perhaps both of you can learn to harvest spices."

No wonder Asher looked like a piece of hard wood. He knew this was the queen's plan. A picture of Asher's cottage tore through Jane's mind. The carefully painted shutters, the strong planked floor, the meticulous furnishings. Asher's life was here in the home he had built for his family.

Jane dropped the prayer book on a small table near her chair and fell to her knees in front of Mary. "Please, Sir Asher belongs here. I would rather that you take my life than force him to do this awful task."

"Force!" Laughter erupted from the queen's throat. "I assure you that is not the case. He is the one who suggested this outcome. Not I."

Asher wanted this? Jane peered up at him, looking for an answer.

"My Queen, may I speak to Lady Jane alone?" Finally, the monolith opened his mouth and spoke.

Queen Mary ran her hands over her opulent gown and then touched her brow. "'Tis quite warm in here. I shall take a breath in my garden. You will meet me there, dear Asher. Do make this girl understand 'tis matrimony or the ax with no pomp this time."

With great splendor, Queen Mary left the chamber, leaving Jane and Asher alone in a cavern of silence.

"Jane," he finally said, helping her to rise.

She pulled away from his all-consuming touch. "The queen must be mad. How could she think this would work?"

"If you marry me, you are no longer a threat to the Crown."

"How so?" Jane cried. "You are a knight. There will be talk."

"Knighted in secret and not noble," his voice low with an edge of bitterness. "No one in England would want a Catholic merchant's son married to the Queen of England. Once we are wed, you will never be a threat to her or Princess Elizabeth."

"I cannot allow you to make this sacrifice. I have seen your cottage and your land. I know your dreams. You have built a place for your parents and your sister." *And your future family.*

Asher lips flattened. "My parents will have a fine place to live, but my sister will be placed at court. One of Queen Mary's ladies."

A deep sorrow filled Jane. The poor girl. "So then, she will still be used as a pawn in case you do not abide by the queen's wishes and marry me."

"Queen Mary is also interested in having her 'own man' in the east, bartering for the Crown."

Her heart gave a sickening lurch. How many more would suffer on her account? *Please God, make it stop.* Jane walked to the open window and took a fresh, life-giving gulp of air. The sun shone bright in the blue sky, and small puffy clouds floated across the heavens. Birds twittered, and in the distance, a moo of a cow made her think of Matilda. Jane sighed. "I cannot marry you. The ax will free us all."

Asher came to stand behind her, placing his hands gently on her upper arms. "Queen Mary will send me to the east anyway. Greed has whetted her appetite."

"But your sister—"

"Would be held regardless if I stayed or went." He squeezed Jane's arms. "I believe Audrey will flourish at court and perhaps make a good match. The queen has promised as much."

Jane turned, tears pricking her eyes. "Promises can be broken. And even if the queen is good on her word, I cannot marry you."

"Why, Jane? The religious differences can be worked out. If nothing else, we will have lively discussions. We both believe Christ died for our sins."

Unable to look at his handsome face a moment longer, Jane broke free of his grasp and walked back to the table and rested her hand on the leather prayer book. "I was in a loveless marriage once; I shall not be so again. I cannot marry a man that does not love me."

Again, he stepped behind her. "Perhaps you mean you cannot marry a man *you* do not love."

Hot tears rolled down her face. *No more intrigue. No more lies.* She turned. "There is the different folly. I do love you and probably have from the moment Otto Werner brought your broken body into the cottage. Why God allowed my heart to stray your way, I do not know. Even if you are sent to the east, you deserve to find someone who can fill your heart with love."

"Oh, I wholeheartedly agree." Asher pulled Jane into his arms and kissed her.

She closed her eyes and let her mind and heart swim in his kiss. For a brief moment he was hers, and she would hold this intimacy deep within her heart until her neck met the ax. He broke the kiss and hugged her. Jane took in his earthy scent. This too she would carry.

"Jane," he choked. "Do you not understand? I am the one who suggested moving away. I am the one who desires this marriage, for I love you to the core of my soul. There is no world I want to live in if you are not there also."

Jane pulled away and looked into his loving face. A bloom so joyous filled her soul. "You speak the truth." He nodded at her statement. "Then God has blessed me more than all the crowns of this earth." A worry entered her heart. "But what of Mrs. Ellen?"

Asher laughed and pulled Jane closer. "Fear not. Your nurse comes with us. Queen Mary wants no loose lips left in England."

A warmth and peace so great filled Jane's heart. "Then let us begin this new adventure in love and in faith."

They sealed their bond with a kiss, and the Heavenly Father knew it was good.

Epilogue

Audrey sat under a large oak tree, staring at her prayer book. Outwardly she looked serene, but inwardly chaos ruled her soul. Most women would consider being a lady's maid to the queen a great gift from God. Yet she could not muster the pleasure. Neither noble born or of great wealth, she was looked upon by most at court as an oddity—the sister of the mysterious Sir Asher Hayes.

She sat alone while the other ladies sat in groups of two and three chattering away. No doubt salivating over the gossip that brought Audrey to court. Oh, she could not fault them. Would she be any different had she been raised in privilege? So deep in her melancholy, she did not hear the approaching steps.

"How fares, my dear sister?" Asher asked as he stood by her side.

"Much better now that you are here, brother." Audrey closed the book and patted the spot next to her. "Come, sit with me. Tell me, do you have news of Mother and Father?"

The prayer book tumbled to the ground when he took her hands in his. "They are fine and thriving at home."

A wistful longing crept into her heart. "I am so glad. I do not think that Mother could have lasted much longer in that awful cell."

Asher frowned and squeezed her hands. "Rest assured she is gaining weight and seems to enjoy the country life."

"Now if only Father would enjoy the same." Audrey glanced around at the whispering women with big ears. "Come, let us walk."

Asher picked up the prayer book and handed it to her before helping her to rise. "We can only hope Father has learned his lesson. Even if he does throw away his good circumstance, Mother will not suffer the same fate."

Audrey took his arm. "And why is that, brother? Have you suddenly become a man of great means?"

He lowered his gaze to the ground and shook his head.

"Rumor has it, you are one of the queen's favorites. That she is in great debt to you." As they passed, the titter of the ladies rose and a few giggled looking his way. Audrey stiffened. How fortunate he was to not endure their senseless prattle.

Asher cleared his throat. "I hardly know the queen."

A cool western wind rustled through the trees, and strands of Audrey's black hair blew across her face. Gently her brother removed them. "If that were so, then I would not be here, would I?"

"How goes it for you?" A look of concern knitted Asher's brow.

She took pity on him, hiding most of the truth. "I have made one friend. The rest are very shallow, and it is hard for me to work up any enthusiasm for their conversations," she whispered with a smile.

"A smart woman is not appreciated at court," he whispered back. "At least you are trying to be happy in your new life."

"Indeed, as I hope you are?"

His smile warmed, his gaze drifting off to a satisfying thought. "I am so truly blessed."

Then it was true. He was leaving once again. He must have read the dread on her face because he stopped and turned to her. "Listen to me. The queen will not release you as long as I remain in England. I must leave."

"Ah, as I suspected. I am to be used as the pawn to keep the knight secure. Tell me, what task does she wish you to complete now?"

His lips twitched, and he looked about before turning his gaze back to her. "What I tell you now I speak in confidence and should never be spoken of again. I am going away to be married."

"Nay, I do not believe it. I am sure the queen has ordered it." Audrey stepped back, letting her gaze assess him as he began to smile. "But I can see you are not at all displeased with the decision. Pray tell, who is it? Someone of importance I wager."

Asher grabbed her hand and pulled her close. "Shh. Do not be so loud. I cannot tell who. It was wrong for me to tell you as much as I have already. Know that I am happy with this arrangement. I love the woman deeply."

Though a tightness of loss gripped Audrey's chest, she pulled her hand free and lifted it to his face. "Oh, no one deserves this more than you. I am so pleased. I shall love getting to know your mysterious wife, my new sister, when you return."

The wind whipped around them, turning up a fresh fragrance from the summer blooms. A dark shadow crossed his face. The sweet smell quickly soured in her nostrils.

"Audrey," he whispered.

A coldness swept over her. "You are not coming back, are you?"

He shook his head.

She fell into his arms. "Nay, brother. I cannot bear the thought of never seeing you again. Say it is not true."

"This marriage is best for all of us. For England as well. I promise, when things have settled down, I will send word."

She gripped his shoulders. "How will Mother and Father survive without your comfort? How will I?"

He pulled back and held her at arm's length. "Be strong and wait on the Lord."

"You quote scripture. If you were not getting married, I would think you were going to become a priest like Robert." The mention of their dear departed brother sent a cloud of gloom over them, and Audrey did not want to spend her last moments with Asher in sad memories. "I am sorry. Let us speak of happier times."

He nodded. "Aye, when you smashed Robert in the face for snatching up that rag of a cloth you always carried around."

"It gave me comfort, and what did you do but help him, tossing it back and forth as if it were a cheap piece of soiled lint."

"It was a piece of soiled lint." Hearty laughter spilled from their lips until it gave way to warm, sad smiles. He pulled her into his arms and gave her a great hug. "I will miss you."

Large tears trailed down her cheeks. "I too," she whispered into his shoulder. When composed, she pulled back and fixed a smile on her face. "You deserve happiness, but I cannot stop my heart from breaking. I love you, brother."

Again, he pulled her into his arms. "I love you too, and I will pray that God will give you the same joy as I have."

"Then go and be fulfilled. Worry not about me for I am certain I shall find joy too."

They spent the afternoon reminiscing about merrier times and making promises to see each other again, which they both knew would never happen. There was no doubt when he left that God had finally given her brother peace and a chance to live in the light away from the shadows. For this she could not be more thankful, for no one deserved a life full of bliss more than her brother and his lady, whomever she may be.

Audrey again took a seat under the large oak and opened her prayer book. There written in Asher's handwriting were the words that had given her great comfort in times of need. *Be strong and of a good courage, fear not, nor be afraid of them: for the Lord thy God, he it is that doth go with thee; he will not fail thee, nor forsake thee. – Deuteronomy 31:6*

A soft breeze kissed her face, and a bright ray of afternoon sun warmed her cheeks. Birds chirped merrily above her head. Indeed, all was in God's hands.

Author Note

The words used by Lady Jane Grey in the prologue are her actual words as recorded by J.G. Nichols (1850 reprint), ***Chronicles of Queen Jane, and of Two Years of Queen Mary, and Especially of the Rebellion of Sir Thomas Wyatt, Written by a Resident in the Tower of London,*** *Llanerch Publishers.*

There is a difference of opinion as to who led Lady Jane Grey to the block once her blindfold was secured. I chose to use John Feckenham as her guide since the opening scene is told from his point of view. After the prologue, all truth to the story was cast to the wind and what followed in, ***A Life Renewed*** is only a possible "what if" Lady Jane Grey had lived.

Although the term "Bloody Mary" is used in this story, it should be noted that Queen Mary was not called such during her lifetime. The term did not take hold until after John Foxe wrote, ***Actes and Monuments*** (known by many as ***Foxe's book of Martyrs***) in 1563. The term later became an effective Protestant propaganda tool.

Finally, you will notice I rarely use the titles *Herr, Frau, and Fräulien.* They were not used in their present form until much later in history. Occasionally, I did use the term *Herr Doktor* which was a term used to describe an educated man or preacher. All other terms, some historically accurate and others not, were used to give flavor and dimension to the story. All other historical errors are mine alone and are not meant to give offense.

Dear Reader,

I hope you enjoyed *A Life Renewed*. The journey into Tudor England and Germany was an adventure for me too. I hope you will join Asher's sister, Audrey in book two, *A Life Redeemed*. We will be heading to Scotland for most of the story. Please come along and meet the Clan Armstrong. It should be a wild tale.

If you love historical romances and haven't read *The Sword and The Cross Chronicles* this would be a great time to do so. You'll meet Templar knights, Richard the Lionheart and other exciting historical figures. Or if you like contemporary romance, check out *Joshua's Prayer* and make sure you have a box of tissues—it will tug at your heartstrings. You may find all these books on my website oliviarae.books.com

As always, at the end of all my letters I make a request for book reviews. If you enjoyed any of my books, consider reviewing where you purchased them. A few kind words can go a long way, and we all know kindness is a wonderful thing to spread around. Thanks so much for reading my books.

Until next time…abundant blessings,
Olivia

Excerpt from

A LIFE REDEEMED

SECRETS OF THE QUEENS · BOOK 2

OLIVIA RAE

CHAPTER 1

April, 1559
Outside of London

Cool spring air filled Audrey's lungs; so fresh, so welcoming, so much better than the stale air of London. Delicate wildflowers were starting to dot the meadows and the brown earth had given up its winter chill. Birds flitted and fluttered from tree to tree and branch to branch. Now she was like them—free from the bonds of Queen Mary's court. God had been merciful and returned her to her family. She should be rejoicing, but she wasn't.

Her family. That wasn't quite so. A tinge of sadness entered her heart and troubled her mind, chasing away her jolly mood. Aye, her mother was here, but her father had died over a year ago. Born a merchant, he could not fathom working the land, yet that became his life since his release from debtor's prison. Now he was gone and her brother Asher, who had bought the land and built this fine cottage, was living somewhere in a distant eastern country with his wife. Though he promised to return someday, Audrey knew she would never see him again.

Audrey pulled a shawl tight around her shoulders before she picked up the basket at her feet. She strode down the hill to where her stepfather and stepbrother had begun to plow the fields. Neither stopped to give her a look, so hard they were at their task. "'Bout time ye got here, girl," her stepfather chided when he finally looked up. "Place the basket on yonder rock and we will eat when this row is done."

Her stepbrother Jacob looked longingly at the basket, but did not gainsay his father. At six and ten, you would think he would have grown a backbone, but no, he was as weak as the rest living at the cottage.

"What ye standin' like a limp saplin'? Do as I say and then fetch us a cool drink from the river." Her stepfather spat on the ground before putting his shoulder to the plow.

Audrey shook her head and stared at his back as he struggled on. The man never had a pleasant word to offer. Truly only loneliness could have prompted her mother to marry such a person. Leaving the basket, Audrey picked up the empty jug her stepfather and Jacob had discarded. What freedom was this doing the same thing over and over every morn? 'Twas not much different than attending to Queen Mary's needs.

With a heavy sigh, Audrey made her way to the river. Her brooding would serve no purpose, better to focus on the joy she had just a few moments ago. She had a roof over her head and food in her belly, what matter if the tasks were mundane and the company chafed? Things could be far worse. "At least I am far away from the deadly games of the court."

A crow cawed and flew away when a woman dressed in a dark cloak and heavily veiled stepped out of the foliage. "Aye, they can be bad?"

The hair on Audrey's neck rose as a band of men dressed like peasants, yet carrying swords common with the royal guard circled around her. Audrey straightened her spine. "What do you want? I have no coin or goods except this empty jug. If you think it is of worth, then it is yours." Audrey hefted the jug above her head and threw it at the woman, who deftly stepped out of the way. The jug hit a rock, fracturing into pieces. The guard charged forward as Audrey dodged left desperately seeking an escape route.

"Stop." The cloaked woman waved a gloved hand in the air. "Can you not see? You are scaring the girl."

The men halted and did not take a step closer, nor did they retreat. Audrey stalled her steps. How fast would it take Jacob to come if she called out? But what could his presence do against these armed men?

The veiled woman moved to the edge of the circle and held out her hand. "Come walk with me. I promise no harm will fall you."

"Nay. I shall not. You mean to harm me. There is nothing I can give you. Leave me be." Audrey folded her arms across her chest.

The woman huffed. "Good heavens. If I wanted you dead, you would not be drawing breath. I just wish to have a private word with you."

This woman was not a leader of a band of thieves, no indeed. Her speech was that of a lady's. Her gait and straight back bespoke of noble breeding. There had been many such women at court. Why this one would create such an elaborate disguise was a bafflement. And unfortunately, Audrey's curious nature was starting to get the better of her.

"What do we have to talk about?"

"Why your family, what else?"

The hook set. Audrey took a deep breath. "My past family or my present one?"

"Come walk with me and find out. The others will stay here." The woman held out her hand.

One of the men rushed forward. "But my—"

"Stay here and say not another word." She then turned to Audrey and motioned with her hand. "There is a smooth path up ahead. Let us stroll there."

Audrey cast her gaze around the circle. What choice did she really have? This woman was going to have her way. Besides it would be easier to escape one female than a band of armed men.

Audrey nodded.

Her mind racing, she walked on in silence surveying the woods around her wondering if there were other hidden attackers. Audrey dropped her gaze to the stones at her feet. Could she strike the woman before she alerted her men?

"So, tell me, have you heard much from your brother recently?" The woman did not break her stride and carried on as if they had been acquaintances for some time.

Audrey's stomach curled inward. This was about Asher. But of course, being a spy for the late Queen Mary, who else lived a life of such intrigue? Audrey took another deep breath to still her racing heart. "Mistress, I have not seen my brother in years and I rarely receive word from him. I cannot help you find him for I do not know where he is."

The path widened to a small opening; rays of sunlight filtered through the leafy canopy. The woman stopped and sat down on a large boulder that graced the side of the path. "I know where he is. That is not why I have sought you out."

The woman raised her veil and Audrey's blood turned to ice. How could she have been so stupid? She curtsied deep and reverent. "Your Majesty."

A layer of fine sweat rested on Queen Elizabeth's pronounced cheek bones. A brightness shown in her dark brown eyes. She looked so much wiser than a woman of five and twenty. "Hush. Do not use such terms here. And do stand up straight. Do you wish to alert the whole of England where I am?"

They were alone on a forest path with no one present except for a few twittering birds and perchance a rabbit or two. "Your...um. If you know where he is, then why have you come to me?" Audrey wiped her sweaty hands on her skirt, knowing her bold words could send her to the Tower.

"I know you were one of my sister's ladies. And I know you were one of the first to leave court after she died. So eager you were to return to your family. But what I do not know is are you as astute as your brother?"

A small creature rustled in a layer of last year's leaves that covered the forest floor. Perspiration slithered down Audrey's back. Oh, how she wished she could as easily slip away. "I do not know what you mean?"

"Come, come. We both know he was a spy who helped my sister root out Protestants. I hear he was quite sneaky and crafty, but all that changed a few years back. He just up and left with my sister's blessing. I thought nothing of it until I came across some of my sister's scribblings. My, my, they were a busy pair—my sister and your brother.

What she ranted about was a mystery. Uneasiness twisted Audrey's gut. One thing she did learn at court: if a royal fumed, best to keep silent. She dropped her gaze to her feet and clenched her jaw.

"But none of that matters now. What I want to know is do you have the same skills as he?"

"Skills? What skills do you mean?"

Queen Elizabeth rose and put her hands on her hips. "Are you dull or are you being crafty?"

Audrey's hands curled into fists and she fought not to glare at her queen.

"I think you are the latter. Do not think I hold that against you. Before I became queen, there were many a time I had to hold my tongue and play the dull maid in order to keep my head upon my neck."

Audrey lifted her head and saw a merry twinkle in the queen's eye. The royal just nodded.

"You and I are not that different. Our survival is due to our wits." The queen circled the clearing and seemed to be distracted by a wren's sweet song. But then she leveled her gaze on Audrey. "Are you happy here, living as a peasant?"

A wave of wariness weaved through Audrey's stomach. Surely, she was not being summoned back to court? "This is where my family lives."

Queen Elizabeth sniffed. "Not true."

"My mother needs me," Audrey snapped.

"Does she? She has a new husband and three new children. Must be crowded in that little cottage, especially since you are used to the comforts at court."

Audrey began to shake. The queen must have had her spies about to know so much. Whatever the queen wanted Audrey refused to be trapped in a royal cage again. "What would a Protestant queen want with a Catholic maid at court?"

"Hush, girl. Keep your voice down." Queen Elizabeth looked about. "Good heavens, the last thing I want is a papist around me. I have enough of those lurking about already."

The anxiety that had whirled around Audrey's insides receded like a wave at low tide. "Then why do you seek me out?"

The queen let out a heavy sigh and sat upon the boulder once again. She looked upward as if contemplating how to proceed. Settling on her course, she stared at Audrey. "I told you of my sister's writings. They were most disturbing. One in particular. There is a lord, on the northern English boarder whose loyalties may not be true to England. His wife has just recently passed away leaving him with two sons and an aging mother."

Uneasiness began to creep up Audrey's spine again. She could feel the intrigue and lies of court suffocating her. "If all this just happened, then how could this information be in Queen Mary's writings? She has been dead for some time."

Queen Elizabeth glared. "Do not contradict me. Just listen."

Audrey rolled her tongue in her mouth and tightened her lips. She was never good at holding her words before her betters. "Forgive me, Your—"

Elizabeth cleared her throat. "This man, Gavin Armstrong a lesser laird, has an interesting heritage. He has an English Protestant mother and a Scottish father, who claimed to be loyal to the English Crown, a member of the Lords of the Congregation, a most prestigious Scottish Protestant group." Her skeptical tone relayed a different thinking. She rose and strolled around the boulder. "I came to throne with the goal to be tolerant of those of the Catholic faith, but there are some who still do not view me as a legitimate queen."

She spoke of the marriage of her mother with King Henry VIII. Some in England, mostly Catholics did not recognize Elizabeth as the true queen. They would prefer to see Mary Queen of Scots, who was married to the French Dauphine sitting on the English throne.

As was her way, Queen Elizabeth got right to the point. "I cannot trust the Scots. Some claim to be my loyal servants and others do not. The border lands are in constant disruption. That is why I need you."

"Me?" Audrey regretted her outburst the moment the syllable left her lips. The queen's brow wrinkled. "Forgive me. I just do not understand how I could be of help."

"Do you not?"

Audrey met the queen's glare.

Elizabeth looked away. "You served my sister. If Armstrong is a Catholic sympathizer who wishes to put Mary of Scots on the English throne, who better would he confide in than another Catholic who has been oppressed by the illegitimate Queen Elizabeth."

Audrey's lifted her chin. "I have never been disloyal to you."

"Aye, I know. That is why I am sending you. I know you will be loyal to me as I am sure you would want me to protect your mother and her brood of stepchildren."

The lashing though heavily coated with sweetness was well taken. However, Audrey could not imagine that this laird would tell all his secrets to her. Nonetheless, she could not reject the queen's offer. "My Queen, you give me more honor than I deserve. I am neither noble or a man, why would this Gavin Armstrong confide in me?"

Elizabeth raised a well-manicured brow. "An act of birth nor one's sex makes someone loyal. I would rather sup with an honorable digger of ditches, than a prince who would sell his devotion for a babble. It has all been arranged. You will go to Liddesdale in the Debatable Land between England and Scotland in the guise as a companion to Laird Armstrong's mother. There you will keep your ears open. You shall correspond any threats to the Crown. I want to know who the man corresponds with, were he goes, who he confides in. I want to know everything that is going on with that clan."

A sinking feeling of defeat settled in Audrey's stomach. Oh, she should have not complained earlier of living a mundane life, for now that life looked sublime. "And if there is nothing out of the ordinary would you like me to talk about the weather?"

The queen narrowed her eyes and pointed a thin finger in Audrey's face. "Do not taunt me. Your very life and of those you love are in my hands."

Indeed. Audrey's emotions and tongue had got the better of her. Why could she not be cool and calm like Asher? Why did she spout off when she should be silent? No good could come from insulting the queen. Audrey lowered her gaze. "I am sorry. My words were vile."

The queen laughed. "You speak your mind and you have a strong spirit. You have just forgotten to choose your words wisely as you did at court. A few weeks back there should cure that."

The Tower would be more preferable. But this was not just about her, it involved her mother and Jacob and her step-sisters. Audrey swallowed hard. "Aye. I am sure it will."

"It has been all arranged. Once you are in Liddesdale, you will write weekly and send your missives to a Mistress Pittman on Levey Lane."

"Levey Lane? I have never heard of such a place. The messages could get lost."

"That is not your concern. Just try to gain Gavin Armstrong's confidence. Learn and report everything he does. Even if it seems minor to you. Perhaps this could be done by keeping an eye on his boy."

About the Author

OLIVIA RAE is an award-winning author of historical and contemporary inspirational romance. She spent her school days dreaming of knights, princesses and far away kingdoms; it made those long, boring days in the classroom go by much faster. Nobody was more shocked than her when she decided to become a teacher. Besides getting her Master's degree, marrying her own prince, and raising a couple of kids, Olivia decided to breathe a little more life into her childhood stories by adding in what she's learned as an adult living in a small town on the edge of a big city. When not writing, she loves to travel, dragging her family to old castles and forts all across the world.

Olivia is the winner of the Golden Quill Award, New England Readers' Choice Award, Southern Magic Contest, and the American Fiction Award. She is an Illumination Award Bronze medalist and she has been a finalist in many other contests such as the National Readers' Choice Awards, and the National Romance Fiction Awards. She is currently hard at work on her next novel.

Contact Olivia at Oliviarae.books@gmail.com

For news and sneak peeks of upcoming novels visit:
www.oliviaraebooks.com

Made in the USA
Middletown, DE
26 April 2020